# An IMPOSSIBLE PRICE

# Books by Davalynn Spencer

## Historical

### THE FRONT RANGE BRIDES SERIES

Mail-Order Misfire - Series Prequel
An Improper Proposal - Book 1
An Unexpected Redemption - Book 2
An Impossible Price – Book 3

### THE CAÑON CITY CHRONICLES SERIES

Loving the Horseman - Book 1
Straight to My Heart - Book 2
Romancing the Widow - Book 3
The Cañon City Chronicles - complete collection

### Novella Collections

"The Wrangler's Woman"
- The Cowboy's Bride Collection
"The Columbine Bride"
- The 12 Brides of Summer
"The Snowbound Bride"
- The 12 Brides of Christmas

## Contemporary

The Miracle Tree

## Novellas

Snow Angel
Just in Time for Christmas
A High-Country Christmas – complete collection

Sign up for my Quarterly Author Update
and receive a free historical novella!
https://bit.ly/3b4eavB

# An IMPOSSIBLE PRICE

Front Range Brides

Book 3

Davalynn Spencer

ISBN 978-0-9989512-9-4



All Scripture quotations are taken from the King James Version of the Bible.

The characters and events in this book are fictional, and any resemblance to actual persons or events is coincidental.

Book cover design by ebooklaunch.com

Wilson Creek Publishing

www.davalynnspencer.com

~

For the wounded and scarred.

~

~

*It is of the Lord's mercies that we are not consumed,*
*because his compassions fail not.*
*They are new every morning; Great is thy faithfulness.*
Lamentations 3:22, 23

~

# CHAPTER 1

# OLIN SPRINGS, COLORADO

## Late March 1885

The bay stallion pawed at the stock-car wall and tossed its head.

Quick as a rattlesnake, its back leg struck. A partition splintered, sending wood fragments showering over crates and barrels.

The horse had fought its constraints for the last four hours—all the way from Denver. It was only a matter of time before the battle between bolted wood and brute strength was decided.

Clay's money was on the horse.

The rhythmic clack of iron wheels began to drag, and Clay pushed to his feet, bracing against the louvered wall of the car. Already heavy with horse sweat and manure, the air thickened at the screech of steel on steel, fear tainting the mix. A long blast of the whistle drew his horse's ears forward.

"It won't be long now, Duster. We're almost home."

His buckskin's dark eye widened with uncertainty. Its shoulder and leg muscles bunched for balance. Clay took hold of the rope that tethered the gelding and rubbed its neck and shoulder, telegraphing calm.

A general stock car wasn't his first choice for either himself or his horse, but the Denver & Rio Grande had nothing else for livestock. He'd chosen the speed of a train over the length of the trail between Kansas City and Colorado, but he'd refused to ride with human passengers and risk injury—or worse—to his unattended horse.

The bay stallion was a perfect example of why.

The car jerked against its couplings, sending a nearby horse to its knees. Billowing steam hissed along the rails, and the train inched toward a full stop.

Olin Springs.

Clay eased out a tight hiss of his own. They weren't off the train in one piece yet.

Memories of his first arrival rose like smoke from the stack—riding into town beaten, broke, and bitter. His outlook now was a whole lot better than it had been four years ago.

Expectation rippled through him, as well as the mixed bunch of horseflesh tethered to rings on the walls. Clay had secured a forward corner, farthest from the stallion and somewhat protected with the outer wall on one side and a flimsy partition on the other.

Anticipating the slide of the car door, he untied Duster and turned him to face daylight.

Behind them, the stallion reared against its rope. Any minute now.

Freight crewmen slid the door wide, and Clay led his horse down the stock ramp into sunshine and fresh air. They'd been too long cooped up.

As they hit solid earth, a panicked whinny sent a chill up Clay's neck. He looked for someone to hold his horse and took a chance on an older boy in tall boots.

"Hold him steady and I'll make it worth your while. And get back out of the way."

The boy took Duster's rope with a silent nod and seasoned hand.

In the same instant, a brutal crash from inside the car froze everyone on the station platform as well as those waiting for livestock.

Clay tugged his hat down and rushed to the open cargo door, finding exactly what he'd feared. The stallion had broken loose but had punched through the stock-car slats with a back leg and was wildly trying to break free—sawing deeper into its leg with every lunge. Frenzied, it bit and struck at whatever it could reach. There'd soon be a blood bath.

Arms wide, he whirled on the men who had crowded the loading ramp hoping to see the show. "Get back!"

Those close to him gave way, looking as uncertain about him as they did the commotion inside the car.

He swung up through the open door and flattened himself against the wall.

The lathered stallion blew and struck, head high, eyes wide and wild. Fear and pain were a volatile mix, Clay well knew. Who in their right mind would send a hot-blooded horse like this on a train without a handler?

A crewman came up the ramp and quickly led two horses out. Clay untied a half dozen more, looped their leads around their necks, and slapped them toward the door. After pulling his hat off, he dragged his sleeve across his forehead, then screwed the hat down hard. He had to come at the horse from the side—not unseen, but not straight on either. Setting his voice at a low, easy tone, he stepped away from the wall and eased toward the stallion.

If he survived, he might be the worse for wear. If he didn't, at least he'd die doing what he loved.

~

Sophie Price stood at the window inside Eisner's tailor shop, her curiosity growing with the increasing number of people rushing toward the depot.

"What could it be?" Abigail Eisner, mere weeks from the birth of her first child, laid a protective hand on her swollen abdomen and joined Sophie at the window. "Please, go see and come back and tell me. I cannot go. Not like this." She was clearly as eager to know as Sophie, her lively eyes sparkling with anticipation.

"All right, but I'll return quickly. We have more to discuss." She set her satchel on the floor at the end of the store counter. "I won't be long."

Hurrying out the door, Sophie almost felt guilty running after others who had dropped whatever they were doing to ogle an incident at the depot. A holdup? A shooting?

Spring fever, perhaps, drawing everyone outdoors, but she didn't slow her steps until she rounded the Western Union office, where a crowd gathered near a stock car, its side door open at the loading ramp.

She pressed through onlookers and passengers who still lingered, all mesmerized by the rocking rail car. Her flesh crawled at the chilling screams of a horse, but a sudden silence disturbed her even more, eerie after such an uproar.

"I hope he's not dead." A fashionably dressed woman clung to her male companion's arm. Both appeared to be travelers who had either just arrived or were ready to depart.

"Did you see him go in there alone? I doubt he survived from the sound of that demon he's facing."

The man pulled his arm free and encircled the anxious woman. "It's a horse, Martha, not a demon."

Sophie's curiosity pushed her past social propriety. "Someone went in the car?"

"A cowboy," the woman said, her voice struck through with awe. "At least he looked like a cowboy. That's his horse over there." She pointed to a saddled buckskin, held by the livery's tack and stable boy. The horse stood with ears and eyes alert, watching the car.

At its whicker, Sophie's attention returned to the loading ramp, where a man appeared in the doorway. He eased a lathered, wild-eyed horse to the edge of the ramp—one of the finest horses she'd ever seen, and clearly terrified. The man's sweaty shirt clung to his back and broad shoulders, but he murmured to the horse in low tones, stroking its neck while leading it down the ramp.

Almost sure she could feel his calming presence herself, she worked her way closer for a better look.

Something about his manner sent a thrill rippling through her. His unquestionable ability to influence the horse, as if it drew peace from his gentle command.

A hush settled over the onlookers, and those closest to the ramp eased back. The rest of the crowd ebbed with them. And then the sea parted for this unlikely Moses as people opened a path for him and the lathered horse.

Turning, he skimmed the crowd on each side, as if looking for something or someone—and his eyes locked on Sophie.

Startlingly blue.

Her breath caught. One hand fisted into her skirt.

He didn't smile, or nod, or touch the brim of his hat. But recognition fired as sharply as if he'd spoken her name.

Passing by, he jerked his head for the livery boy to follow, and that's when she saw the ugly gash on the stallion's back leg. Blood pumped with every step and trailed to the hoof, calling for sutures.

A twinge at the corner of her mouth drew her fingers, but she tucked her hand under her arm. That beautiful animal would die a horrible death if the wound were left untended and became infected.

Following the two and their horses, she brushed past the crowd as it closed behind them. The handler spoke to the stallion in soothing tones, his voice steady and deep. *Familiar*. She knew of few who worked such miracles with wild or frightened horses. Deacon Jewett at the Parker ranch was one. The other, a young man who'd honed his gift at Deacon's side.

Anticipation veined through her as she made the corner at Main Street, still following the livery boy and the stranger. Could it be? On occasion, Deacon's young protégé had turned her head and set her mind to wondering if she'd remained unmarried for a reason not yet revealed. But *young* was the word that snagged. He'd been a boy of sixteen, she a woman of twenty, and that fact had quashed her musings in those days.

Craning her neck to better see the stranger, she noted his long stride and the slightest hint of a halting gait. Her heart reared like a horse itself, and she pressed a hand to the base of her throat.

The voice, the subtle limp. *Those eyes.* Only one person had all those traits, and when he'd left, he'd said nothing that made her think he'd ever return.

Far from an unseasoned youth, the confident stranger leading the fiery stallion might be no stranger at all.

Had Clay Ferguson come home?

# CHAPTER 2

Torn between desire and duty, Sophie paused at the Eisner's window, where Abigail still watched, and held up a finger. "One more minute," she mouthed.

Abigail nodded excitedly as she motioned Sophie on.

Thank God the woman wasn't in labor. Of course Sophie would not have asked under those conditions, which was the reason she was in town in the first place. At the very moment that man—whoever he was—led an injured, frightened, yet powerful animal off a train and through a crowd of people without anyone being harmed.

She shuddered at what *could* have happened and quickened her pace, holding her skirt as she stepped from the boardwalk to the street.

Few stragglers had followed from the depot, so she had an unobstructed view from the livery's wide entry where she stood eavesdropping.

Not exactly eavesdropping. Merely listening.

*Shoot.* All right, eavesdropping.

She faded to the left, pressing against the door frame and into the building, feigning invisibility in the shadows. "Never be a target," Deacon had once told her on one of his many visits to the farm on some trumped-up mission so he could see Mama.

But Sophie simply had to know more about this horse handler—confirm her hunch—for he certainly dwarfed the person she thought he might be.

She hadn't seen Clay Ferguson since Betsy and Garrett Wilson's wedding reception three years ago. The reception *before* the wedding. Only Maggie Snowfield with her exquisite home and refinement could have pulled off something completely unheard of without raising a single matronly eyebrow in town.

Erik came from his forge, hammer in hand, leather apron circling his substantial girth. Doubt narrowed his eyes as he took in the new arrivals.

"Erik." The handler spoke calmly, as if he knew the smithy, and the deep timbre of his voice rippled over Sophie's skin like warm water.

She moved a step closer.

"I need a stout beam and large box stall for this fella. He requires sutures, and I doubt he'll stand for it without … *assistance*."

At the mention of sutures, Sophie's hunch burrowed deeper. All Clay had ever talked about was becoming a horse doctor. A veterinarian.

Erik set his beefy hands at his hips and scowled. "And you might be …"

Without taking his hand from the stallion's neck, the handler tipped his head toward its hind quarters. "I might be in a hurry to save this horse's life."

Blood still pulsed from the deep gash on its right back leg and now pooled around the hoof. Time was not on their side.

Erik took a closer look and gave one stout nod, then motioned for the stranger to follow. "I have what you need."

The stable boy held the buckskin inside a stall near the front.

As the stranger passed, he slowed. "Unsaddle him for me and bring me the saddle bags. Then give him a can of oats."

Two steps on, he glanced over his shoulder. "Obliged."

The boy drew himself up, as proud as if Napoléon himself had commissioned him to care for his war horse, Marengo.

Sophie wanted nothing more than to follow the parade, but she had an obligation to an expectant mother. And this whole affair really wasn't any of her business. However, that didn't keep her from approaching the boy.

"Do you know that man? The man whose horse you're holding?"

He draped the saddlebags over the edge of the stall and set to unsaddling the buckskin. "No, ma'am, I don't. But after what I just witnessed, I'm happy to do what he asked."

Secretly she agreed but kept that opinion to herself and left.

By the time Sophie returned to the store, Abigail had abandoned her vigil at the window and was busy with a feather duster on a wall-mounted shelf of men's hats, gloves, and other accessories. She turned at the click of the door.

"Was anyone hurt? I saw that beautiful horse."

Sophie picked up her satchel from where she'd left it. "That beautiful horse was a handful and, thankfully, was the only one injured. The man who was leading him is tending to his wound at the livery."

"Is he from town? He wasn't Dr. Weaver."

"I don't know for sure where he's from, but he seemed to be in charge." Very much so. And apparently, very capable. Even Erik hadn't challenged him beyond an initial question.

She angled her right side forward, conscious of Abigail's curious glance when they'd first met. "Is Mr. Eisner around to watch the store while we talk privately? Perhaps at the back?"

"Oh yes. He is sewing. Come with me."

The poor woman actually waddled ahead of Sophie, raising questions about when this baby might be making its entrance into the world. Sophie's instincts said sooner rather than the assumed later.

Beyond a curtain at the back, a treadle sewing machine hummed off and on. Abigail drew the curtain aside. "Hiram, this is Sophie Price, my midwife." She blushed as she spoke.

Hiram looked up and then stood with a stilted bow, acknowledging Sophie's presence. "It is my pleasure to meet you,"—his eyes flicked to her cheek—"*Miss* Price?"

The unintended jab hit its mark.

"Yes. Miss Price. But you may call me Sophie since I will be here so often, working closely with your wife."

He glanced aside as if he could not consider such a breach of manners.

"Hiram, can you watch the front while we discuss … things?"

"Of course." Another brief bow. "Excuse me." He left as if fleeing imminent attack.

Abigail drew the chair away from the sewing machine for Sophie and took another for herself, then fell heavily onto it. "We could go upstairs to our apartment, but I try to make the trip only once a day. It is becoming more difficult for me."

Concerned, Sophie walked to the railing that disappeared around a wall, and looked up at the narrow stairway to the second floor. No handrail beyond the first few steps. Completely unacceptable.

"About that," she said, seating herself a safe distance from fine woolen fabric held in place by the machine's needle. It looked to be the sleeve of a man's suit coat. "How far along are you exactly? When did you have your last monthly time?"

Abigail blushed again, obviously with child yet clearly uncomfortable discussing the details that led to her condition. No wonder she didn't want Doc Weaver's help.

"I believe you say August?"

"Do you know the exact date?"

Abigail's dark brows pulled together as she considered an answer. "The end."

"All right, that's good. That means that you are between thirty-eight and forty weeks along." She laid a reassuring hand atop Abigail's. "Your baby will be here soon. Very soon. Do you have family anywhere nearby?"

The woman blinked rapidly and shook her head, tears gathering in her lovely eyes. "In Chicago."

"I see." Sophie gave her another pat. "Everything will be fine, don't you worry. I will be with you every minute."

In as assuring a tone as possible, Sophie conversationally plied Abigail with questions to determine her understanding and readiness. They discussed clothing and flannels, early signs of labor, and what to do should things come on quickly. But rather than overwhelm the young mother-to-be all at once, she promised to return for another visit and picked up her satchel.

"I will call again in a day or so. Until then, I want you to rest as much as possible. Perhaps you can go up early and lie down while Hiram closes the shop. You are wise to not attempt the stairs more than once each day. And no lifting anything other than a fork of food to your mouth."

"A cup of tea?"

Encouraged by the spark of humor displacing earlier tears, Sophie laughed as she drew aside the curtain. "Oh, if you insist. Chamomile tea, preferably."

At the front of the shop, Hiram took the measurements of a man who stood with his back to them, arms out like a scarecrow.

Sophie stopped several feet away, unwilling to cloud happy expectations with unnecessary worry, but neither did she want her client falling down the stairs.

She lowered her voice. "Does Hiram have time to attach a railing to the wall along the staircase, all the way from the bottom of the stairs to your apartment?"

Abigail shook her head, lifting wisps of wavy black hair at her temples. "Oh no. He is very busy. And not so good with building things other than clothes."

"Of course." Sophie smiled at the image of building clothes. "Perhaps he knows someone who could do the job. I really don't like the idea of you climbing up and down without a handrail. If he doesn't know anyone who can do the work, I'll see if I can find someone."

"I would be happy to help in that department."

Scarecrow Man turned around, his sleeves bearing marks from the tailor's chalk, his eyes roaming Sophie's person as if he sought ownership.

She shuddered but held tightly to her poise. "Mr. Thatcher. I didn't realize it was you being fitted."

He dipped his head in greeting, never taking his eyes off her, like a snake watching its prey. "Please, call me Clarence. And forgive me, but I couldn't help overhearing what you said."

*Overhearing my eye.*

"The part about the stairs needing a handrail," he hastily clarified at Sophie's less-than-friendly stare.

No doubt he'd eavesdropped on the entire conversation, and here she was casting the first stone, as guilty as he. But this was a private conversation of a personal nature between women. He should be ashamed of himself, regardless of how close the quarters were.

He drew himself up. "I did quite a bit of the repair on my hotel following that devastating conflagration a few years back. Stair railing is something I am quite good at if I do say so myself."

And of course he would say so himself. The man irritated the fire out of her and made her skin crawl. Mama's training alone held off what she really wanted to say.

"I'm sure I can find someone not quite as busy—"

"Oh, but I insist."

Sophie managed to hold her tongue and not insist that he mind his own business. She glanced at Abigail, who was nodding appreciatively.

"Thank you, sir."

Sophie wanted to gag, but she managed to hold that back as well. Turning away from the men, she whispered, "I will check with you the day after tomorrow, right after church. Is that convenient?"

Abigail glanced at her husband and leaned closer. "We do not attend the services on Sunday."

For a moment Sophie was at a loss, but the couple's accent and now this bit of information all served to explain.

"Of course," she said, laying her hand atop Abigail's, which rested habitually on her stomach. "Would you mind if I knocked on your door late Sunday morning?"

"Not at all." A quick smile. "Knock loud."

Sophie left without speaking again to Mr. Thatcher—her second breach of social propriety in less than an hour—but the man's untiring pursuit drove her to distraction. She refused to do or say anything that might be construed as encouragement.

At twenty-four, her opportunities were dwindling, but Clarence Thatcher cornered her at every church function, reminding her how challenging it was to run the Olin Springs Hotel *all alone.* She was no stranger to *all alone,* and if he mentioned that phrase to her one more time, she might throttle him in front of God and the whole congregation.

Encountering him today in such close quarters left her feeling boxed in. Like that stallion must have felt in the railroad car.

A clear image of the strapping handler left Mr. Thatcher wilting in the shadows and Sophie thinking things she had no business thinking.

Her old mare waited good-naturedly at the hitch rail, where she secured her satchel, swung up, and took the cross street leading to Maggie Snowfield's mansion and Betsy Wilson. It wasn't really a mansion, but that's what she and Betsy had called it as schoolgirls, dreaming of romantic encounters with suitors in the cupola atop the magnificent house.

An old barb pressed deeper into Sophie's breast, throbbing like a lesser heartbeat.

Betsy, as most women their age, had a family. But for some unknown reason, the Lord had gifted Sophie not with a husband and children of her own, but with delivering the children of others. Doc often sent for her when mothers preferred another woman at their side, as in Abigail Eisner's case.

Helping the helpless filled Sophie with a sense of purpose. But the longing never went away. It remained silently permanent. Just like the scar on her left cheek.

She rode around to the back of Maggie's home and tied the mare in front of the small barn and buggy shed Clay Ferguson had helped raise after a fire here. *He* could make a handrail for the Eisners.

That quickly, the handler strode through her mind, fast on the heels of a gangly young man who'd landed in town on the wrong side of the street. Sheriff Wilson had taken an immediate liking to Clay after jailing him for being "drunk and disorderly." Yet his quick turn-around had made her sit up and take notice. Like the day he joined the men of Parker ranch to gather mares.

With a sudden flush of heat, she recalled the bright blue of his eyes on that brisk fall day, the same flashing blue that held her a breathless moment at the depot.

Tamping down the memory, she palmed her damp forehead and took the five steps to Maggie's back stoop. The door opened before she had a chance to knock.

"Sophie! What perfect timing." Betsy Wilson thrust her chubby infant into Sophie's arms. "Would you please hold George for a moment while I dash to the water closet?"

Betsy hurried out of the kitchen and down the hall to a door beneath the stairs.

Sophie wrinkled her nose at the youngster in her arms, and he responded in kind. "I'd rather go out to the privy, wouldn't you?" she whispered conspiratorially, nuzzling his neck and drawing a giggle.

When Betsy returned, George was in his highchair gumming one of Maggie's ginger thins, hands and face sufficiently gooey. His mother wiped his mouth and chubby fingers with a rag from the table. "Why don't you move to town, Sophie? You could stay here. Maggie has several empty bedrooms upstairs, and I'm sure she'd love to have you."

"I'm grateful for the invitation, and that's one of my reasons for stopping by."

Betsy gave her a subtle glance and set the kettle on for tea. Maggie Snowfield's tact was clearly contagious.

"I stopped by Eisner's Tailor Shop and Haberdashery today and met with his wife, Abigail—the expectant seamstress you mentioned last Sunday." Sophie helped herself to two tea sets from the cupboard and set them on opposite sides of the small kitchen table, preferring the incongruent intimacy in the large kitchen rather than the sprawling dining room or formal parlor. "You were right. She is very much in the family way."

Feeling remiss, Sophie took down another tea set.

"We won't need that. Maggie is resting." Betsy's voice betrayed uncommon concern.

"Is she ill?"

"I don't believe so, though she wouldn't tell us if she were. She sleeps quite a bit these days. 'Resting her eyes,' she calls it, though when I check on her, she is always sound asleep and curled into a ball like a kitten. A quilt covers her, regardless of the season."

Betsy brought another tin of ginger cookies from the pantry and placed them in the center of the table. "Between you and me, I worry about her. I've no idea of her age, nor have I the courage to ask."

Sophie laughed. "No courage—you? After fighting fires, winning shooting matches with men, and being held at gunpoint? Not to mention, marrying the sheriff."

The kettle hissed, and Betsy brought it to the table with a hot pad. "Compared to wrangling private information out of the petite but formidable Margaret Snowfield, all those accomplishments pale pathetically." She took the chair next to George and gave him another ginger thin. "I don't know what I'll do if she passes." Her voice had thinned to match the cookie.

Based on the intensity of her friend's emotion, Sophie made a note to check on the elderly woman herself and, if necessary, ask Doc Weaver to stop by. Betsy wasn't one to puddle up so easily, though childbirth had softened her to some degree.

"I might take you up on your offer to stay in town, at least for a week or so."

Betsy brightened. "Is Abigail Eisner that far along?"

"She is. And I'm concerned about the stairs she has to use between their second-story living quarters and the shop. There is no handrail."

"Can her husband make one?"

"In Abigail's words, he builds only clothes."

Betsy laughed quietly and wiped George's face and hands yet again.

"Just let the boy enjoy his food, for heaven's sake."

Betsy scowled. "You've no idea how tiresome it is to constantly wipe down the walls or chairs or my own clothing from grimy little hand—"

The barb hooked flesh before Betsy realized what she'd said.

Her eyes widened. "I'm sorry. I didn't mean to—"

"Please don't apologize. I refuse to let everyday conversation ruin my life." The life that had turned out quite unlike Sophie's cupola dreams. "And I've no doubt I will be able to afford room and board."

"You know there is no charge, Sophie. You are always welcome here."

She dipped her head, acquiescing to her friend's insistence, but determined to pay her way regardless. "Well, with the only clothing store in town, aside from what the mercantile offers, I believe the Eisners are doing quite well."

Betsy sipped her tea. "And?"

Sophie looked across the narrow table.

"You said *one* of the reasons you came was to discuss staying in town. What is the other?"

Now was not the time to bring up her suspicions about a handsome stranger. But evading Betsy's inquisition was right up there with querying Maggie Snowfield on her personal life.

Sophie returned the dainty cup to its floral-edged saucer. "There was a disturbance today at the train station. I doubt you heard it this far from the depot. But from Abigail's store window, we saw what seemed like the entire town rushing toward the ruckus, so I went too."

A smile tipped her friend's mouth. "Of course you did. What was it?"

"When I got there, everyone was watching a stock car from which came chilling screams. Screams of horses. More specifically, *one* horse. A stallion."

A ginger thin stopped halfway to Betsy's mouth and her eyes flashed with alarm. "What did this stallion look like?"

Surprised by the response, Sophie chose her words carefully. "It was a dark bay. One of the most beautiful horses I've seen. But it had a deep gouge in its back right leg, I'm guessing from kicking through a wall."

Betsy groaned. "Did you see Cade there?"

"No, why? Was he expecting a horse on the train?"

Betsy laid the cookie on her saucer. "Yes, he was. But if he wasn't there, it must not have been his. He bought a stallion sight unseen from a breeder in Missouri—quite unlike Cade. But he wants new blood for his mares, he told me last month, and this breeder has a sterling reputation." Lifting the teacup to her lips, she added, "Evidently, the expected horse cost a pretty penny. Prettier than my brother was inclined to pay at first."

Sophie's collar grew tight and she slipped the button free at her throat. It could still be the expected horse. Perhaps Cade had simply missed the train's arrival.

"A man led the horse off the car, through the crowd, and to the livery stable without incident. According to a woman I spoke with at the depot, his handling of the animal was near miraculous. Erik's tack and stable boy felt the same way." As did she.

"So you followed them to the livery?"

Sophie took a cookie from the tin. "I did. I had to know."

"Know what?" Betsy raised one eyebrow. "What did this man look like?"

At Sophie's hesitation, Betsy leaned forward in expectation.

Sophie snapped her cookie in half, seeing the tall handler as clearly as if he stood in the kitchen with them. "He looked very much like a grown-up Clay Ferguson."

# CHAPTER 3

*It was her.*

Clay studied the horse before him, its right back leg bent, keeping weight off the injury and breathing more calmly than it had in the stock car.

But Clay wasn't. The sight of Sophie Price at the front of the crowd lining his exit from the train station had burned into his brain.

He stroked the stallion's neck, murmuring as he eased the lead rope around a support beam, but not snubbing it tight. Confinement had nearly driven the horse mad, and it needed a little slack in its life at the moment.

Sophie had been staring like everyone else, but the moment her eyes connected with his, her reaction gave her away—an event he'd long anticipated, though it clearly caught her by surprise. For some reason, that pleased him.

If he'd had any doubt about her identity, the slight tilt of her mouth would have confirmed it. She hadn't smiled, but a faint scar lifted the left side of her lips. He'd always sensed it made her self-conscious, but it was as much a part of her as her caring nature and summer-brown hair. Like his limp was a part of him. More so when he was stiff and tired like today.

Pushing her image aside, he focused on the injured horse. Rather than throw it down right away, he wanted to hobble its front legs and scotch-hobble the back left. He'd run a cotton rope through the halter, allowing some lateral movement but preventing it from bogging its head enough to buck and kick.

Time was something they didn't have, not with every beat of the animal's heart pumping blood onto the straw-covered floor. If it came to a fight, the horse would win. Clay had to win its trust instead, and he knew from firsthand experience that trust was not easily won.

Keeping his voice low and calm, he asked Erik for a can of oats. "Sprinkle them along the top of the wall brace here above his head. And if you have a rawhide lariat, tie it high around this first beam, but not out of reach."

"You think to distract him?"

"Hope is more like it. There's no distracting him from the pain, but maybe we can take his mind off it for a minute. If not, we'll need to cast him down. But we'll have a head start on it by scotching up his good leg."

"Where do you want your saddlebags?"

Clay glanced at the boy outside the stall. A couple years shy of manhood, he'd handled Duster well. "Hang 'em over the stall door here, then bring me a pan of soapy water. If you can warm it first at Erik's forge, that'd be good. Make it as soapy as you can get it." Looking at him straight on, he added, "You do have soap here, don't you?"

"Yes, sir."

He'd not been called *sir* when he was here last, and the word felt misplaced. The boy was a mirror image of himself at that age.

Clay washed his hands, then cleaned the wound, as well as his needle and surgical instruments, with carbolic acid before attempting to probe for splintered wood. Erik's brute strength anchored the rope holding up the tied leg. Without leverage, the horse couldn't fight as well, but they had to throw it anyway.

An hour later, Clay washed his hands and instruments again and rolled his sleeves down. A slippery elm poultice for swelling and pain lay snug against the sutures, held in place with twisted rags tied around the stallion's leg.

"Is *gut*." Recognition had fired in Erik's eyes halfway through the procedure, and now he offered a meaty handshake. "You are a fine doctor. *Willkommen zuhause*."

"It's good to be home." Not many men would call a livery *home*, but it'd been Clay's for a good while. The familiar smell of hay and grain, the warmth of the animals, their shuffling and whickering. It all added up to an odd sense of security.

They loosed the stallion slowly, and it lunged to its feet. Clay kept a running murmur going, his voice smooth and even, and when the horse grew accustomed to the bandages, he brought fresh water and forked hay into the rack. "Do you know anything about this horse? Who it belongs to?" He rolled his instruments into a leather pouch and returned it to his saddle bags.

"*Ja*, I think it is Cade Parker. He has been waiting for a stallion."

The news surprised Clay, for Parker hadn't been at the depot. "He'll need to be told the horse is here."

He pulled two newly minted Morgan dollars from his pocket. "Until the owner shows up, this should cover boarding for a couple of days."

Erik shook his head and stepped back. "*Nein.* It is *gut.* You are here. The horse is here. I have much to do. Settle with me for your horse later."

On the surface, the old softy was as tough as the thick leather apron he wore. He returned to his forge, where the ping of hammer on anvil again sang a familiar tune.

Erik's helper approached. "Does your gelding need anything other than the usual?"

Clay held his hand out, inviting the boy to respond in kind, and dropped a dollar in his palm. "Nothing other than good food and care."

The kid looked at the dollar as if there were fifty of them lined up, all gold.

"What's your name?"

"John Borden, sir." The boy pocketed the coin. "And thank you."

"I used to work here, John. Erik's a good man, and he'll treat you right if you hold up your end of the bargain."

John studied his boots longer than necessary, seeing as how he'd probably been wearing them for a year or two.

"You have a question?"

"Uh, yes, sir." He met Clay's eye with open honesty. "Are you one of those veter … veter-an…"

"Veterinarian." Clearly the boy had a little more respect for the profession than many folks Clay had encountered. *Quack horse doctor* was the term he'd heard most often.

"I thought so. It was mighty impressive the way you calmed that stallion, then sewed him up."

"Appreciate it, John." He swung the bags over his shoulder and reset his hat. "Let me know if anyone comes in looking for a veterinarian. Or horse doctor, as the case may be. I'll be in town for a while, staying at the hotel, but I'll check in every day, see how things are going."

"Yes, sir. I will, sir." John bobbed his head.

Clay touched his brim. "Obliged."

The hotel was at the opposite end of town, giving Clay a chance to see how things had changed. He couldn't have missed the Olin Springs Hose & Reel Company if he'd wanted to, housed across the street in a red brick building right next to the feed store. Definitely a necessary addition since his earlier days here. The tailor shop had a fancy sign painted on the window and looked to be faring well, and the *Olin Springs Gazette* was still churning out weeklies. A block down, Bozeman's Café was doing a hearty business, though the blue-checkered curtains were gone from the windows. He caught a good look at himself in the glass.

He hadn't eaten in twenty-four hours, but he couldn't very well sit down in a public place covered in blood and grime as he was. No wonder people were eyeing him on the boardwalk and whispering among themselves. He looked like he'd been dragged up the side of a mountain, and the ache in his leg said he had.

The jail sat ahead on the left, but he wanted to clean up before he saw Sheriff Wilson. He needed a hot bath, a good meal, and a clean bed. Hopefully in that order. He'd never had occasion to visit the hotel, but the way things stood, it'd be his lodging until he found a place of his own.

The ornate front door opened without a squeak or a bell, and the place seemed quiet and proper, with parlor chairs and tables set up on one side of the lobby. Fancy green-and-gold flocked wallpaper raised his hopes for a bath. He hit the brass call bell on the registration desk.

A narrow door opened behind it, and a man came out, spectacles riding his nose. A quick appraisal lifted his head a notch, and Clay got the impression the man's nose turned up a notch as well.

"How may I help you?"

Clay thought it obvious, but he'd give the fella the benefit of the doubt and hope the favor would be returned. "I need a room for at least a week."

A hasty once-over. "That will be five dollars. In advance." He didn't offer the registration book or dip pen until after Clay laid a Garfield note on the desk.

"That includes baths, correct?"

The clerk opened his mouth and closed it before the words on his face fell out between his teeth. He took a key from a rack next to the door and exchanged it for the five-dollar bill.

"It does. The bathing room is at the end of the second floor on the right."

Clay looked to his left. "Is that a café?"

Another once-over, this time with a sniff. "It is the *restaurant.* Our dinner specialty today is seasoned roast beef, glazed carrots, and julienned potatoes."

Clay picked up the key with a nod. The fella would likely faint dead away if he knew Clay thought slivered spuds didn't live up to that highfalutin' name.

At the stairs, he waited for a man descending, who stopped and looked at him curiously. No wonder, considering Clay's blood-smeared shirt. He thought the gent was Clarence Thatcher, though he'd grayed some at the temples and had a hard look around his mouth.

"Welcome to my hotel." His eyes said otherwise.

Clay didn't take kindly to liars. "You have a question, Mr. Thatcher?"

The man's white hands took hold of his lapels and his gaze narrowed. "I usually remember a face, and something about you is familiar. Have you stayed here before?"

"I'm staying for a while this trip." Since he'd signed the book, he didn't see the need to repeat himself, especially since he was now giving serious consideration to the lodging at the livery instead.

"Very good." Doubt flickered, and Clay saw the question before the man voiced it. "Did you by any chance come in on the train this morning—with a horse?"

Good old Olin Springs. Didn't take long for word to spread.

"After that trip, I'm looking forward to a hot bath." He stepped up one riser.

"Yes, of course. As I'm sure my clerk told you,"—he cut a look to the front desk—"the bathing room is at the end of the hall on the right. Running water is piped into the room. Just light the gas heater under the tub and it will quickly warm." He looked at his pocket watch and glanced toward the dining room. "We will be serving dinner in an hour and supper at six."

"I hear roast is on the menu."

The man's chest puffed against his green brocade vest, remarkably like the wallpaper, and he offered a polished smile. "Indeed. I hope you'll join us."

Clay continued up the carpeted stairs, certain he'd be visiting Hoss Bozeman before he'd eat his potatoes julienned. He preferred 'em mashed with gravy.

~

Maggie Snowfield did not wake before Sophie left for home, so she stopped by Doc Weaver's office and asked him to check on the elderly woman. More than likely, it was merely the years creeping up on her, but there was no reason not to take every precaution.

Temptation pulled hard as Sophie rode through town. The livery called. She was itching to know how the situation had worked out with the stallion and the stranger, but what would she say if she bumped into him? Best let things play out in their own time and not set herself up as a busybody.

As she passed the hotel, she looked squarely at the sheriff's office across the street, avoiding any chance sighting of Clarence Thatcher. She wouldn't put it past the man to be standing at his overly large front window, hoping to snag her on her way out of town so he could further discuss a railing to the Eisner's apartment.

"Miss Price!"

Lord, help her. Hurried footsteps followed his voice into the street.

Heeling the mare for a fast getaway would only land her in the back of a slow-moving farm wagon ahead. Could she simply ignore the man? Pretend she hadn't heard?

He reached for the mare and it shied to the left, into the path of several riders who yelled at Sophie for not watching where she was going.

Digging her heels in, she turned the mare's backside against the interfering oaf. He stumbled back.

As annoyed as she was, Mama hadn't taught her to be rude. "Mr. Thatcher—I didn't see you." Which was true at first.

He gathered himself, tugging on the bottom of his waistcoat, clearly put out and a bit unbalanced. "I hoped to speak with you before you left the tailor shop."

She bit the inside of her cheek, stifling words that rushed toward escape.

He reached again for the mare's headstall, and she reined back. "Please don't grab her, Mr. Thatcher. It makes her nervous when strangers do that." Which was not true at all. It made *Sophie* nervous, though *irritable* was a more accurate word.

"My apologies." He raised both hands shoulder high, as if being held at gunpoint.

She stifled the image.

"What do you need, sir?"

"Please, call me Clarence." He pushed up a stiff flap of fading hair that had fallen across his forehead. "I thought we could discuss the Eisner's need for a handrail over dinner at the hotel. I don't believe you've had the pleasure of dining here, and today's specialty is most delightful."

"Thank you, but I'm on my way to an appointment. Perhaps another time."

She squeezed her legs, signaling the mare forward.

Mr. Thatcher hopscotched ahead.

"But doesn't Mrs. Eisner need the railing as soon as possible. I thought you said—"

Her glare cut him off, and he fumbled for his verbal footing.

She did not consider herself mean or cruelhearted, so she regrouped, shortening her hold on the reins as well as her manners. "Mr. Thatcher, it would be best if you discussed this with Mr. Eisner. He can show you the stairway and work out a time schedule with you. As you say, sooner would be better than later." He clearly missed her darted look. "Your concern for Mrs. Eisner's safety is noted. Good day."

The mare sensed her eagerness to leave, but Sophie held a tight rein, walking rather than galloping away from the fuming man standing in the middle of Main Street.

# CHAPTER 4

From the window of his hotel room, Clay had a good view of several businesses, as well as the saloon, jail, and Clarence Thatcher running out in front of a horse on Main Street.

Sophie's horse.

Protectiveness fired through Clay, hot and hair-triggered.

Was Thatcher a fool?

Sophie Price knew how to sit a horse, and she handled the situation well, though he couldn't be sure if she'd deliberately turned the nag's hind quarters into the man or not. The idea brought a smile to Clay's lips.

He ran his fingers back through his damp hair and over his shaved chin. It felt good to feel clean. He hadn't seen a laundry on his walk from the livery, but he'd ask around. He'd also pick up a copy of the latest paper and inquire about available land in the area. Not inclined to open an account at the bank, he left his money in a hidden pocket of his saddle bags, grabbed his hat, and set out for Bozeman's.

As he closed the hotel's front door behind him, Sheriff Wilson came out of his office. Clay adjusted his course and crossed the street.

"Sheriff." He stepped up onto the boardwalk and offered his hand. "Good to see you again."

Garrett Wilson gave him a guarded look, taking in his boots, clean shirt, and lack of a sidearm. "Do I know—" His expression relaxed, and he gipped Clay's upper arm and tightened his handshake.

"Clay Ferguson."

His obvious pleasure struck a note of welcome. The second one that day.

"I didn't know if I'd ever see you again."

Clay swallowed the knot trying to block his words. "It's good to be back."

"I'm headed to Bozeman's. Care to join me?" Garrett slapped him on the shoulder and took a step in that direction.

"Don't mind if I do. I'm goin' the same way."

At the top of the noon hour, Bozeman's was brimming over. Apparently, not many locals took to glazed carrots and julienned potatoes. Even so, Garrett found a table in the corner and took the seat with his back to the wall.

"I thought you'd be goin' home for dinner," Clay said, hanging his hat on his knee.

Garrett did the same and uprighted his cup on the table. "I do about half the time. But Olin Springs is growing fast, and I'd just as soon keep an ear to the ground and an eye peeled. This is about the best place to do it."

Hoss Bozeman approached with his camp-sized coffee pot, and Clay turned his cup over.

"I got beans with side pork and hot buttered cornbread, Sheriff." He nodded at Clay, then took a harder look.

"You remember Clay Ferguson?" Garrett grinned like he and Clay were blood kin. In Clay's book, they might as well be.

The cookie's face split with a wide grin. "I thought you looked familiar. Had me goin' for a minute there. I pride myself on knowin' everyone who eats here."

"It's been a few years."

"I seem to recall how you cottoned to my bear sign, but I'm fresh out today. Come back tomorrow for breakfast and I'll fill your gullet."

Clay nodded, spilling a smile. "I'll be sure to do that."

After Hoss left, Garrett took a swig of hot coffee and winced. "His cookin's passable, but his brew gets a might thick by dinner."

Clay lifted his cup. The smell alone could sterilize his surgical instruments.

"When did you get in?"

"This morning on the train."

Garrett's attention slid to a man cutting through the tables toward them.

"Excuse me, Sheriff." He turned to Clay. "Ain't you the fella led that locoed stallion off the train this mornin'?"

Garrett's eyes narrowed a degree.

"He's not locoed. Just scared and hurt is all. We got him settled down."

The man stuck his hand out, and Clay shook it.

"Fine job is all I can say. I was there. I seen what you done. So did half the town, I'd say, by the crowd. It's an honor to meet you."

Unfamiliar words, at best. "Appreciate it." Now was as good a time as any. "If you know of anyone needing a veterinarian, leave word at the livery. I'll be checking in there a couple times every day."

The man chuckled, then cut it off as if caught making a rude joke. "Sorry, son. But most folks around here do their own horse doctorin'. But if I come across a snot-slingin' bronc, I'll be sure to stop by."

He stepped back and nodded at Garrett before going back to his table.

A few stares followed him, then swung back to Clay. He went for his coffee again.

"So you're the one." Garrett's gray eyes smiled a little, and he leaned against the back of his chair. "Heard all about what you did."

Clay took a swallow and let it burn a path to his empty stomach. "I'm sure the story grew by the time it reached your ears."

"You singled-handedly dragged a bleeding, screaming stallion off a cattle car and through a crowd of onlookers without injury to yourself or anyone standing by. Made quite an impression on folks. I'm sure it made the paper too."

"I didn't exactly drag him, but I have Deacon Jewett to thank for that skill."

"So what really happened?"

Clay leaned his arms on the table. "Someone put that hot-blooded horse on a stock car with no handler. Tied it to the wall for who knows how long, and by the time the train pulled in this morning, it was terrified, frustrated, and kicking at anything it could reach, including the louvered car walls. I think I might have been lathered up too if I'd been in that condition."

Garrett's low laugh revealed his agreement. "So why were you on the car?"

"With my horse. I wasn't about to leave him in there unattended."

The sheriff's keen eyes skimmed the room, and he deftly switched leads on the conversation. "So you finished school."

Not a question. A man like Garrett Wilson knew everything about his town, so he probably knew who'd paid for Clay's schooling. "And worked a year in St. Louis with a veterinarian there who taught me more than I learned in two years at Iowa State College.

"Why'd you leave and come back here?"

Clay didn't mind the sheriff's third degree, but he was happy to see Hoss bring two plates of beans and cornbread. The smell of it settled in around him like a promise kept.

They set to, and talk gave way to hungry men enjoying a hot meal. A better meal than Clay'd had all the way from Kansas City. But from what he remembered about the Snowfield place, where Garrett and his wife were living when Clay left, Bozeman's cooking more than likely came in just under the high-water mark.

Before they finished, three more men stopped by the table to comment on the morning's excitement at the depot. The last fella congratulated Clay on his skill with a needle, and he wondered if Erik was charging admission to see the sutured stallion.

By then, his cornbread was cold and Garrett's eyes were permanently crinkled from holding in his thoughts. "Next time, we'll go home," he said with a teasing edge. "Less traffic."

The reference jerked Clay's mind to the near collision this morning in front of the hotel. "Speaking of traffic, there was a close call earlier in front of the jail. You happen to see it?"

Garrett filled his mouth with the last of his cornbread and nodded, then washed it down with coffee. "Sophie Price is more horsewoman than most, and Clarence Thatcher is lucky she didn't run him over. He'll do just about anything to get her attention."

Clay's jaw clenched.

Perceptive as always, Garrett registered the reaction. "So that's why you came back."

"Not entirely." Clay took another swig of coffee. He owed Garrett Wilson. The man had saved his young stubborn hide four years ago.

*Works on horses and dogs—it'll work on you*, Garrett had said of the ointment he spread on a sixteen-year-old's torn flesh. From what Clay knew now about infection, the sheriff literally as well as figuratively gave him a fighting chance. And he'd trusted Clay when he didn't have to.

"This is home. More home than I've ever had. I intend to settle here, buy my own place, and pay back the folks who gave me a leg up."

Garrett sobered. He remembered. He remembered everything, Clay was certain.

The voice quieted, gray eyes softened. "Seein' you turn out on the right side is all me or anyone else wants."

Hearing it from Garrett Wilson himself soothed a wound in Clay that ran deeper than skin and bone. Just like the man's salve had soothed his lacerated back in that jail cell.

His sense of direction solidified. Now all he had to do was convince Sophie Price he was worth her attention.

~

Once Sophie made the outskirts of town, she'd nudged the mare into an easy lope, but not for long. The old girl was nearly Sophie's age, which, thinking of it in those terms, made Sophie feel decrepit and slow the horse to a walk. She leaned over to pat its neck. Some things aged better than others. And some things blossomed with the years. Like her mother.

Deacon Jewett had seen to that. The man lit up Mama's face like a robin's breast every time he rode out to the farm.

Deacon was a bright spot in all their lives for certain. If not for him, much would remain undone around the farm, and their windmill would not be patched up, pampered along, and nursed back to health. She knew Mama didn't like him climbing up to work on the persnickety old thing, but they needed water, and he'd horse-traded Todd into digging a ditch to the garden once the windmill worked consistently.

That was miracle enough. Her little brother avoided sweat like hogs avoided butchers.

No, Mama didn't like Deacon working on the windmill. Sophie wasn't fond of the idea herself, for a rotted board on the platform had caused her pa's fall to his death. The memory cowered like a wounded animal at the back of her heart, and she fingered the corner of her mouth, wondering if Deacon knew.

Of course it was allowed that he was sweet on Mama, but it made Sophie feel like an ugly spinster sister. What if he proposed before Sophie heard a similar question from anyone other than Clarence Thatcher?

She had no prospects other than the ever-insistent hotelier, and she shuddered, preferring to end up like the mother she adored rather than that man's wife. Travine Price had survived the last decade and more as a proud, wrinkle-cut farm woman, alone aside from her children.

The only difference was Sophie had no children.

Meadow larks called from one side of the road to the other, two echoing the first in a springtime trio. The lilting song lifted Sophie's heart as she turned off the road where Parker Land and Cattle spread itself green and speckled with wildflowers. She'd promised Mae Ann she'd stop in on her way back from town.

Doc Weaver had encouraged the visit as well since Sophie lived nearby. For a professional man, he did a poor job of hiding his concern over Mae Ann's condition. But Sophie was glad to help. She'd grown fond of Mae Ann—so close to her own age—and the Parkers' little boy, Willy. William Cade Parker, III, to be precise. There was no prouder papa than Cade Parker, unless it was Sheriff Wilson over little George.

The sheriff hadn't come home while Sophie visited Betsy, and it was just as well. Betsy would have certainly asked him straight out if he knew whether Clay Ferguson had returned to Olin Springs, and Sophie wasn't prepared to avoid the man's discerning eye.

The mare broke into a trot, jarring Sophie from her musings that had clearly spread to the horse. If the mare knew, how easily would everyone else pick up on her pathetic pretense?

In the brief year she'd known Clay before he left, she'd never heard him mention his own parents. Not a word about a mother who might have smoothed a boy's rough ways and taught him gentle words. Nothing about sisters or brothers. It was as if he had no past, no connections. Yet one thing she knew for certain—he connected with animals. His kindness was evident. A firm kindness that stirred confidence in the horses he handled. Just like the stranger had with the stallion that morning.

The man's quiet strength eddied through her, drawing her to him in an unexplained way. But the memory of his blue gaze sent a shiver up her spine.

The Parker barn rose ahead of her, its roof mimicking mountain peaks that rose to the west. She'd always admired the Parker ranch, its neat, sturdy buildings and corrals. Not a lazy thing on it as far as she could tell. Even the windmill worked. Maybe that boded well for Deacon's help at her family's farm.

She looped her reins on the hitch rail at the big log house, much more impressive than her meager home at the farm. A flagstone porch spread invitingly before the wide front door, and unlit lanterns hung on either side, inviting and offering respite.

The ranch dogs, Blue and Mae Ann's Cougar, flagged about Sophie's skirt, whining and squirming their welcome, happy as only dogs can be about a familiar guest willing to stoop and rub their backs.

She looked up as Cade Parker came out the front door, disheveled and agitated, Willy in his arms and concern riding his features.

"Sophie. I'm glad you're here. Mae Ann's upstairs not feeling well. Would you mind going on up? I'll tend to your horse and bring in your bag."

Her pulse skipped. Mae Ann's delivery of Willy had been hard, and Sophie had believed it was because he was the first baby. But maybe Doc Weaver was right to be concerned.

She let herself in, relishing the cool shadows of the great room with its broad stone fireplace and hide-covered floors. A piano stood against one inside wall, and a large desk sat beneath a front window, bookcases lining the remainder of the wall. She took the log stairs that climbed to the second story, paying special attention to the peeled railing that edged them on both sides all the way to the landing. More had gone into this home than into an upstairs apartment in town.

She knocked quietly on the master bedroom door and peeked in before entering. Mae Ann lay propped against several pillows, eyes closed. The window curtains wavered in a tepid breeze.

"It's Sophie."

Mae Ann's eyes fluttered open as if she'd been in a deep sleep, but she reached out.

Sophie pulled the rocker close to the edge of the bed, pleased to find Mae Ann's hand neither clammy nor too warm.

"Thank you for coming. I know you must be busy."

"Not too busy to check on you. How do you feel?"

"Weak as water." Mae Ann's less-than-enthusiastic smile underscored her choice of words.

Sophie had previously calculated the due date, which, if Mae Ann went the full forty weeks, would be early May. "Are you resting most of the day?"

"Just as you and Doc Weaver ordered. Plenty of bed rest."

"And what about your food? Is Cade preparing meals for you?"

At Mae Ann's sideways glance, Sophie guessed the answer.

"He has so much he needs to do. I hate to ask him to do more."

"I happen to know the man can cook. He survived before you came, remember?"

Mae Ann laughed weakly, but no color flushed her cheeks.

Sophie pulled her hand away and brushed Mae Ann's temple. No fever, but a listlessness filled Mae Ann's eyes. The woman was wearing herself out, and if she weren't careful, Cade Parker would be cooking his own meals again, this time permanently.

Sophie refused to let that happen.

"May I have a look at you? See how you're progressing?"

Mae Ann nodded. "Then we can go to the kitchen for coffee."

"Or I can bring chamomile tea to you. Right now, I'd prefer you not try to maneuver the stairs until you get your strength back."

She didn't want to frighten the woman—just as she hadn't wanted to frighten Abigail Eisner. But neither seemed to realize what a fall could do. To both the mother and the unborn child.

Sophie washed and dried her hands at the washstand and satisfied herself that Mae Ann was not facing a premature birth. Not yet anyway. The babe had not dropped into position, as best she could tell, but going up and down stairs had to stop. Which meant Sophie might be moving into Betsy's old room at the end of the landing. She could prepare things here for Mae Ann and Cade, giving herself time to visit Abigail in town and be back by nightfall.

And she'd pray that both babies didn't come at the same time.

# CHAPTER 5

The laundry was a block south of the hotel, so Clay stopped by the newspaper office and the mercantile before going back for his soiled clothes. Sure enough, a front-page headline read:

**MYSTERIOUS STRANGER RESCUES INJURED STALLION**

**Avoids Disaster at Depot**

So much for mention of a veterinarian in town.

With the paper tucked under his arm, he entered the bell-topped entrance of Reynold's mercantile and straight back to his earlier days in Olin Springs. Tobacco, pickles, oiled leather, and spices filled his senses before he stepped around a display of fancy soap and into a gal bent over, unpacking a box.

"Oh!"

Without thinking, he grabbed her arms and helped her straighten. "My apologies, miss. I wasn't watching where I was going."

She brushed herself off, then looked up with a scowl that quickly faded into wonder. "Clay? Is that you, Clay Ferguson?"

He wasn't sure, but he thought she might be Fred and Willa Reynolds' daughter, a gal in pigtails last time he'd seen her.

"Yes. Miss Reynolds, is it? Clay Ferguson." He doffed his hat. "Pleased to make your acquaintance. Again."

She offered her hand and with the other pushed at the back of her hair. "It's Sarah. Please call me Sarah."

Her father cleared his throat—audible across the store.

She batted her eyes. "I heard you went away to school. Veterinary school, is that right?"

More batting.

"Yes, ma'am. Miss."

"Sarah."

"Of course." He tugged his hand from her not-so-gentle hold and took a couple steps back. "Just stocking up." He plunked his hat on and headed straight to the canned goods for a few tins of fruit, then filled a sack with jerked beef.

Fred Reynolds waited behind the counter drawing a bead on Clay's every move. Either he'd seen the incident at the depot or he was keeping tabs on his daughter.

"Afternoon, Mr. Reynolds. I'll take a can of Bickmore saddle soap and a box of matches." He eyed a black Stetson in a side display and a cotton-backed wool vest with deep pockets, but settled on another shirt and leather gloves from a glass-topped case. Recalling spring in Colorado, he also picked out a couple pairs of socks.

While Reynolds wrapped his purchases, he snatched up the vest and tried it on.

"You look very fine in that vest, Clay."

The sing-songy lilt of her voice made him skittish, but he managed a polite nod. He paid his tab and escaped the mercantile without getting corralled by Sarah Reynolds or shot by her pa. He wasn't sure which would have been worse.

After stashing his food and clothes in his hotel room, he took his laundry down the street and decided to pay Maggie Snowfield a visit.

The trees in the woman's apple orchard filled the air with perfume, in full blossom and promising a good crop if a late freeze didn't kill things off. He opened the spired gate, recalling the last time he'd walked through, leading Garrett's roan out with that sleazy lawyer draped over the saddle—Rochester. What a night that was.

Mounting the steps to the wide porch, he hoped things were well with Mrs. Snowfield. He wanted to thank her while he had a chance.

Her doorbell buzzed—another memory from his recent past—and soon footsteps approached the finely carved door that opened at Betsy Wilson's hand.

She stared, slack-jawed, then clapped her mouth shut and moved aside, all mannerly and proper. "Clay, please come in. I heard you were back in town."

He took off his hat and stepped into the entryway, taking in the fine furnishings, polished floor, and oak banister that led to the second floor. All the same as he'd left it. He and Garrett had dragged Rochester down those very stairs, out cold as a dead fish.

"Mrs. Wilson, ma'am."

"Oh, for goodness sake, Clay, come here and let me give you a hug."

Betsy Parker Wilson always had been unconventional, and he guessed this was his day for meeting progressive women.

"Betsy, did I hear you say Clay Ferguson?"

A thin but authoritative voice cut out through the parlor doorway, and Betsy pointed him in that direction.

Maggie Snowfield reclined on the settee, her white topknot in place and a shawl around her shoulders. Her face bloomed into a smile, and she extended both arms.

"Clay, it *is* you. Come give this old woman a hug and let me have a good look at you."

He took a knee by the velvet couch, and she cupped his face between her cold hands. His heart hitched at the signs, and he was glad he hadn't waited to stop by.

"I'll get another tea service while you two chat," Betsy said behind him. "Or would you prefer coffee, Clay?"

He stood to face her. "Coffee, if you have it, ma'am."

She raised her chin and plunked her hands at her waist. "Call me ma'am or Mrs. Wilson again, and I'll lace that coffee with licorice root."

He laughed, inwardly cringing at the thought of such a mix. "Thank you, Betsy."

When she left, he pulled a fancy chair next to the settee and took Maggie's hands again. "I want to thank you for what you did."

"Oh, posh." She fussed and shook her head. "It was my pleasure. I have no grandsons of my own to encourage along in their future, and to see you here, looking so well, simply does my heart good. I know you finished your schooling, because the registrar kept me up to date. I couldn't be more proud."

He swallowed around a lump big enough to lame a sound horse and had to clear his throat a couple of times. "I'll never be able to repay you."

Pulling her hands free, she waved his words aside. "Say no more, young man. That is as it should be. You can keep an eye on my Lolly for me. She's getting up in years, you know, just like me. And take a good look at my barn. See if it needs any repairs."

"I'd be happy to." As he stood, he leaned in and kissed the top of her head.

She blinked several times like she had something in her eye, and he pulled the chair to the foot of the settee as Betsy returned with his coffee.

"Where are you staying, Clay? You know I have several empty rooms here in this big drafty house."

"I'm at the hotel for the time being, but I appreciate your offer. I'm looking to get my own place soon, but I'll let you know how things go."

He tried the coffee and was relieved that it hadn't cooked down like Hoss Bozeman's.

"A place of your own, you say? I have a friend on the Library Committee who is thinking of selling her small ranch. Her husband has passed on, you know, and it's too much for her to look after and keep her hired help in line. I'll ask her more about it and let you know. May I leave a message at the hotel?"

No telling what *small ranch* meant to Maggie Snowfield, but he'd not turn down her kind offer. "You may, ma'am, and I appreciate it."

Feeling Betsy's bold stare, he cut a sideways glance and confirmed his suspicion. "Good coffee."

She checked herself, as if she'd drifted off on some wild goose chase. "Pardon me, I'm just so surprised to see you. Especially after what Sophie said earlier—"

Her fingers fluttered at her mouth, attempting to snatch back the words. But they'd already flown around the parlor and perched on his shoulder, echoing in his ear.

*Sophie had told her.*

~

The day's spring warmth dwindled into the cool of early evening, and Sophie let her tension slide away with it. At the mare's gentle plodding, she loosened her hold on events, slowing her thoughts to the same unhurried pace, looking at each one individually, rather than bunching them all together in a wild stampede. She could do only one thing at a time. Why did she always try to do more?

The mysterious yet familiar stranger.

Abigail Eisner's timidity.

Clarence Thatcher's idiocy.

And Mae Ann's weakness.

She drew in the sweet breath of evening—her favorite time of day when earth and animal settled and night birds laced their lonely songs through scrub oak and cedar. A coyote called not far away, answered by another, and soon was joined by a yipping crowd, no doubt celebrating the demise of a hapless rabbit or two.

And the deeper the sun slid into the western peaks, the deeper her conviction that the stranger was Clay Ferguson.

She shook her head to clear his image. He should be the least of her concerns, the one that deserved the least of her attention. But he hovered above all other thoughts like an insistent hummingbird refusing to sink into the shadows where it belonged.

She kept clear of rock outcroppings where snakes sunned themselves by day and cougars ambushed at dusk. But she also kept one eye on the mare's ears, for the horse would tell her if danger lurked nearby.

The country was never predictable. Gentle grasslands on one hand, a predator's lair on the other. Everything around her seemed to sigh in expectation of rest, and she relaxed in her seat, unprepared for a dash from the left that set the mare back with a snort.

Sophie yanked on the reins, and a doe bounded from a thicket and across the trail, two fawns on its heels. She waited, leaning forward to pat the old mare's quivering neck, and two more mule deer sprang across in front of them. A family.

So much for paying attention.

"Easy, girl. We just got in their way. Best be getting on now."

She heeled the mare into a trot, and soon the windmill rose against the horizon, catching the falling sunlight on its wide blades. The slow churning came to her before she made the yard, its metallic moan a rough imitation of her own emotions.

Daylight slipped undercover as she dismounted at the barn, and their old hound ran to greet her, baying his welcome, tail flailing to beat the band.

"Good boy, Dudley." She scratched his back and patted her approval, then unsaddled the mare, brushed her, and turned her out in the near pasture.

*Take care o' your horse afore yourself.* Another of Deacon's lessons. The ornery old cowboy was full of stories and proverbs, and often kept the family laughing of an evening around the supper table. Riding home in the dark didn't hinder him from staying as late as possible.

Truth be told, Sophie could no longer imagine her mother without him.

Two sides of her heart tugged against each other, threatening to tear in half as she mounted the back-porch steps. How could she be so double-minded where her dear mama was concerned—jealous on the one hand and happy on the other? *Sweet water and bitter hadn't ought to flow from the same spring*, Pastor Bittman once said.

"Sophie. I was worried about you." Her mother looked up from the table, where she was setting plates and cups, lamplight rinsing her grayed temples with a soft ochre glow. "It's near dark. Did everything go all right in town today?"

Sophie left her satchel on a stool in the corner by the shotgun, washed her hands at the sink, then tied on an apron. "Yes and no."

Todd and Deacon stomped in the back door before she could elaborate.

"You boys wash up." Her mother tipped her head toward the sink. "Then help yourself to coffee. Supper will be ready in no time."

"We ain't *boys,* Ma. We're men." Todd took offense at any comment he considered a slight to his manhood, delicate though it was in Sophie's opinion.

"Speak for yourself," Deacon said, blue eyes sparking as if he were fourteen with peach fuzz on his face rather than a full silver mustache.

Mama swatted his shoulder as she passed behind him, failing to hide her Deacon-smile, as Sophie called it, though not out loud.

"I forgot to bring in more milk." Her mother dashed out the screen door.

Deacon caught it before it slapped shut. "I'll help."

Todd rolled his eyes and dried his hands, then poured a mug of coffee. His reaction to the pair was the one opinion he and Sophie shared without reservation.

She broke sausage into the skillet Mama had heating, then pulled the flour canister closer to the stove.

Laughter danced through the screen as Deacon opened it. Mama entered first and set the milk jar on the counter, her cheeks blooming like summer roses in the lamp's orange glow, tempting Sophie to jealousy.

Shamed by her self-centeredness, Sophie sprinkled a handful of flour over the crumbled sausage, stirred until it browned in the hot grease, and added milk, salt, and pepper.

Biscuits fresh from the oven, hot coffee, and a bowl of sausage gravy would help them all sleep well until sunup.

Seated next to Mama at the table, Deacon held out his hands, one to her and one to Todd, and Sophie caught the little squeeze he pressed into Mama's fingers. "Thank you, Lord, for this family, this food, and this farm. 'Men."

Sophie kept her head bowed an extra beat, repeating the brief prayer, burying it deep within her for future reference. She had much for which to be grateful.

"Who did you see in town today?" Mama took a biscuit and passed the pan to Sophie.

*Clay Ferguson.* "Mrs. Eisner, the tailor's wife. She's near her time, and I stopped by Betsy Wilson's to see if I could stay with her for a week or so to be closer. All the Eisners' family is in Chicago."

Deacon glanced up in the subsequent silence. "Cade's missus is nearin' her time as well." He mumbled in his mustache, plainly uncomfortable about the subject. So why had he mentioned it?

Sophie knew for a fact that he'd delivered foals and calves himself, but talking about such things with women at the table made him squirm like bait on a hook, worse than Abigail Eisner.

Sophie was doing her own share of secret squirming. "You're right, Deacon. I stopped there on my way home. That's why I got in so late."

"Just so's you know, spring brandin's comin' up and then Cade's goin' to Denver to talk beeves with a buyer up there for this fall. Last he said, he'll be pullin' out in a week and gone for two or three."

The news didn't help supper settle, and again Sophie felt herself pulled in opposite directions.

"I wanna help gather," Todd said, looking all of six begging for an Arbuckles' peppermint stick instead of his full sixteen years.

Deacon met his gaze. "I know ya do, son, but your ma needs ya' here while we're tied up." His pale-blue eyes shifted to Sophie. "And the missus is gonna need you with her at the ranch."

"Oh dear." Mama said.

Sophie's thoughts exactly. How could she stay down-the-hall close for Mae Ann and in town for Abigail Eisner at the same time?

# CHAPTER 6

Sunday morning, Sophie packed a carpet bag with extra clothes and tied it with her satchel to the mare's saddle just in case.

Todd had brought the wagon around to the house, and Mama climbed in, none too happy about everyone not riding together.

Deacon had left last night after dark, insisting Cade needed him. Sophie's guess was he needed Deacon to ride for help if the baby came early.

"It's better this way, Mama. If Abigail is as far along as I believe she is, I'll be staying in town. And I'll be more comfortable knowing I can ride out to the ranch if Mae Ann needs me. It's simply easier to ride than drive the wagon."

"I know." Mama smoothed her skirt and fussed with her hat pin. "I just don't like it is all."

Her mother had always kept the family close and together, ever since Pa died, but times were changing. Sophie was a grown woman, and it wouldn't be long before Todd made his own decision about staying on at the farm. Honestly, Deacon was the only thing Mama had to look forward to. Sophie wouldn't be giving her grandchildren anytime soon.

They all set out for town, riding into the sun. Sophie lagged behind the wagon, and every so often Mama looked back, no doubt making sure she was still there.

Wild primrose, pasqueflower, and sagebrush buttercups sprinkled pink and yellow and white across the greening countryside. A few meadow larks called to one another, but the closer to town, the farther apart their melodic echoes. They sang where noise and activity were silenced, and Sophie missed their song as she rode onto Main Street.

The field next to the church was packed with buggies, and horses lined the hitch rails. She looked for a handsome buckskin, realizing both Deacon and the horse handler rode one, but none were there. She tied the mare to the back of the wagon.

Todd handed Mama down, and the three of them entered together. Sophie hadn't expected Cade and Mae Ann, due to Mae Ann's condition, but Maggie Snowfield wasn't there either, for Betsy, Sheriff Wilson, and little George sat by themselves in the back row.

Antsy throughout the songs and sermon, Sophie couldn't keep her mind from wandering from Mae Ann to Abigail to Clay Ferguson. She itched to know if he'd come in late and stood at the back but couldn't bring herself to turn around and look. Sometimes decorum was just plain annoying.

Clay used to come to church when he lived there before, but he and his past habits were not the topic of the morning. What was that Scripture Pastor Bittman just read? She glanced at her mother's Bible, open to Isaiah 66. Something about peace like a river.

Shamefully overflowing with impatience rather than peace, at Bittman's closing *amen*, Sophie was out of the pew and marching toward the back.

And there, next to the door, stood the horse handler, hat in hand, watching her.

She stopped and stared. Clay Ferguson in the flesh, shoulders straight, feet planted wide. Today there was no doubt.

A near smile eased into his blue eyes, but they sobered as his gaze shifted beyond her.

"Excuse me, please."

Startled by the voice, she glanced back to apologize for blocking the aisle, only to bite down on the words. Clarence Thatcher smirked like he'd won the ring toss at the country fair.

"Miss Price. How fortuitous that we meet this way." He extended his hand toward the exit as if she might not find her way otherwise. "Perhaps we could visit for a moment about the Eisner's handrail."

When she looked ahead again, several men had corralled Clay, and her expectations wilted. Passing by, her eyes drifted his way and found him deep in the moment, discussing fever and punctured lungs.

It was just as well. What would she say? *Oh, Clay, how you've grown!* Heavens.

Once outside, she turned rather abruptly, lacking societal grace and completely devoid of Christian charity.

"Mr. Thatcher. I believe I explained the situation quite plainly to you earlier. Take the matter up with Mr. Eisner. Good day."

If he followed her around the side of the church, she might inflict bodily harm.

Fortunately for the hotel owner, he did *not* follow her.

By the time Mama and Todd reached the wagon, she was in the saddle gathering frowns from church matrons who clearly disapproved of her riding astride in her Sunday best. She blew a kiss to her mother who waved and nodded, and then turned down the street toward the Eisners' shop.

At the corner, she opted for the alley entrance. The stairs were closer to the back door than the front.

She tethered the mare to a hitching post, climbed two steps to the small stoop, and banged on the door, still riled over Clarence Thatcher.

After a few moments, Mr. Eisner appeared.

"Miss Price." His tight greeting was no less comforting than the pinch of his brows. "Thank you for coming. Abigail is upstairs …" He rubbed his left arm. "It is good you have come."

Satchel in hand, Sophie hurried up the stairs fully appreciating the lack of railing that would have provided some comfort at the sharp turn near the top. The treads diminished into pie-shaped slices, leaving less foot space on each one than the already narrow passage offered. The situation was intolerable. Abigail Eisner was the one who belonged at Maggie Snowfield's spacious home, not Sophie.

The stairs led not to a landing, but into an open area that served as kitchen, sitting room, and bedroom. Abigail lay on the bed in obvious agony, clutched in the tight grip of birth pangs. Hand railings were no longer important.

"Mr. Eisner." Sophie placed her satchel at the foot of the bed and faced Abigail's husband, short on time and chit-chat. "Heat water and pour it in the wash basin.

Bring me a bowl of cool water and whatever towels you have, then go downstairs and wait until I call for you."

The man stood nailed in place, mouth ajar, eyes wide.

"Now, Hiram, if not sooner."

Once he started moving, Sophie closed her eyes and whispered an urgent prayer. Something was not right. "Oh, Lord, I know You are with us in our hour of need. This is Abigail's hour."

A high-pitched squeal brought her about, and she leaned close to the woman, taking her hand. "Don't push, Abigail. Not yet."

As was always the case regardless of a woman's strength or stature, the young mother's grip would have shamed the blacksmith. Sophie wrenched her hand free, twisted one of the towels Hiram brought, and wrapped Abigail's fingers around it.

He set the washstand near and poured water in the basin, then pulled a small table closer, upon which he set the bowl of cool water.

"Thank you, Mr. Eisner. I will call for you soon."

And she did. Much sooner than she'd hoped.

~

Clay welcomed the local inquisition after church, but the men blocked his view of Sophie and kept him from speaking to her outside. They also kept him from shoving the sneer down Clarence Thatcher's throat—the one he'd thrown at Clay as he followed Sophie out the door. Clay desperately wanted to turn the man's other cheek, but that was likely a misinterpretation of a Scripture he'd heard a few years back.

Sophie and nearly everyone else was gone by the time he left to walk back to the hotel. He hadn't seen Maggie at the service, though the Wilsons were there. Concern skirted the back of his brain, and since witnessing her frailty the other day, he changed course and walked to her home on Saddle Blossom Lane instead.

Garrett met him at the front door, as did a waft of roasted beef and homemade bread.

"You're just in time, Clay. We intended to invite you for dinner, but you were pretty well cornered at the church."

Clay hooked his hat on the entryway hall tree. "Much obliged. I came to check on Maggie. Is she still not feeling well?"

"Still?" Garrett threw a look toward the kitchen.

Clay filled him in on his earlier visit as they made their way to the dining room.

"Have a seat and I'll get coffee." Which translated as "sit down while I talk to my wife."

Not much had changed since Garrett and Betsy's reception. The same massive table anchored the room, covered in a fancy cloth and surrounded by matching chairs. Three place settings were laid in the center of the table rather than at the ends, and he took a chair facing the kitchen door.

"Hello, Clay." Betsy entered with a platter of sliced roast.

He stood. "Betsy," he offered, recalling her threat if he used *ma'am* or *Mrs. Wilson.*

Garrett followed with a gravy bowl and mashed potatoes, and Betsy went back for green beans with salt pork and onions, and that fresh bread Clay had smelled.

Clarence Thatcher's fancy chef could learn a thing or two.

A squall sent Betsy upstairs, and she soon returned with a tow-headed youngster who lit up Garrett's face at the sight of him.

He took the boy and dragged a highchair from the corner in between two seats on the opposite side of the table. "George, say howdy to Clay Ferguson. Olin Springs' new veterinarian."

Mussed hair framed two watery eyes that stared across the table at Clay.

He chuckled. "Howdy, little fella. Looks like you just woke up."

Serious as an undertaker, the boy never blinked.

A half hour later, after eating enough to fill his saddle bags, Clay thought he might not make it back to the hotel. He hadn't eaten so much in he couldn't remember how long. "As fine a feast as I ever had, Betsy. Thank you."

"She's a good cook," Garrett said with a wink at his wife. "Had to let my belt out."

She blushed as she wiped off the baby's hands and face. "I learned everything I know from Maggie."

Clay figured he was sitting in the widow's seat. "Does she miss many meals?"

Betsy flicked her husband a look. "She's been overly tired lately. I'll take a little something to her room when she wakens."

Clay laid his silverware on the plate and rose. "I'm gonna check on Lolly and then poke around the barn. Maggie charged me with keeping them both in good condition."

Garrett lifted George from his chair. "We'll go with you."

Tied to an iron bench behind the house, Garrett's gangly dog lunged as they skirted the length of its lead.

George slapped his hands against Garrett's head and squealed.

Garrett grabbed the youngster's hands. "Pearl. Can you say Pearl?"

Surprised to see the dog, Clay laughed. "I see she's still with you."

Garrett huffed. "Much to Maggie's delight but not Betsy's. I keep Pearl with me at the jail during the week, but Maggie dotes on her ever since she snagged the fire bug who torched her barn."

Clay remembered well. He'd nearly been mistaken for that bug himself.

The afternoon sun cut through his new vest with a summer-like intensity, and he hung the vest on a nail in the barn and rolled up his sleeves. Lolly was a sweet old mare that had definitely seen better days, and in Clay's line of work, he understood all too well the inevitability of old age.

He checked her teeth and felt for heat in her legs. She was sound in spite of her age, but an aloes drench would help against parasites, and she could stand to be exercised more regularly, though not overworked. A buggy ride around town once or twice a week would do.

Garrett shifted George to his shoulders, and the little fella's legs bowed around his daddy's neck.

Clay shifted his focus. *Daddy* was a term he'd never used himself. He hadn't known a man like that, and George was too young to understand how lucky he was.

"Why don't you stay here in my old room?"

Clay laughed. "You mean that screened-in porch, with spring snows guaranteed for another month or two? I don't intend to freeze to death."

"It's not that bad, and the shutters are on. In fact, you can come back and help—"

Garrett flinched and shrugged George from his neck with a disgusted look. "He sprang a leak."

Clay laughed and gave a mock salute as Garrett headed to the house. If he'd done that to his father, the man would have …

Leaving the thought in the past where it belonged, Clay started in on the loose boards. He appreciated Garrett's offer, but wanted his own place. If he got too comfortable, he might quit looking. He hadn't gotten rich from selling the farm, but with that and what he'd saved from his year working in St. Louis, he had enough for a small stake, a place with no memories of a past he'd just as soon forget.

By early evening, he had most of the loose boards nailed down. He'd come back and finish in daylight. The idea of a lantern in the barn didn't set well.

He returned the hammer and nails to the storage room, then went to the water trough, where he pumped out a clear, cold dousing and drenched his head and arms. Not as soothing as the hot bath he'd soaked in the other day, but good enough to wake a man after a few hours' work and inspire a walk back to the hotel.

The sun snagged on the western ridge, giving notice that the day was over. Clay flung his hair back, needing a haircut—and stopped short. A steady plod on soft ground behind him brought him round to a silhouetted rider. He could tell from the outline it was a woman, but that was all he could tell.

Aware that he was clearly lit by the setting sun, he held steady and watched her approach. When she rode through the shadow cast by the house, he saw it was Sophie. She looked right at him, like she had at the train station and at church that morning, but instead of stopping, she rode on by and dismounted at the hitch rail.

If his memory served him, that was the same old nag she'd been riding earlier, as well as the first time they met four years ago, and it was just as worn out now as it had been then.

She came around the back of the horse, her left arm curving over its rump, and kept walking toward him until she stopped a couple yards out.

"Hello, Clay."

Her voice came weary, heavy. Like she'd worked all day plowing a field, but he knew better.

"Sophie. It's good to see you." A regular speech-giver he was. His dripping hair and wet shirt probably didn't make much of an impression either.

She took a step closer and tipped her head, as if to see better in the fading light. "Are you staying here at Maggie's?"

"No, I just stopped by to look in on her and ended up staying for dinner and—"

"Look in on her?" Another step. "Is she all right?"

Her brows worried themselves together, and he fought the urge to smooth them. Brush the loose hair from her temples. Hold her.

He rolled down his sleeves to give his fingers something to do other than what they shouldn't. "She was resting earlier. I've been out here most of the day checking on her mare and tending to the barn. I don't know if she's up and around."

Sophie's frown eased on its own and she let out a tired sigh.

"Are *you* staying here?" Depending on her answer, he might take Garrett up on his offer. Then again, that'd be a bad idea.

"Yes. For a day or so. I was in town helping Mrs. Eisner who …"

Her voice trailed off and she looked past him to the pasture, dark now and quiet, and a ragged whisper finished her sentence. "She was with child. Until today after church."

That was an odd way to put it. Was Sophie midwifing?

Her breath stuttered and a shaft of falling light caught a single tear trailing her right cheek.

Unchecked pain cut through him, and against his better judgment he closed the distance between them, wrapping his arms around her. She melted into him as if she had no bones. No strength. A wrenching sob broke loose, and he cradled her head against his chest.

Her fingers fisted into the back of his shirt, and he held her as she cried. He knew what it was like to lose new life—a foal or calf or lamb. But never a child.

He brushed his lips across the top of her hair, catching the scent of lamp oil and the wintergreen tinge of willow bark. His voice rose like a burning whisper from deep inside. "I'm so sorry."

# CHAPTER 7

Sophie could barely breathe, much less resist the strong arms of this man who'd caught her when her legs gave way. He carried her inside Maggie's house, set her gently in a chair at the kitchen table, then knelt on one knee in front of her, brushing hair from her face.

His eyes ached. She could see it, as if they were drawing out her pain. What kind of man had compassion like that?

At Betsy's arrival, he rose and spoke close to Sophie's ear. "I'll see to your horse."

She hadn't asked. She *wouldn't* have asked. But he was out the door before she could object.

Betsy pulled another chair next to her and glanced at the closing back door. "What happened?"

Sophie rubbed her temples, scouring her memory for details, but Clay's comforting embrace pushed all else aside. All but one thing. She squeezed her eyes against a rising flood of tears and buried her face in her hands.

"Did he hurt you?" Betsy's whisper sliced deep.

Sophie couldn't fault her, given the circumstances. She shook her head and spoke into her hands. "No. Quite the opposite."

"Tell me, Sophie. What's going on?"

With a jagged breath, she lifted her head and faced her friend's worry. "I'm not the one who needs your concern. Abigail Eisner—"

At the name, she saw the young woman's grief-stricken face. Heard the keening wail of a heart-broken mother. Held again the body of a lifeless child.

Sobs heaved from her chest.

Betsy reached for her. "Oh, Sophie."

She straightened, pulling away from her friend. She was not the one who needed sympathy or comfort. She'd done nothing. *Nothing.*

She'd not sent Hiram for Doc Weaver quickly enough.

She'd not gotten to Abigail early enough.

She'd not warned her sternly enough against pushing too soon.

But would any of those things have made a difference? She'd never know.

Spent and empty, she shook her head. "I can't do this anymore."

Betsy handed her one of Maggie's embroidered napkins. "I'll put on some tea." She didn't press, but waited for the kettle to whistle, then brought china cups and chamomile tea to the table. "Is something wrong with Abigail or the baby?"

Though soft as goose down, Betsy's whisper tore through Sophie's heart. She squeezed her eyes tight and drew a searing breath. "I told Abigail I would stop by today after church." She looked at her friend. "Maybe if I had come in yesterday …"

Betsy took her hand and leaned close.

Raw and burning, the words came. "Their son was stillborn."

Soundlessly, the back door opened, and Clay brought her satchel and carpet bag and set them on the floor by the table. Then he laid his hand on her shoulder as he passed and left as quietly as he'd come.

His gentle strength nearly overwhelmed her.

Tears filled Betsy's eyes. "You don't hold the life of a child in the womb, Sophie. You're not God."

"But I depend on Him to help me. To help the mother and baby. Why didn't He?"

"How do you know He didn't?" Betsy's tone had squeezed to a hush.

At a knock on the back door, she rose.

Doc Weaver's voice slipped through the opening, and Betsy stepped aside for him to enter. A wiser man Sophie had never met, and by the deep lines carved in his features, he'd experienced much loss himself. He took the chair Betsy had vacated and leaned forward on his knees. "You did everything you could, Sophie."

At the kindness of his tone, she shook her head, refusing to accept absolution.

He took her hands in his. "You did what I would have done and no different. Can you breathe life into a babe before it enters the world?"

With burning eyes, she looked into his and saw the comfortless truth of his words. "I would have if I could."

He patted her hands—his own worn and wrinkled from caring for others, but still tender. "We don't give life, but you know that. We give help and we give comfort. And what you need to do now is give yourself time to grieve but not to blame. You will heal, as will Abigail and her husband, though the scar will remain on their hearts and yours."

She flinched at his metaphor but didn't draw her hands from his.

"There will be more babies, I assure you."

She stiffened, anticipating something she did not want to hear.

"But not all babies live. Not all children grow up, and not all adults see old age. It is the way of man. We can only do our best, and trust those who survive, as well as those who do not, to the hands of a loving God who knows all."

*Not all babies live.* If he had said that to her when she first became a midwife, she would not have continued.

Heart heavy with truth that did not ease her pain, she saw clearly the high cost of her calling. She must choose whether to trust again, but tonight she didn't have the strength.

When the doctor left, Betsy picked up Sophie's bags. "Let's get you to your room. I'll bring your tea once you're dressed for bed."

She followed Betsy upstairs, feet leaden, each tread of the stairway a mountain. How could she take the risk again? How could she ever assure another woman that all would be well?

Betsy led her into a darkened room, then quickly lit a lamp on the dressing table. "I'll be back shortly." After a hug, she quietly clicked the door closed.

Sophie fell across the bed as she was and stared up at the ceiling, where yellow lamplight flickered and thinned into the corners. Rolling onto her stomach, she buried her face in the feather pillow and wept until sleep overcame her.

~

Clay stood at the window of his hotel room, staring across Main Street rooftops to the second floor of Maggie Snowfield's grand house. A pale light shone in one small square, and he wondered if it was Sophie's room.

He wondered if he'd ever hold her again.

He wondered if Mr. Eisner was holding his wife.

No doubt he was.

Clay pulled off his boots and laid his trousers and shirt over a chair, realizing he'd left his vest at Maggie's barn. He'd get it tomorrow after he checked in with Erik at the livery.

He lifted the window, relieved not to hear the Pike's off-key piano banging away. Sunday night in Olin Springs was a sight quieter than Friday and Saturday nights. He knew that from experience.

Lying back on the bed, he bunched his pillow and linked his fingers beneath it. Things hadn't gone as he'd expected, but then again, he hadn't known what to expect. Certainly not a remarkable stallion cutting itself open on the train. Or finding Maggie Snowfield so frail. Or holding Sophie in his arms as she cried her heart out.

If he could, he'd take her pain on himself. And if he were a praying man, he'd lift her name to the Almighty. But it'd been a while since they'd talked, and it'd probably be a long while until they did again, in spite of his attendance in church this morning. He'd been there for one reason, and that reason was Sophie Price.

Clarence Thatcher had thwarted that purpose, and an overwhelming need to protect Sophie nearly raised Clay to his feet. He didn't trust the man and he didn't know why.

But one thing he was sure of. He didn't want Thatcher anywhere near the woman he'd come home to find.

~

Clay's internal clock woke him as the sky grayed in the east. Something about approaching dawn had him up to see it most mornings, and he was dressed and downstairs before anyone else.

As far as he could tell, no help stirred at the hotel, and only the case clock in the lobby made any sound at all. No coffee brewed in the restaurant, and it was just as well. He wouldn't drink it anyway.

The sweet morning air carried spring on its breath, and the brisk walk to the livery got his blood flowing. The big front doors were closed, which meant John was still asleep in the loft and Erik hadn't come in yet. But the crack between the doors let Clay lift the bar that held them shut, and he slipped inside, lowering it behind him.

Duster stuck his head over the stall door and whiffled a greeting.

"Mornin', old boy." He rubbed the gelding's neck and shoulder and up under its forelock, then scooped a can of oats from the feed barrel nearby.

Scuffling in the loft dropped a dusting of straw. A wry smile tugged Clay's mouth. He'd scrambled like that plenty of times. The boy's feet hit the ground near the forge and soon a lantern flared to life. Made Clay jittery.

"Morning, sir. I thought I heard someone talking down here."

"Just me and Duster. Good to see you're up and at it so early."

"Yes, sir."

John tucked his shirt in with one hand while holding on to the lantern.

Clay jerked his head at the light. "Works better if you hang that on a nail."

He walked back to the stallion and found it standing calmly, its right back leg cocked to keep pressure off the wound. The poultice patch remained in place, and that was what Clay had hoped for. When daylight streamed through the stable, he'd check the sutures and reapply the poultice.

"He was quiet as a mouse all night," John offered. "I didn't expect that."

"He felt safe here. Plus you don't have any mares. That always helps."

The boy smiled self-consciously. "Yes sir. I suppose it does."

"Did anyone come in yesterday asking about this fella?"

"No, sir, but a few stop by just to look. Word's got out about what you did." He reached into his pocket. "And I've got the name of a man here who wants you to come out for his mare about ready to foal. Her first time, he said, and he wants you to look her over, make sure everything's all right."

Clay palmed his eyes and the side of his face. There was no guaranteeing anything, as yesterday's situation with Mrs. Eisner proved. "Tell me where he lives, and I'll ride out there today after breakfast."

"Yes, sir. I'll have Duster ready when you get back from Bozeman's."

Clay cocked his head at the boy. "What makes you think I'm goin' to Bozeman's?"

With a sheepish look, John kicked at the dirt. "I didn't figure you as someone who'd like the hotel's food."

Clay slapped him on the shoulder. "You figured right. I'll bring you some bear sign."

He perked right up. "Thank you, sir."

By the time Clay had checked on the horses and walked down the street, Hoss Bozeman was up to his elbows in customers. Clay took the nearest table, a full helping of steak and eggs, and a bag of bear sign back to the livery for John.

Duster waited at the hitch rail, tacked up and ready to go, and he swiveled his ears at Clay's approach. The stable doors were opened wide, both front and back, and daylight shot through the interior.

John stood in front of the stallion's stall, either talking to the horse or someone inside the stall with it. An uneasy feeling worked up Clay's back and along his shoulders. He set the paper bag on a feed barrel and closed in on the conversation.

The man was running a hand over the stallion's injured leg.

Clay's hackles rose. "Don't touch the horse."

Shoulders squared and tightened. "And you are ..." The man's tone and stance said he'd know who or what for.

Clay checked his pocket for the poultice packet he'd brought, then flexed his hands. He didn't go huntin' fights, but he'd defend his work as well as the animal if it came to that.

"I'm the one who stitched up the stallion and applied that poultice, and I'll see that you don't undo what I've done."

"Will you now." Gravel edged the voice, and the man turned, hat brim low, shielding his eyes. He stepped through the stall door and thumbed his hat up.

"And it's a fine job you did, Clay. What do I owe you for saving my horse?"

# CHAPTER 8

The dressing-table mirror in Sophie's room told her to get back in bed and hide under the covers until her eyes looked normal. But that might never happen, so she splashed her face with tepid water from the washstand and did the best she could to make herself presentable.

At the stairs, the aroma of frying bacon drew her stomach as tight as a reticule cord. Food was not what she needed. Hot coffee was.

Maggie sat at the kitchen table sipping tea and attempting to spoon mush into George's rosebud lips while Betsy prepared breakfast.

The baby grinned a toothless welcome, dribbling his mush, and pounded the tray of his highchair. Sophie was helpless but to smile at him.

Two hand-painted teacups waited upside down in their matching saucers.

"Good morning, dear." Maggie turned over the nearest cup and scooted it closer to the chair at her left. A flush brightened her cheeks, but Sophie suspected a rouge pot had something to do with it.

Betsy glanced over her shoulder. "You're just in time. Biscuits are almost done."

Sophie held up a hand that Betsy missed. "Coffee is all I need. If that's a pot of it on the back of the stove, I'll help myself."

Maggie shook her top-knotted head and approached George with another spoonful. "I'll never understand you stout-hearted country women drinking coffee in the morning rather than tea." She waived a frail hand. "But to each his own."

Sophie filled her cup and added sugar from a matched set at the table. "I'm glad to see you up this morning, Maggie. It looks as though George is as well."

He screwed up his little face and expelled the previously introduced mush.

Sophie laughed. "Give him a piece of bacon to suck on. I wouldn't want mush either with that smell wafting right under my nose."

"I thought you said you weren't hungry." Betsy leaned across the table with a cooled slice for her son.

"I'm not, but someone else is."

Halfway through breakfast, a particularly sober look settled on George's face, and he turned beet red and grunted.

"Oh no." Betsy shoved from the table and snatched up her son. Hurried footsteps on the stairs drew laughter from both Sophie and Maggie, but Sophie's was short-lived.

Abigail Eisner was not enjoying such antics this morning, nor would she for quite some time. Sophie'd best be leaving to check on the poor woman. She scooted her chair back.

Maggie stopped her with a touch and a look in her eye that said she knew what happened. Sophie needed sympathy like she needed a plateful of bacon in her traitorous stomach.

"There is a two-sided coin in the Bible that I have always considered quite valuable, though at times difficult for me to hold."

So much for dreaded sympathy. True to her nature, Maggie had successfully garnered Sophie's attention, for she could not imagine anything being difficult for the resolute Maggie Snowfield.

"You are a bright young woman, Sophie, and gifted. As such, I am sure you have noticed that I've never mentioned children or grandchildren of my own."

Sophie's throat constricted as tightly as her stomach, and she hid her hands in her lap.

"I once had a son."

Sophie stared at the woman who seemed to age before her very eyes.

"His little body lies in our family plot in Illinois." One thin hand fluttered to Maggie's bodice. "But he *lives* here. In my heart with his father."

Sophie couldn't move. She couldn't rise and run from the conversation, nor could she sit at the table upright without quaking with grief.

Maggie's eyes filled with tears, something Sophie had not witnessed before. "'Weep with those who weep and rejoice with those who rejoice.' That is the coin, my dear, and you are gifted with this treasure. It is one that women crave when they are at the peak or valley of their careers as mothers. Remember that when you visit Mrs. Eisner today. The gift is beyond price and will help soothe what cannot otherwise be soothed."

A knock on the back door turned them both.

"Would you get that please, dear?" Maggie patted Sophie's arm and then brushed at her own eyes.

Opening the door, Sophie faced the last two people she expected to see that morning.

"Come in, come in," Maggie called from behind her.

Sophie pulled the door wider and stepped aside, at a complete loss for words. A malady she rarely suffered.

Cade Parker and Clay Ferguson doffed their hats and stood awkwardly by the door, filling the kitchen with their presence and diminishing its spaciousness.

"Coffee?" She managed the single word with as much effort as it took to keep her eyes off Clay and on Betsy's brother.

"We'd be obliged, Miss Sophie. Maggie." Cade Parker nodded politely to each of them.

Sophie removed the two teacups and saucers and searched the cupboard for mugs she'd seen earlier. Chair legs scraped the floor behind her as the men took their places at the table.

And a frightful cry from the second floor drew them all to their feet.

Sophie ran up the stairs and straight to the nursery, followed by Clay. Betsy was leaning over George's crib, where he lay screaming.

"Oh, Sophie, he's burning up." Betsy attempted to lift him, but he screamed all the louder.

"Strip him down and I'll get water and rags." Sophie unbuttoned her sleeves and pushed them up. "We'll give him a cooling bath."

Clay was already down the stairs and in the kitchen when she got there, filling a pitcher with cold water from the tap.

She went through drawers for towels and rags, then lifted the warm tea kettle from the stove.

Clay took the kettle from her and she let him. Now was not the time to argue.

His long strides took him up the stairs ahead of her, but he waited for her to enter the room first.

Betsy had George stripped down, holding him against her chest.

Clay poured cold water into the washstand basin and added warmer water from the tea kettle.

Sophie spread a large towel on the crib bottom. "Let me have him," she cooed as she took the feverish babe from Betsy's arms. She laid him on his back on the towel and accepted wet rags as Clay soaked and squeezed them out. Without her saying a word, he knew what she intended to do.

Cade Parker assisted Maggie into the room, and she slipped an arm around Betsy's waist.

Sophie draped George with a thin cloth and then another, amazed as always at the effect on the baby. Releasing a stuttered breath he looked up at her, his big green eyes pools of trust.

With his screaming stopped, he didn't feel as feverish, and she gently ran the tip of her finger along his gums. He bit down hard and then whimpered.

Clay handed her another thin rag, and she twisted it into a soft knot and placed it over the baby's gums. Immediately he started chewing and grabbed the cloth with his chubby hands.

Triumphantly, she smiled at Clay, who captured her with a look that left her as feverish as George had been and more than a little shaken.

~

Sophie's eyes were puffy, and Clay could guess why. But in spite of that, she was prettier every time he saw her.

She dropped her gaze and turned to Betsy. "He's still a bit warm, but I think he cried himself into that. He's cutting a tooth. Comfort is what he needs right now."

Her calm demeanor inspired confidence in everyone in the room, including Clay. He wasn't close to being a medical doctor, but he'd learned about fevers in foals, and Sophie had headed in the same direction as his instincts for cooling the child.

They'd made a great team.

As that thought stampeded through his brain, he picked up the pitcher and kettle and made tracks downstairs.

Sophie wasn't far behind him with a pile of wet rags and towels that she set in the sink. "Thank you for your help."

"I'm glad I was here." *In more ways than one.*

With her hands on the sink's edge, she leaned against her braced arms and looked over her shoulder. "Why did you come?"

*To see you.* "To finish in the barn and get my vest. I left it here last night."

She blushed and fingered the back of her hair—remembering, he hoped. The moment they'd shared had been one of empathy more than intimacy, but he had no regrets. "And Parker wants to talk to Betsy about the stallion."

The change of subject brought her around. "So it *is* Cade's horse. Betsy wondered when I told her, but when I said he hadn't shown up to claim it, she thought perhaps ..."

Apparently she'd said more than she intended and shifted her gaze to the stovetop.

He filled the empty space. "I saw you there. At the train station."

She met his eyes then, but cautiously. "You handled that situation well."

"Thanks to Deacon."

That brought a smile to her lips in the lopsided way he remembered.

"The coffee has overcooked, but I can add a little water to it if you'd like a cup."

"Suits me fine." Nothing could be as bad as Bozeman's brew this late in the morning.

Parker came in with Maggie on his arm, followed by Betsy and the baby. Clay pulled out his chair for Maggie.

"Thank you, dear. Would you please bring another from the dining room so we can all squeeze in here? If there's one thing I like, it's a full kitchen."

He complied and kept the extra chair for himself, sitting back from the small square table. He had yet to understand why Maggie didn't have a decent-size kitchen table. It wasn't like she couldn't afford it.

Sophie filled a mug and brought it to him before serving the others, but kept her beautiful eyes to herself.

Betsy settled George in his highchair, his pudgy fingers still gripping the knotted rag. "I'm so glad you were here, Sophie. I wouldn't have known what to do otherwise."

Sophie dodged the comment and busied herself at the stove.

"So what brings you men by this fine morning?" Maggie was in her element, and it flushed her cheeks. Clay hoped all the fuss wasn't too much for her.

"I came to get my horse and heard quite a tale about its arrival," Parker said.

"Why weren't you there at the train station after what you had to pay for that stallion?" Betsy voiced everyone's question but Clay's. He wanted to know why it came without a handler, but he'd hold on to that for another time and place.

Parker rubbed the back of his neck and studied the tablecloth. "Mae Ann wasn't her usual self that morning. I was afraid to leave her. Today she's better, and I told Deacon to keep an ear to the door and ride for Travine Price if need be." He cut a look at Sophie. "I'm hoping you'll come out and stay for a while. I've got calves to brand and a trip to Denver, but with her time so near, I'm afraid to leave her alone."

Sophie's face blanched, and she swallowed so hard Clay could see the effort.

"I … can't come … for a few days. I … have someone else I must see to first."

She glanced at Maggie, who smiled in an odd way and slowly nodded her head.

"I need your help too, Clay." Parker looked right at him. "You can hold things down at the ranch while Deacon and I sort and brand. Then I'll be leaving for a couple weeks or more. Depends on how things go in Denver."

Clay's turn to swallow hard.

Parker stood and set his mug in the sink. "Thanks for the coffee." He chucked George under the chin. "Tell your mama to come out to the ranch and take a look at Xavier."

"Who?" Betsy's voice pitched high enough to draw her son's attention.

"The stallion. Not a name I'd pick, but that's what his papers say. He's good blood for the mares, and I think he'll give Blanca a fine foal."

He motioned for Clay to follow him out.

"Miss Maggie, thank you again. Sophie." Hat in hand he paused at the door, addressing her. "I know you have other women who need your help, but as soon as you can come, I'd appreciate it if you'd stay with Mae Ann while I'm gone."

On their way to the barn, Clay considered what Parker was asking, entrusting Sophie with his wife in his absence and Clay with the ranch. He found his vest where he'd left it, and met Parker standing beside his horse, one hand on his saddle horn as he looked across the seat to Clay.

"Will you do it?"

Clay stepped up and reined Duster around, facing one of the men who'd given him a hand when he needed it most. He reset his hat with a single nod.

Parker pulled a roll of bills from his pocket and held it out. "A month's wages, plus what I owe you for Xavier. If the trip takes longer, I'm good for it. And keep track of anything extra you need for the stallion's care. You're in charge." He mounted and held his horse in check. "You'll bunk in Deacon's cabin. If you can be at the ranch by tomorrow, you can help us bring in the saddle horses the next day."

Clay didn't know *how* he'd do it—start a business, hunt a place of his own, and look after the Parker ranch for a month—but he'd do it. And Sophie Price living on the same spread takin' care of Mae Ann didn't hurt his outlook any.

They headed for the livery, where Parker took possession of a horse called Xavier and Clay settled with Erik. After the maiden mare call, he'd come back to Maggie's and finish what she needed.

On his way out of town, he stopped by the mercantile for dried beans and coffee in case he'd be cooking for himself. He also bought a few tins of peaches and a sack of barrel crackers, and since Miss Sarah wasn't working, he made it out of the store unscathed.

But his neck and shoulders knotted as he approached the hotel, where an old mare waited at the rail, a satchel tied to her saddle. He stepped down and laid rein, standing between the horses, clearing his head and flexing his hands. No reason to go in half-cocked, not seeing things as they really were.

And he sure enough needed to see what Sophie Price was doing at the Olin Springs Hotel.

# CHAPTER 9

"No, thank you. I did not come for brunch or anything else from your restaurant."

Sophie's already taut nerves stretched even further at the offended look on the desk clerk's face.

"I came simply to leave a message for Mr. Thatcher."

"Excellent!"

Her tightest nerve twanged at the hotelier's appraisal ringing from the staircase he casually descended.

"Ah, Miss Price. I see that you have finally agreed to let me show you Olin Springs' finest." He offered his arm expectantly.

She did not take it.

He was so bold as to reach for hers, and she stepped back, astounded by the man's audacity.

"I believe the lady has other plans."

At the deep voice from behind, her knees weakened with relief, and she fought to hold her position.

Mr. Thatcher's features hardened to stone, then quickly veiled with an ingratiating smile. "Mr. Ferguson, I believe. Am I correct? How may I assist you this fine morning?"

Clay stood beside her, and she drew strength merely from his presence, something she'd never experienced with anyone and for which she had no explanation.

"I'll be checking out today."

Thatcher's expression brightened. "I see. You may take that up with my assistant here who will prepare your bill for you."

"You mean refund. I paid in advance for a week."

The muscle in Mr. Thatcher's jaw flexed. "As you wish."

"But we don't give re—"

Thatcher's brusque turn startled the clerk. "See to Mr. Ferguson's request." With a tilted nod to Sophie, he added, "Another time, then, Miss Price."

"I came to let you know the Eisners will not need your assistance with stair railing."

A light snapped in his eyes as if he'd found a chink in an opponent's armor. "How unfortunate that you lost their child." He shook his head, tsking.

Clay took a step forward.

Sophie grabbed his arm, hard as steel above his clenched fist. "How unfortunate that you believed misinformation, Mr. Thatcher."

The man visibly bristled at her rebuke.

Clay rested his hand at the back of her waist and addressed the clerk, whose mouth hung open like a carriage door. "I'll be back for my refund." Then he gave Thatcher a cold stare and with the lightest pressure, urged her toward the door.

Once on the boardwalk, Sophie rushed to the hitch rail and braced herself, shaking with fury over Clarence Thatcher's callous remark.

She dragged in as much fresh air as her lungs would hold. "You have an uncanny sense of timing."

Clay moved in, shielding her, his hand on her shoulder. "He had no right to say that to you."

Deep, yet soft as a baby's breath, his voice warmed her as much as his touch, seeping through the fabric of her dress, her skin, and slipping into her veins.

For the briefest moment she relished the idea of a man like Clay Ferguson in her life. A man of strength, character, and compassion.

Loosing the mare's reins, she moved from his protective stance and around to her horse, facing him with the hitch rail between them. Earnest eyes met hers, as blue as the sky, yet capable of icing into steely gray when focused on an enemy. He was not looking at an enemy now.

"I'll see you home if you want me to."

Oh, how she wanted him to. His manner, his tone made her want it very much, but she shook her head. "I suspect you have other things to do, like collecting your refund." She attempted a smile.

He returned it, his glance flitting to the left side of her mouth and back to her eyes.

Inwardly, she cringed, recoiling from such pointed notice, and stepped to the saddle. "I'm not leaving for a few days, and then only if Abigail Eisner is doing well. But I appreciate your offer."

She turned the mare toward the north end of town and the tailor shop. Some things she needed to do alone. Grieving with Abigail was one.

Grieving over a scar she couldn't hide was another.

~

Since it was a business day, she tied the mare on Main Street and entered the shop's front door, satchel in hand. No call had ever been harder, but she kept running Maggie's words through her mind—*weep with those who weep*. Clearly, that would not be hard to do.

Hiram came from the back, older than he'd appeared yesterday. He had difficulty meeting her eyes.

"Mr. Eisner, I'm here to check on Abigail. She is still in need of care …"

He turned away before she finished and indicated that she precede him. At least he hadn't chased her off.

Taking to the treacherous stairs, she clutched her satchel with one hand and trailed the other along the unforgiving wall, breathing easier once she stepped into the couple's apartment.

Abigail appeared to be sleeping, but as Sophie approached the bed, the young woman turned a tear-ravaged face to her, eyes swollen and red, yet she was smiling.

*Smiling*? How could that be?

Sophie pulled a spindle-backed chair close, set down her satchel, and reached for the limp hand Abigail held out to her.

"I hoped you would come." Tears welled, her voice coarse and broken from crying.

"There are still things for you to be aware of, and I want to help you in your recovery in every way that I can."

A slight pressure on her fingers had power to break Sophie in two.

"You have been with me in my grief, as has Hiram, though his wound may take longer to heal than mine.

Not that I love our son any less than he does, but I have found comfort in the words of a very wise man."

Had Doc Weaver returned this morning? Regardless, Sophie could not imagine anyone bringing comfort to this poor woman other than God Himself.

Abigail's eyes closed and her hand relaxed. Sophie thought she had drifted into a healing sleep, but in moments, they opened.

"I know your Bible has some of the writings favored by people of our faith. One is called Job."

Sophie was not very familiar with the Old Testament book, but she opened her heart to hear what Abigail wanted to share.

"'The Lord gave, and the Lord hath taken away.'" Tears quivered at Abigail's lashes. "'Blessed be the name of the Lord.'"

"Blessed be His name." Hiram's hushed tone drifted across the room.

Sophie let her own tears fall as she held Abigail's hand, unsure as to whether God had taken the baby and more inclined to believe He had received it. However, the words rang with the same mystery that Doc Weaver had mentioned. Yet she hesitated to tell Abigail there would be other children, especially when the wound was so fresh. How did she know? How could she or Doc Weaver himself make such a promise? They didn't know the future.

*But you know Me.*

Sophie stilled at the unspoken words, then glanced behind her, finding only Hiram in another spindle-backed chair at a small table, head in his hands.

Oddly soothed by the voice, she spent the next half hour with Abigail, listening to her talk about her life and dreams. Then she told her what to expect in the following days and left her with a packet of elderberry as well as willow bark tea and instructions for brewing them. She felt no childbed fever in Abigail's brow or body, but things could shift suddenly, and the next few days were critical.

"The willow helps with pain and tenderness, and elderberry fights fever. But should you have any difficulties this evening, send Hiram to the Snowfield home on Saddle Blossom Lane. I'm staying there for a day or so."

After promising to return the next morning, she bid them both goodbye and saw herself out.

Grateful she'd ridden the short distance to town rather than walked, she rode north past the church and the library, out where the meadowlarks sang and the sun warmed the grass and wildflowers. Out where no one but God would hear her cry.

~

Clay wanted nothing more than to feed Clarence Thatcher his teeth—*julienned*—but the man had been conveniently absent when Clay went back for his clothes and saddle bags. The desk clerk returned half his money, more than he'd expected, and Clay took the road east for the Hickman farm and a maiden mare.

This was where his and Sophie's work overlapped—assisting life into the world. His fingers tightened on the reins. He'd like to assist a certain hotel owner *out,* but taking life was not what he did. In spite of what his father had told him.

Clay heeled Duster into an easy lope, leaving ugly memories behind. He'd come to Olin Springs to start living, and that meant getting a grip on his thoughts.

"We feed our souls like we feed our bellies," the old veterinarian in St. Louis had told him, right before he started quoting Scriptures. Clay bought the first line and stopped listening to the rest. He knew good feed made the difference in an animal's condition as well as a person's, so it stood to reason that what a man fed his thoughts would affect them the same way.

As he approached the neat house and barn of Cyrus Hickman, his hopes rose for the mare. The outbuildings were modest but well kept, as was a kitchen garden and the fencing around the near pasture. Neglect did not appear to be part of the picture that he'd seen at many a farm.

A boy, no bigger than eight or ten, walked out from the barn in dungarees and a straw hat and waited until Clay reached him. "You the horse doctor?"

Clay chuckled to himself and stepped down. "Yes, sir, I am. And you are …?"

"Peter Hickman. But you can call me Pete."

It was all Clay could do not to laugh at the boy's seriousness, but he held a tight rein. "Nice to meet you, Pete. You can call me Clay."

The young face scrunched up. "Like dirt?"

That fast, the dart hit dead center. He hadn't seen it coming. He shook his head, dislodging an echo and separating the youngster's curiosity from an adult's sneering disdain.

"Pete."

The boy whipped around. "Yes, Pa?"

"Go on inside for now. Your ma wants ya."

Downcast and shoulders drooping, the boy glanced up at Clay and whispered, "He always says she wants me when he *doesn't* want me seein' somethin'."

Clay stooped and met the boy eye to eye. "You got a ma. That's the best thing you could see."

The doubtful look on Pete's face said he wasn't buying it, but he did as his pa told him and dragged himself as slowly as possible to the house.

"Mr. Ferguson?" Hickman offered his hand.

"Yes, sir."

"Cyrus Hickman. I appreciate you coming out. I couldn't very well bring her in to the livery, seein' as how she's already waxed over and bagged up."

"You made the right call. Is she kicking and nipping at her belly? Rolling around and acting fidgety?"

Cyrus screwed his face up like his son had. "How'd you know?"

*Three years' experience.* "Just a hunch. Show me where she is."

The yellow mare had a roomy stall to herself with plenty of water and the fresh smell of clean straw bedding. She stood with her hindquarters facing them and threw her head around with an expression that was none too happy. From the looks of things, she'd be dropping any day.

"I'd say you've done all you can for her. She's ready, but I'll check the foal's position. More than likely, she'll take care of things herself, and soon you'll come out some morning to find you've got another horse to feed."

The mare was good-natured, as far as mares in her condition went. Clay palpated her and believed the foal was positioned well. He encouraged Cyrus to keep the stall clean, water and feed fresh, and when the foal came, to make sure it got first milk right off.

"The sooner the better. If it won't nurse, you can milk the mare, but that may not be easy. If need be, send for me at the Parker ranch. I'll be staying there for the next month."

Clay left confident that the first foal in the area under his watch would be standing on its own within the week, and he had a hunch the Hickman boy would appoint himself the proud guardian.

A sore spot on his chest throbbed, and he dug the heel of his hand into it not sure if it was from Sophie's grief over the Eisner baby or Pete's innocent jab.

~

Abigail Eisner was sitting up when Sophie called the next afternoon, a cup of willow bark tea on the bedside table with a biscuit and jam. Her brow was cool, her hands dry. Hiram rose a notch in Sophie's estimation. However, she managed to earn Abigail's agreement for Doc Weaver to stop by—not for an examination, but merely to see how she was doing and answer any questions.

With the verbal promise, Sophie visited the good doctor on her way out of town and rode easily the rest of the way home to the farm.

Todd was splitting and stacking firewood, and Mama was breaking ground in the garden. She paused, wiping her brow as Sophie rode up to the hitch rail by the house. Dudley welcomed her as if she were a long-lost pup.

"Are you here for a while?" Mama's eyes asked more than that, but she was wise enough to tackle only one issue at a time.

"A few hours."

Her mother leaned the hoe against the garden gate and gave Sophie a hug. "Then we have time for coffee and fritters."

Either Mama knew how to read minds, or she had an uncanny knack for detecting sorrow. More than likely, both.

The security of home and the comfort of things familiar dropped Sophie's defenses, and she spilled out every detail. Mama's eyes filled, and as Maggie had suggested, shared grief was easier carried than grief borne alone.

"Nothing else hurts quite as much," Mama said, her wrinkle-cut features bearing witness. "Hopes and dreams of the future die with a child, and you feel like you're unable to live as well. Depression can overwhelm the mother, and a close eye must be kept. But the midwife suffers too, as you have learned." She covered Sophie's hand where it lay on the table.

Sophie felt a twinge of betrayal.

Her mother rolled her lips, thinking in that way she had, scrolling through all the things she could say and finally choosing the best.

"Rarely—if ever—is the loss of a child due to the midwife. Don't let this discourage you and stir fear in your heart. Not enough women do what you do, and more are needed. More like you, with a healing touch."

Mama insisted they eat while Sophie was there, and she called Todd in for an early supper of fried potatoes, sausage, and onions along with biscuits and strawberry preserves.

"I'll send a few jars with you," she said as Sophie cleared the table after their meal. "I doubt Mae Ann has been up to cooking much, and she may be running short on last year's stores."

Sophie packed all of her clothes—from dresses and stockings to shifts and chemises—even a pair of Todd's trousers he'd outgrown, just in case. Just in case of what, she wasn't sure, but better to have something and not need it than to need it and not have it. She also took her boots, heavy cloak, straw hat and a felt, following the same line of thinking as she had with the trousers. Just because it was spring didn't mean it couldn't be snowing and blowing by tomorrow.

With a little mashing and rearranging, everything fit into a carpet bag, and she lashed it to the mare's saddle.

"Are you sure you can't stay longer?" Mama's eyes pleaded, loneliness peeking through at the corner creases.

From atop the mare, Sophie leaned down and cupped her mother's cheek. "You know I need to be there. But do you know I love you?"

Mama brushed at her eyes and handed over a bundle that smelled suspiciously like stockpiled fritters. "See that Deacon gets a few of these if you would. I promised him I'd make another batch just for h—" She waved the words away.

Sophie gave a soft laugh and stuffed the fritters in her bulging carpet bag. "You spoil him, but he'll be tickled."

Mama hugged her arms around herself and stepped back, her stance the picture of a woman letting go of things she wanted to hold on to. Sophie rode through the yard and out across the pasture shortcut, praying she'd have such wisdom when she needed it.

Watching for deer this trip, she kept the mare at a lively clip, and when they reached the Parker ranch, lights winked on either side of the ranch-house door and barking dogs welcomed her to the second home in one day. People expected her, needed her. Again she prayed, but this time with more urgency, that she would have what Mae Ann needed when her time came.

A rustling deep inside told her that time would likely come while Cade and Deacon were gone.

At the thought of Deacon, she glanced toward his cabin huddled in the dusk with a dim light warming his window. She'd give him the fritters tomorrow at breakfast. No horses stood tethered out front, and she couldn't tell if Clay was already there or not. Not that it mattered.

Why would it matter? She had come for Mae Ann and no other reason.

Heart pounding strangely, she tied up at the house, loosed her satchel and bags, and let herself inside.

Cade slumped in a leather chair in front of the cold hearth, head tipped to the side and Willy asleep in his arms. Surprised that the dogs hadn't roused him, she hated to do what they had failed at, but he needed to know she'd arrived.

She touched his arm. "Cade. It's Sophie."

He startled, but without waking Willy, and rubbed his eyes with his thumb and fingers. "Go on up," he whispered, "and I'll see to your horse."

"I can do that. I just wanted you to know who was tiptoeing around in your home." She took her things upstairs and set her bags on the bed in the room at the end of the hall—Betsy's old room. Shadows scurried under the furniture when she lit a lamp on the bed table. She hung her dresses and shifts on pegs and filled two drawers in the bureau with the remainder of her clothes. Her hairbrush and comb, tooth powder, and other things took their places on the dressing table, and she tucked her boots beneath it.

On her way downstairs with Mama's preserves and fritters, she paused at Mae Ann's door, listening for sounds of discomfort but hearing none.

Cade had fallen asleep again, and she touched his arm. "Go on to bed. I'll take Willy if you want."

He stirred. "No, I'll take him rather than wake him up handing him over. Glad you made it tonight."

She watched him climb the stairs, still wearing those old moccasins of all things, as quiet as a Ute on a sand bar. Anxious to take stock of the kitchen for the next morning, she left the mare a few minutes longer while she checked on what was where and what was needed.

Satisfied that she could serve coffee, eggs, biscuits, and preserves, she heated a kettle of water and set to washing the dishes left in the sink.

~

It had been dark with a saucer moon rising when Clay rode in. Lights were burning in the house, and a tired old horse stood slouching at the rail, a back leg bent.

Across from the house about fifty yards, Deacon's cabin hunkered next to the barn on one side with a shed on the other. The door opened, spilling the old codger and a thin wash of light into the yard. Clay tied up at the barn but went to the cabin before unsaddling.

"Boss said you was comin'. Get your soogans, and I'll show you where you're bunkin'."

Deacon wasn't much on speech-giving, but his manner made Clay feel welcomed just the same. He unlashed his bed roll and slicker from behind his cantle and tossed them with his saddle bags on the nearest of four bunks in the room off the main cabin, then went back to unsaddle Duster. After brushing him down, he set fresh water in a stall, filled the trough with hay, and led him in.

"This is home for the next month or so."

The gelding flicked an ear and drank his fill, then raised his head toward a familiar whinny.

Clay walked through the barn and out the back. A high-sided round corral sat a hundred paces out, and the dark stallion tossed its head and whinnied again. Clay approached with an eye to its right back leg, watching it travel. The sides of the round pen angled out slightly, and the top pole laid at just above his six feet. A snubbing post sprouted dead center, and the stallion circled it like a wheel around a hub.

"Looks like we'll be sharing the same spread for a while, *Xavier*."

The horse stopped across the corral and watched him without watchin' him.

Clay waited, keeping up a low, steady stream of talk, until curiosity won the day. The stallion came around from the side and blew into Clay's outstretched hand, then trotted away, head high, tail swishing.

Good signs, all.

At the cabin, Deacon had coffee cooking, and some kind of fried bread on the stout-built table that centered the room.

Clay was hungry enough not to be picky.

"Travine's fritters. I saved back a few." A lamp on the table lit a gleam in the old man's eye.

Clay read sign as well as the next fella. "She make 'em special for you?"

The handlebar mustache puffed at Deacon's fluster. "I'm glad you took the job. Roundin' up the herd'll be easier knowin' you're here seein' to things."

Clay valued the remark and helped himself to a fritter. Deacon Jewett didn't scatter compliments like seed corn.

One bite of fried-apple goodness set things right. "These are good enough to make a man wanna tie down." He almost felt guilty baiting his mentor.

Deacon snorted, but it didn't hide that look in his eye or the twitching mustache.

"You ask her yet?"

The question earned Clay a hard-eyed glare. "I'm fixin' to."

"Before or after branding?"

"Don't rush me, boy."

Clay washed one fritter down with a swig of coffee and reached for a second.

Deacon did the same.

The old cabin had a homey feel—stone fireplace, cook stove, sideboard, and cupboards. The bed in the corner was a real bed with a tick mattress and quilts, not just a leather-strapped bottom and ground sheet like the bunks in the spare room. No water at the sink, but the hand pump outside at the trough served.

Deacon noted the survey. "Got this place ready for you. Good stove, good bunk. All the chinks filled. Be a nice little setup for you to get your doctorin' goin'. After we leave, you can bunk out here if ya' want."

Well, that answered one question. Clay agreed—the place would be a good start for him. He heard the unspoken offer, but he hadn't come back to sign on with the Parker Land and Cattle. He wanted his own place. Needed his own place. Helping out was one thing, but filling Deacon's boots wasn't in the plan. And as far as that went, he figured it'd be near impossible.

The old cowboy didn't have the schooling Clay had, but that didn't mean he had no education. He'd learned firsthand what worked and what didn't. Spent his life around livestock and had taught Clay how to gentle yearlings and steer clear of locoed broncs. It'd take a lifetime to catch up to Deacon Jewett.

"How long you been here?"

A river of memories washed through pale-blue eyes. "I trailed the original Parker herd up from Texas right after the war. When Cade's grandpap passed, his pa asked me to stay on."

Clay'd been alive as long, and he couldn't help but wonder how things might have been if a man like that had sired him.

"The Colonel was a good cow man, but he had the temper of a mossy horn bull."

That bit of news stopped the coffee halfway down Clay's throat. Not what he'd expected to hear about the Parker clan, but a lot of deep water passes under some bridges. "You been married before?"

Either stalling or stoking his courage, Deacon swigged his coffee, refilled his cup, and took the last fritter. "Before the war I had my eye on a gal, but I dallied around and lost her to a fancier gent."

Clay waited for more, but Deacon only gave him one of those eye-full looks that said more than a Sunday-morning preacher.

"My rough-string ridin' days is over. But I can still drive a chuck wagon, heat an iron, and help Travine at her place." What little showed of Deacon Jewett's face above his handlebars turned berry red. "Way I see it, she needs a hand and I know just the one."

Courting was serious business, regardless of a man's age.

That night Clay lay fully dressed and awake on his bunk, looking into his own future—and nearly as many stars through the roof as he'd seen out on the plains. Easy to forget about patching over a spare room rarely used. A spring storm meant trouble for the roof and anything underneath it. Clay'd better have it repaired sooner rather than later.

He rolled to his side, a sight fewer miles on his trail than the old cow puncher. But he knew the cut of loneliness when the night gathered round and supper was a solitary affair. He too had a gal in his sights. A girl with soft brown eyes and a crooked smile.

He got up and stole into the main room, where Deacon was snoring like that mossy-horned bull he'd mentioned. At the window over the dry sink, Clay pulled back the canvas. The old horse was still out there.

# CHAPTER 10

Sophie couldn't see the barn from her bedroom window, but dawn was graying the sky and shimmering pink along the horizon. She quickly finished with her tooth powder and washed her face, then dressed, twisted her hair into a bun, and quietly went downstairs.

The house was chilly, and she rubbed her arms, deciding against a fire on the hearth, for she'd soon have the cook stove heating the kitchen. On her way through the great room, she stopped at one of the wide windows and checked the yard for activity.

Last night after cleaning up, she'd gone out with a lantern from the pantry to take care of her horse, but the hitch rail was empty. She'd stood there a moment, baffled, the lantern throwing a dim circle around her. Nothing stirred. There'd been no sign of a scuffle, and she doubted the dogs had frightened the old girl off. And then she saw movement across the yard, the mare's tail swishing as she plodded into the barn, led by a man as tall as Deacon Jewett but not Deacon Jewett.

A tingling sensation had danced over her left shoulder—and did so again. The place Clay's hand had rested when they stood in front of the hotel.

Had he been watching for her last night, or was it merely his uncanny sense of timing?

Rousing herself from such fanciful reflection, she found one of Mae Ann's aprons, started the coffee, and stirred up a batch of biscuits. Then she remembered the smoke house. Surely Parker Land and Cattle had a side of beef hanging from which she could slice steaks. With a pie pan and a good-sized knife in hand, she went out the back and around the end of the house.

By the time she returned, Cade and Willy were at the sink washing their hands.

"I hope you men are hungry this morning."

"They're always hungry."

Sophie turned at Mae Ann's voice, sleep-edged and forcefully cheery.

"I'm surprised to see you up and around." Worried more than surprised, Sophie tempered her concern. "How are you feeling?"

Mae Ann took the nearest chair and smoothed her skirt over her swollen belly. "Absolutely useless and hungry as a bear."

Bear was good. "I'll make you some chamomile tea."

Willy climbed onto a chair next to his mama. "Tea."

"Tea, *please*," she said, leaning close to his tousled head.

Cade joined his family. "My guess is those are your ma's preserves on the table."

"And it's your beef steaks I'll be frying up with gravy for the biscuits. I helped myself to the smokehouse this morning."

Mae Ann attempted to stand. "There are a few potatoes in the pantry—"

"Never you mind. You sit right there and I'll take care of breakfast. If I'm going to go to the trouble of making you tea, the least you can do is savor it."

"Tea!" Willy clapped his hands.

"Oh, but I could get used to this." Mae Ann sighed, doing her best to smile.

Sophie heard the strain.

Willy jabbered on, and Cade took off on a parental oratory about the intelligence of his firstborn. The sounds of family swirled around Sophie—meat sizzling in the skillet, childish chatter, parents boasting. The front door opening.

Her pulse leaped into double time at boot steps crossing the great room on their way to the kitchen. Deacon? Clay? Neither should cause such a reaction, but the possibility of one certainly did. And she certainly best squelch it immediately.

"Smells mighty good in here."

Turning a steak, she relaxed at Deacon's crusty voice. No need to see him to know. But she'd have to turn around and set food on the table sooner or later. In the meantime, she retrieved potatoes from the pantry and sliced them into another skillet.

The tea kettle boiled over, and she grabbed it without thinking.

Wincing with pain, she gripped her wrist, angry for being so foolish. More heat closed in behind her and a long arm reached around with a hot pad and slid the kettle to a cooler spot.

*Lord, may I melt into a puddle on the floor and evaporate.*

The Lord did not accommodate her. She pressed her hand against her bodice and glanced into Clay's questioning eyes. Not laughing, but close to smiling. And close to untying her as if she were a loose apron string.

He reached for her hand and, in spite of her resistance, turned it over, revealing a pink blotch sure to blister. Lifting the pump handle at the sink, he spoke to her in low tones as if they were the only two people in the room. "Hold your hand under the water for a few minutes." Then he turned to Mae Ann. "Do you have any honey?"

"Yes." Chair legs scraped the wooden floor.

"Stay right there," he said. "Just tell me where it is. I can get it."

Though Sophie felt ridiculous standing at the sink doing nothing, she did it. "Deacon, would you please transfer the steaks in the skillet to the platter I have on the counter, start two more, and stir the potatoes?"

"Consider it done."

More chair legs scraped. Willy chattered like a jay. Cade took the coffee pot from the stove—with a hot pad—and filled the cups she'd set on the table earlier.

Clay returned with a crock of honey and shut off the water.

She lifted her apron to dry her hand, but he stopped her, and with a clean flour-sack from a drawer, gently pressed the palm of her hand dry. Using a fork to spear the hunk of honeycomb, he held it over her hand until it dripped like liquid amber onto the blister, then finished by tearing a strip from the toweling and wrapping her hand.

With a gentle press of his fingers and a warm smile, he broke through her flimsy self-consciousness.

"You'll be good as new in no time. Just keep it clean. No pitchin' hay or roughhousing with the dogs." His eyes snapped with the tease, and a corner of his mouth twitched against the laughter it held.

Why were there no other words waiting than the two she seemed to use over and over where Clay Ferguson was concerned? "Thank you."

Looking her square in the eye, he dipped his head once and let go, then took a seat at the table.

No one had been listening and watching as she'd feared, and Clay joined a conversation she hadn't been aware of.

"Yearling bulls?"

"I bought a couple last spring. They covered a few heifers, but I want you to take a look at them before I retire my old herd bull. Tell me if you think they were worth the investment."

"You'll have a pretty good idea after the first crop," Clay said.

"We will. But Deacon says you've 'got the eye.'"

Sophie could vouch for that, and she pushed straying hair into the loosening knot at her neck.

Deacon laid two more steaks on the platter and turned with a proud grin. At least she thought it was a grin, based on the spread of his mustache.

"Takes me back to my drovin' days. Up from Texas with beeves as far as the eye could see." He set the platter on the table and sat down.

*Life goes on.* But with family and the gentle touch of someone dear, it went more easily. She bunched her apron, opened the oven door, and with her left hand and a towel removed two pans of golden-topped biscuits.

*Someone dear?*

Where had that come from?

~

The smell of fried steak, fresh biscuits, and Sophie's hair had Clay's head swimming so fast he could hardly see his plate.

She'd tried to resist his help but eventually gave way. Like a skittish filly that didn't know if it could trust a man. 'Course he'd not let on that he'd compared her to a horse.

"Thank you, Lord, for this food and the work You give us to do," Parker said.

Caught unawares, Clay ducked his head—quick, like a bronc.

"And the people who help us do it. Amen."

"'Men," Deacon offered.

"Eat hardy. We're bringing the horses down this morning. They're in Echo Valley, so it won't take us long to gather and drive 'em in." Parker paused to chew a bite of steak and throw Sophie an appreciative glance.

She missed it. Sitting straight across from Clay, she watched her food like it might sprout legs and run off. She had no idea how becoming she was with that blush on her cheeks—either from the heat of the stove or something on her mind. He knew which one he hoped it was, but he best not get ahead of himself.

"We'll run 'em in the barn corral, and you can each cut out your mounts. Deacon, take two saddle horses, plus what you need for the wagon. Clay, take two for now. The rest will stay here in one of the lower pastures. The other ranchers we're workin' with will have their own strings, and we'll run ours in with the remuda once we meet up."

From the head of the table, Parker angled a glance. "While you're here, I provide your mounts and your food. Let me know if you need different tack, and I'll see you get it. You're expected to trim and shoe your own ponies, but I supply the shoes. Today you'll carry the tools in case one of us throws a shoe before we get home."

A creased brow. "You can shoe a horse, can't you?"

"I can."

Silence settled over the table as everyone made light work of Sophie's cooking.

Parker drained his coffee and pushed his plate back. "Tomorrow we leave before it breaks light. It'll take all day and then some to get the cattle out of the hills and woods and down to the bunch ground. Deacon'll have the chuck wagon."

At mention of Deacon and the wagon, Sophie took a bundle from the counter and slipped it to him with a quiet word at his ear. From the look in the old codger's eye, Clay would lay money it was more of Travine Price's fritters.

Soon enough, Clay, Deacon, and Parker were sittin' their saddles, riding around the barn to open range.

The horses were grazing in the valley, just as Parker predicted, a smaller bunch than the band of mares Clay had once helped drive down. The weather was warmer, and the horses weren't as haired up as the mares had been, nor as free-spirited. Watching them bunch and travel, he picked two that looked like they'd be strong-hearted—a white-stockinged sorrel and a black.

By midday, they had the horses corralled and Parker rode the perimeter.

"Deacon, you throw first loop. Then Clay."

Deacon snagged a little dun that pretty much let him catch it, and on Clay's first try, he dropped a hoolihan on the sorrel and led him to a separate pen.

Parker went for the black, but it ducked and the loop fell on another horse. Clay watched his face as he settled with the horse he'd collared and led it out. Boss or no, you rode what you caught.

Deacon tried for the black but not with his typical flair. The old man could rope the hair off a wolf without breaking a sweat, and Clay knew it.

He didn't want to be gifted, though the horse *had* ducked. He built a loop, predicted the black's dance routine and threw accordingly. When the loop snugged around its neck, it bogged its head and went to bucking.

Both men hollered and whooped and laid bets on whether Clay would get it saddled.

No gifting to it. He'd been set up.

Parker caught a third one in short order, and in another hour, everything was haltered, handled, and fed a can of oats. Clay was hungry enough to eat a handful himself, but he was counting on Sophie cooking up another storm like the one she'd served that morning.

He wasn't disappointed—except to see that she wasn't there.

Mae Ann said she was putting Willy down for a nap.

He swigged his coffee, afraid his frustration read like a wanted poster. Why else would she explain Sophie's absence when no one had asked?

That afternoon he helped load the chuck wagon with sacks of flour, sugar, coffee, and beans. He checked all the horses' hooves, mouthed them for ulcers and loose teeth, and made sure the team's harness was in good repair. He also threw in a half-box of horseshoes and nails.

Deacon hung a can of axel grease under the wagon, tied a wrapped side of salt pork to the bed, and loaded his chuck box with canned milk, fruit, baking soda, and other fixin's to feed a crew. Clay hadn't looked that hard in the pantry, but chances were he'd be making a trip to town based on the amount of food Deacon loaded.

The next morning, dawn split a cloud-bank on the eastern edge, sparking anticipation in man and beast alike. Though Parker wore a sober expression after kissing his wife and son good-bye, the send-off was anything but solemn. Deacon hollered at his team, the yellow dog howled from the stall where it was locked, and Blue yipped and bounced like a pup, anxious to leave.

Sophie ran out of the house with a covered basket and handed it up to Deacon. Must have been what she'd baked the previous night, for the aroma had lingered in the kitchen this morning—cinnamon and sugar—and she sure enough hadn't served it alongside her eggs and hotcakes.

With a sharp whistle, Parker waved his hat. Deacon slapped the reins on his team, and the chuck wagon rolled ahead, complaining all the way. Clay swung the corral gate wide, and a half dozen horses ran out in a cloud of dust. Parker loped alongside the small herd, Blue close behind.

The thrill of it almost made Clay want to go with them, but he had his own work and plenty of it.

He closed the gate and slid the bar, then leaned back against the poles, surveying his responsibilities. A hot-blooded stallion on the mend, livestock and fences to tend, and a place of his own to find.

Plus two women and a child to look after, with another one about to hatch any day.

And to think—less than a week ago he'd been a man with nothing but his horse, a saddle, and a dream.

Part of that dream stood over by a long bench set back under a cluster of cottonwood trees, arm around Parker's wife, who was wiping her eyes as the parade clamored past.

With a casual turn of her head, Sophie looked over her shoulder toward the outbuildings and barn, the corral and hitch rail, then settled on him.

From the look on her face, he'd lay good money that she could read his intentions, even from a distance.

# Chapter 11

Against all counsel, Mae Ann had refused to stay abed that morning, nor would she be dissuaded from seeing her husband off. Sophie kept a close eye, attentive to the slightest change or halting step.

More restful after the grand departure, Mae Ann settled at the kitchen table with a cup of chamomile tea while Sophie let the chickens out and gathered eggs. Clay was nowhere to be seen. Curious, since he'd been standing by the corral when Deacon and Cade headed out. Looking right at her.

She shook off what she'd read in his eyes but nearly dropped the egg basket when she returned to the house and the door opened right in front of her.

Clay steadied her, one hand on her arm and the other on the basket until he let it go and ran both hands slowly down her arms, settling them at her waist.

Unable to breathe, she merely blinked.

A slow smile lifted one side of his mouth and crinkled his eyes, then he touched his hat brim and strode off toward the barn.

If she didn't get ahold of herself, she'd have no nerves or eggs left by the end of the branding.

In the kitchen, a bucket of milk waited on the sideboard.

Mae Ann sweetened her tea from the silver sugar bowl on the table. "Someone's been busy already this morning."

"Yes." Sophie smothered the single word with as much indifference as possible, still searching for a deep, even breath. She had no desire to discuss someone she couldn't get out of her thoughts. "Since you didn't eat earlier, what is your preference—fried eggs and bacon? Hotcakes?"

"Can you poach an egg?"

She took stock of the mistress of Parker Land and Cattle. "Are you not feeling well?"

Mae Ann gave a half-laugh. "No. I mean yes. Physically, I'm fine. But something less greasy appeals to me right now. Like a plain slice of skillet-toasted bread and a boring, poached egg."

"One boring egg and dry toast on the way."

Sophie knew very well that *fine* was not what Mae Ann felt, physically or emotionally. This wasn't the Parkers' first roundup, nor would it be their last, Lord willing. Yet Mae Ann and Cade were like young lovers. Sophie hadn't seen the like in all the people she knew. Not even Abigail and Hiram made eyes at each other like the Parkers, and Sophie suspected it had to do with Mae Ann's tragic start as a mail-order widow.

Mama said the good Lord worked out that situation in a way only He could orchestrate, and for a while, Sophie had found hope in their unlikely story. But each year, that hope thinned a bit as birthdays ticked by like seconds on the mantel clock. And with each birthday, the hitch in the left side of her mouth seemed to grow more pronounced as well. Not the most encouraging combination.

"I wonder if he let Cougar out of his stall in the barn."

"Who?" Sophie bit her tongue the moment the word escaped. She might have given herself away.

"Clay, of course. Who else?"

"He really wanted to go with the others, didn't he?"

"Who?"

Sophie turned away before rolling her eyes. Was Mae Ann mocking her? "Cougar. I heard him yowling from his prison."

"I know, poor thing. But he'd be no help on a gathering and would probably change his mind halfway up the hills and head back here alone. I'd hate to see him attacked by a pack of coyotes or his name-bearer. Thankfully, Cade has gone to locking him in the barn any time he takes Blue along."

"That's very considerate." Sophie flipped the toast over and removed the egg from its simmering bath.

"Clay seems to have that same characteristic, don't you think?"

Sophie's lack of reply echoed through the kitchen.

"You have to admit, that bucket of milk on the counter is rather considerate, especially since I didn't mention milking the cow to anyone. He seems to just do what needs doing without being asked."

Sophie did not want to agree, but ever since Clay had returned on the train, he'd done exactly that. She laid the toast on a floral-edged plate, topped it with the poached egg, and set it before the weary mother.

Eventually, the morning's excitement caught up to Mae Ann, and she agreed to lie down in her room.

Sophie helped her up the stairs. Again, stairs—the bane of motherhood. What she wouldn't give for a sofa by the fireplace instead of those two worn leather chairs.

Willy whimpered for his daddy, but she convinced him to nap with Mama, then hurried down to start a roast. Dinner would be late, but they still had to eat, as did someone else.

And they needed clean clothes. Sophie had seen the pile of laundry on the back porch by the wash tub, and immediately wondered who did Clay's. She shivered at the disconcerting thought.

Halfway through peeling potatoes, she laid the paring knife aside and listened for a repetitive noise that had worked its way into her subconscious.

There it was again. Tapping. Over and over.

The window above the sink gave no indication of the source, merely a view of the garden, which also needed tending, and the mountains climbing in staggered peaks to the west.

She went to the great room and cracked open the front door. The yard was clear aside from the chickens. Her mare and Betsy's Blanca grazed in the near pasture, and the rest of the horses appeared quiet and unalarmed farther out beyond the windmill.

She stared at the derrick. Was it making that noise?

Again the tapping started, and it drew her ear and eye to Deacon's cabin.

Clay knelt atop a lean-to that very much leaned to the cabin, nailing shingles onto the roof. Rhythmically he hammered, three taps followed by a pause each time he reached for another shingle. A pouch at his side held nails, she guessed, and he worked as if he'd been a carpenter all his life.

Folding her arms, she leaned against the door frame, assessing his measured movements and unwasted effort. He could certainly have made a handrail for the Eisner's apartment, and would not have boasted about it like a certain hotelier. Sophie might hire Clay for the job herself, just to see that it was done and done right.

Was there anything he didn't do?

She eased the door closed and returned to the kitchen, where she moved the tea kettle to the hottest spot and retrieved the honey crock from the pantry. It'd be easy enough to sweeten a starter cup of strong tea, then add cold water from the pump. A cool drink while working in the sun was the least she could do for a man Mae Ann considered so considerate.

A smile tugged at the phrasing.

Another batch of oat cookies wouldn't hurt either. If she couldn't find currants or raisins, she'd dip a spoon of preserves into the middle of each mound.

Within the hour, she had sweet tea in a tin pitcher, warm cookies in her apron pocket, and a roast in the back of the oven. Armed with the tea and a tin cup, she went out the back door and around the end of the house.

*Tap, tap, tap.*

Clay's back was to her, shirtless in the sun where he knelt on one knee atop the low roof. Closing in on him, she slowed her steps, hesitant to simply appear unannounced before a man half-dressed. Not that he was doing anything improper, for the sun bore down with a summer-like insistence, casting irregular marks across his back. Odd, since no trees shaded the cabin.

He stood then and flexed his neck and shoulders, a sheen of sweat defining the stature he'd gained. The muscled strength. The long whip-like scars that ran old and puckered from his right shoulder to the opposite hip.

Cold shock held her in place and her lungs froze on a gasp.

He turned.

~

Some things couldn't be erased. Hopefully, the horror on Sophie's face wasn't one of them.

Clay snatched up his shirt and pulled it on, bothered not so much by what she'd seen as her reaction to it. He jumped the short distance to the ground.

Stone-like, she held a pitcher in one hand, a tin cup in the other, her mouth uncharacteristically ajar.

He buttoned his shirt. "I didn't hear you coming."

Her jaw clapped shut and expressive eyes roamed his face as if seeing him for the first time. Sorrow, wonder, curiosity all played in them, though not the one thing he hated most—pity.

"I—I should have called out. Let you know I had something for you." She raised the cup and pitcher as if they were prizes, but her expression didn't fit the gesture.

He took the cup from her and held it while she poured dark tea. What could he say? Please excuse my brand?

The cool sweetness refreshed him, and he downed it all at once. "How'd you know that was exactly what I needed? It's hot up there."

She gathered herself a little more and refilled his cup. Again he drank it all, while she watched him like he might do something unexpected.

He offered a smile. "One more, if you don't mind."

She poured with one hand and reached into her apron pocket with the other. "Dinner will be late, so I thought you might enjoy something to tide you over until then."

Three cookies covered her upturned palm.

As he took them, his fingers brushed her skin. Warm and smooth and full of caring.

"This will hit the spot." He raised one in a mock toast, then bit into it. Warm and soft, like its baker.

"Are these what you rushed out to Deacon this morning?" Not that it was any of his business, but he had to say something, the way she was looking at him, other than what he knew she wanted him to say.

A near laugh escaped, but not from her eyes. "Whether he shares with the others is up to him, but at least they'll keep him happy while he's driving."

A step took her back, farther away. "I can bring more if you'd like."

He'd like, but she had her own work to do.

"Well, I best be getting inside. Um, keep an eye on Willy, you know. And Mae Ann."

He nodded, holding her eyes with his, wishing she wouldn't go so soon. "How's your hand?"

Puzzlement flashed before she remembered and switched the pitcher to her left hand. "It doesn't hurt at all." She flexed her fingers. "But I should probably change the dressing. It's gotten dirty just working in the kitchen." Another step back, yet still she faced him, opening an invisible door. Waiting.

"I appreciate you thinking of me." He had a lot more to say, but now wasn't the time. Not with the question filling her eyes that he couldn't answer.

"Of course. I mean …" Her brows tucked together and she fumbled with her apron.

He'd never seen her so unsure of herself. So distracted.

"All right, then. Roast for dinner. And potatoes." Another backward step.

"And more sweet tea?"

"Um, yes. Of course. Tea." At that, she turned and walked to the end of the ranch house rather than going in the front door, and at the corner hitched her skirt and ran out of view.

He would never understand women. But it didn't matter, as long as one in particular was somewhere close.

~

Flattened against the back door, Sophie clutched the cold pitcher against her middle and stared up at the hill behind the house. A regal pine spread its arms protectively over two grave markers. Based on the hammering of her heart and head, she might not be far off from that state herself.

Who had done such a horrible thing to Clay? And when? Where? *Why*? Questions bunched like cattle before a storm, but she had no right to ask them. No wonder he'd never mentioned his past.

She fingered the scar at her mouth, instantly hearing the snap of wood, her father's cry, and the sound of his body hitting the ground where she'd been standing. She squeezed her eyes shut against the image of his twisted form, yet still she saw his eyes open in death and the crushed bucket beneath her. Milk pooled on the ground near her head, bright red spots marring its purity. A sting at her mouth had drawn her fingers, and when she lowered her hand, it was covered with blood.

Mama held her tight as a cradle board while Doc Weaver stitched her mouth. And the wagon bed held Papa's body while they took him to the undertaker. All the stitches in the world would not bring him back to her or mend her ten-year-old heart.

She'd borne both scars more than half her life, but in light of Clay's scars so much worse than her own, she cringed. Mama had warned her about comparing herself to others and, as was usually the case, Mama was right. There would always be someone with more or less than she. More skill or less. More insight or less. More pain or less.

*Comparison is futile and self-defeating,* Mama had said. *Focus instead on what God has blessed you with.*

Sophie blew out a breath and rubbed the back of her hand across her eyes. Enough reminiscing. She seldom went to that place in her memories for just this reason. It always left her spent and worn.

Opening the back door into the kitchen, she heard a loud *thud* and set the pitcher on the table. Another *thud*, and she ran for the stairs.

~

Sophie forgot the cup. Clay debated whether to take it to the house or wait until she called for dinner. He never wavered over such simple decisions and, in fact, didn't qualify them as decisions. More like reactions. What made sense. The shortest distance between two points.

And yet …

He tipped the cup to catch the last drop in his mouth and headed for the house.

Stomping his boots on the stones out front, he held the door open, giving Sophie a chance to hear him coming. Then he stepped inside, listening for pots and pans, chairs scraping the floor. A broom. Dishes being washed.

Nothing.

"Sophie?" His pulse picked up and he walked around the dividing wall into the kitchen. Roasting beef tainted the air and the tea pitcher sat on the table, dripping a ring of moisture onto the wood. The back door stood open. He checked the porch and yard but found no one.

*Mae Ann.*

He took the stairs two at a time.

# CHAPTER 12

Sophie forced a calm she wasn't feeling into her voice. "Wait. Don't push yet. Let me see how far along you are."

"I—am—wait—ing!" Mae Ann hissed through clenched teeth.

Willy sat on the floor near a knocked-over chair, a pout quivering his bottom lip. Never had Sophie felt so unprepared. She could not deliver a baby and watch a lively three-year-old at the same time. What had she been thinking?

How could she get Clay's attention—throw her shoe through the window? And thereby teach Willy that such behavior was acceptable?

With a towel from the washstand, she bathed Mae Ann's neck and arms. In less than two minutes, her face reddened, her breathing stopped, and she went rigid.

"Breathe, honey. You must breathe."

Mae Ann's rock-hard belly eventually eased beneath Sophie's touch, and she fell back on the pillows, gasping for breath.

Heavy steps charged up the stairs, and a man's arms snatched Willy from the threshold.

"Oh, Clay, thank God. Please—bring my satchel from the room at the end of the landing. And a pitcher of cool water as well as a kettle of hot. And all the towels you can find."

He delivered livestock, for heaven's sake.

He understood, she told herself.

His mere presence in the house somehow encouraged her. And he had Willy.

In less than a minute, he set her satchel in the room and gave it a shove across the floor, then hurried down the stairs. *God bless him.* Yes, God bless him and Mae Ann as well. It was all Sophie could do to keep images of the Eisners from invading the moment.

"You're doing just fine." She pushed damp hair from Mae Ann's brow and reached deep for that peaceful river Pastor Bittman had talked about last Sunday. Lord, she needed a gushing spring flood.

Lifting Mae Ann's skirt and petticoat, she discovered things much farther along than she'd expected this soon. She discarded stockings and everything else except the loose-fitting house dress and draped the skirt protectively over Mae Ann in case Clay returned.

He'd better return. This baby was coming today.

She patted Mae Ann's arm. "You're little one must be eager to get here and see the world."

Clay charged in with pitchers, towels, and Willy, and set everything except the boy within Sophie's reach. With a reassuring hand atop Sophie's shoulder, he left as quickly.

She was beginning to cherish that gesture.

Mae Ann pulled up again. Sophie went to the foot of the bed and checked once more, then offered her hands.

"All right, you can push on the next contraction. Take hold. I've got you."

Again and again, they repeated the steps. Sunlight shifted on the floor, time inching by and Mae Ann's grip growing weaker with each contraction.

*God, help her. Help me. This is Your plan—life, the way You have set things in order. Bring life. Please, bring rejoicing, not weeping.*

Mae Ann's grip suddenly clamped vise-like onto Sophie's fingers and she pulled as if to dislocate arms from shoulders.

Another clenching squeeze and screaming groan, and the baby swished out onto the bed.

Sophie broke from Mae Ann's grasp, her fingers near numb. Quickly, she cleared the infant's mouth and held it by its heels for a slap to its tiny wet bottom.

No response.

*Oh, God—please.*

With prayer racing as fast as her heart, she repeated the process until a startled gasp ushered breath into newborn lungs.

Sophie held her own until the most beautiful sound in all the world broke through—a baby's first cry. The spring flood she'd prayer for swelled from her own heart and ran down her cheeks. Life—precious life. No moment lived on earth was better than this.

With two narrow strips from her satchel, she tied off the cord, then swaddled the babe in a clean towel. Mae Ann had fallen against the pillows in utter exhaustion, eyes closed, chest heaving.

"You have a little girl." Sophie leaned close, watching Mae Ann's face, praying she was conscious and able to hold her child.

Her eyes fluttered, and Sophie laid the babe against its mother's breast.

"The Lord has blessed you again with the fruit of the womb—His reward."

Mae Anne's tears mingled with sweat as she kissed her daughter's soppy hair.

Sophie's tears continued to fall as they always did at the miracle of birth. And this one truly had been a miracle, the timing so unexpected. Everyone, Doc Weaver included, thought at least a week remained. But this sweet little girl had other ideas.

Sophie's arms and heart ached anew, not only for herself this time, but for the Eisners as well.

"Do you need anything?"

Clay's voice came from the hallway, calm and deep. Strong and comforting like his hand on her shoulder.

"I'm about to cut the cord."

"How?"

*How?* The way she always did. "With scissors from my satchel."

"Wait. Please—I'll be right back."

Somewhat irritated by his request, she followed his uneven but hurried descent of the stairs, the banging swing of the front door, and through the window, his dash to the cabin without Willy, who must be downstairs.

In less than a breath, he was back, running through the great room, then bounding up the stairs. "May I come in?"

She threw an extra quilt over Mae Ann who nodded her consent.

"All right."

Sheepishly he entered with Willy, a giant holding a child's hand, and turned his gaze away as he held out a rolled leather pouch. "You'll find an exceptionally sharp scalpel and a small bottle of carbolic acid. Hold the scalpel over a towel and pour the acid on both sides of the blade. Don't dry it off or touch anything with it before you cut the cord."

She took the pouch, found the short, pointed knife and bottle, and hesitated.

"The acid will purify the blade and reduce the risk of infection." He paused, softened his voice. "Trust me."

Had Clay learned this at veterinary school? She'd never heard of such a thing. Pain was not a factor in the procedure, but the precaution was new to her. Steeling herself, she unwrapped the babe, uncapped the bottle, and poured the sweet-smelling liquid over the scalpel.

*Trust* Me, another voice whispered in her heart.

The cord cut easier than any had before.

Boot steps left the room.

"Clay?"

They paused outside the door.

She wanted to say more than *thank you*. She wanted to fling her arms around him and shelter against his solid chest. "Would you please take the roast out of the oven?"

"Mama?" Willy's little voice called pleadingly.

Sophie went to the door. "Will you wait while I take him to her for just a moment?"

At Clay's consent, Sophie led him to his mama's bedside, too weary to carry the boy.

"I love you, Willy." Mae Ann's whisper drew her son's eyes, so like her own. He looked from her to his sister and back again. "A baby."

"That's right, sweetheart. We love her too."

Bursting inside and fighting to contain it, Sophie leaned toward Willy. "Let's go now so Mama can rest. Would you like a cookie?"

"Yes, and tea, pease."

Sophie's heart squeezed anew, and she led Willy back to the door, where Clay waited tall and powerful and protective.

He lifted Willy with a hidden tickle that drew a little-boy laugh. But his eyes held so much more than she had seen there before, and she laid her hand on his arm that encircled the child. He covered it with his own and gave a light squeeze before turning for the stairs.

Feeling as worn as Mae Ann looked, Sophie washed the baby while Mae Ann napped, then gently laid her in her mother's arms. "Time for dinner, little lady."

Mae Ann opened tired but smiling eyes and held her daughter close. "Thank you," she said, "for being here again."

~

Clay pulled a lidded kettle from the oven. A peek inside revealed a dry roast, but the aroma filled the kitchen and his brain with promise of a meal better than he could make.

"Let's go for a ride." He handed Willy a cookie, took one for himself, and went out the back door. Sophie wouldn't be down for a while, and he had a three-year-old to entertain.

He set the boy in the saddle, then swung up and lifted him to his lap. They climbed the gentle slope to the knoll that overlooked the ranch, Willy laughing at the yellow dog running ahead, flushing rabbits out of the brush. Clay figured the little fella had ridden with Parker, the way he sat easy, hands on the saddle swells. Born to it.

The play of light across the land made it all look different than it did at sunrise. Fewer shadows, greener. Snowy peaks sharper cut against blue sky. Scrub oak huddled beneath an outcrop of red sandstone, and the dog bellied in under an arched branch, sniffing and snuffling. Clay drew rein at the top, taking in the wide sweep of high park between two cedar-covered ridges. Jays squawked, and a fly chased itself around Duster's flicking ears.

"Someday this will all be yours, Willy. Your papa's land. Your inheritance." Clay looped an arm around the boy, who had no way of knowing how good he had it.

Memories shrouded the sun, dimming the view …

*A boot swipe cut Clay's legs out from under him and sent him face down. "You killed her, you no-account dirt-licker."*

*He bent his arms over his head and flinched at every gut kick until he retched and spewed his last meal on the feet of his attacker.*

*"Look what you've done, you good-for-nothing piece of dirt!"*

*A whiskey bottle dropped next to his head, the dregs of what always led to a beating sharp in his nose. A muddled curse, a scuffling step, and a body fell across him, heavy with the stench of sweat and liquor.*

*He shoved against the dead weight and rolled out. Pushing to his knees, he wiped his soiled mouth on his shirt sleeve …*

"Papa's land?"

Clay ran a hand down his face, scraping at the memory, the stink, the taste of bile on his tongue. "That's right, Willy. Papa's land. You have a future here."

His own future lay hidden in his saddlebags, ever since he'd learned his father had drunk himself to death. Not an inheritance, but what was left over. He intended to see things went different for his son if he had one.

They rode north around the pasture with the yearling bulls, and by the time they skirted Pine Hill, Willy was nodding with every step of the horse. Clay stopped at the house and took the boy inside.

"I'm thusty, Mustu Cay."

"Me too."

He helped Willy into his chair and scooted it close to the table with one of Sophie's cookies at eye level. From what remained in the pitcher, he filled a small cup for Willy, another for Sophie, and sat down with the cup he'd brought in earlier.

Footfall on the stairway sounded a welcomed note.

When she came around the corner, he stood. Maggie's instruction all those years ago hadn't fallen on deaf ears, though he'd been nearly as clueless as Willy at the time.

Sophie looked at him curiously, but took a seat, immediately polishing off what he'd poured. Her temples were damp with sweaty hair. Maggie would say she was *glistening*. But he wouldn't. Sweat was sweat.

A question filled Sophie's eyes before she voiced it. "How did you know?"

The same way he knew to move before a cow kicked him to kingdom come. The same way he knew a horse was about to snake its neck out and take a bite from his hide. He just knew.

He scratched his unshaven jaw. "A feeling in my gut?" More question than answer.

She let loose a sigh and leaned back in her chair.

He set the crock of cookies in front of her. "Maybe you need something to tide you over until dinner."

Her crooked smile pulled weakly. "More like supper, now."

Which would be just the two of them eating together if he didn't count Willy.

"What?"

She read him like a newspaper, which wasn't the most comforting thought.

"Just thinking ahead is all. Why?"

"You seemed, I don't know, suddenly surprised by something."

Intuition—a trait not to be taken lightly.

She went to the stove and stoked the fire before moving the kettle to the hottest part.

*Use a hot pad* trailed through his brain, but he held his tongue. This woman would be feeding him for the next month, and he didn't want to sour that proposition by telling her how to do her job. Beans and canned peaches would go only so far in Deacon's cabin, and he'd never baked a cookie in his life.

However, she *had* taken his advice on cutting the cord.

"Did you learn about that acid at school?"

They were running parallel. "Antiseptic is being used more and more. A British surgeon, Joseph Lister, believes germs cause infection. But he also says they can be killed before they invade a patient. He pretty much proved his theory when he used carbolic acid during minor surgery on Queen Victoria."

"Germs." She looked doubtful.

"Those small, invisible things that are easily held at bay by washing our hands as well as surgical areas. I sterilized my instruments and Xavier's gash before stitching him up. So far, no infection."

"I see." She pressed her hands down the front of her apron.

She was right, the dressing on her burn needed to be changed. He got up and took her hand, turning it over in his. "I can change this for you."

He held on gently, yet as firmly as he held her eyes with his. "In a day or so, you won't need one at all."

The kettle hissed, and he pulled it to the front of the stove.

"I'm brewing tea for Mae Ann," she said. "Willow bark as well as elderberry. The herbs are in my satchel." Her voice hushed with a promise. "I'll be right back."

He let her fingers slide from his, realizing he'd change that dressing every hour if it meant he could touch her.

When she returned, he was bouncing Willy on his knee, teasing laughter from the boy's crumb-covered mouth.

"You do well with children." Pleasure wrapped her words. "Did your mother teach you?"

The bouncing stopped. Willy looked up at him, not understanding why. Neither did Clay, completely. He returned the boy to the chair and gave him another cookie.

Sophie stared but kept her thoughts to herself.

Motherhood was not a delicate subject in his line of work. But *his* mother was. The cutting pain attached to her memory was sharper than any scalpel. Of all the agony he'd tried leaving in the past, he had never been able to let go of her.

Just like he hadn't been able to let go of her that night.

"Clay?"

Sophie's touch was a firebrand and he jerked.

She pulled back, confusion clouding her soft eyes. "What's wrong? Are you all right?"

No, he wasn't all right, and too much was wrong to talk about. If he could just keep the memories buried, he'd manage. He *did* manage, most of the time. Until an innocent like Pete Hickman or Willy or Sophie Price tore open the sutures and he started bleeding all over himself.

He tousled the boy's hair, keenly aware that his mother lay abed upstairs with a sibling. Two points in the kid's favor. "You're a big brother now. Maybe you can help your ma come up with a name for your—"

At his glance, Sophie answered. "Sister. Willy has a little sister."

Clay stood, chair legs scraping the floor. "I've near finished patching the roof. And there's a couple other things I need to check on. I'll be back for dinner. Supper." He scrubbed his face. "Later."

*Maybe.*

"Clay?"

He stopped at the gentle way she said his name but didn't turn around.

"Your help today meant everything and … "

He looked across his shoulder but avoided her gaze.

"I want you to know you can talk to me about things. *Any*thing. I'd like to help if I can."

He gave a quick nod and beat a path out the front door and across the yard. At the cabin, he worked the pump handle until water ran cold and fast, then ducked under it, soaking his shirt as well as his hair.

He'd never backed down from an honest fight or allowed some fool to beat an animal. He'd never turned away those who couldn't pay for his services or refused to make the most difficult call of a merciful death. But he couldn't face the pulsing wound within himself. And the one thing he feared more than any other was Sophie's likelihood of making him do just that.

He didn't go back to the house that night. He had to get hold of himself first, and daybreak always gave him a clearer perspective. He'd moved his bedroll from the bunk room to Deacon's bed in the main cabin and plopped down on it fully dressed. Reaching for the lamp, he caught the dull shimmer of gold letters on a black leather book behind it. Now wasn't the time to open it, though he didn't know exactly when the right time might be. He blew out the lamp and rolled into his blankets, waiting for sleep to dull the ache.

In the middle of the night, a cry woke him. A young boy screaming for his ma. Flames licked up the sides of the barn, but he couldn't get her to move. He pulled on her arm, her dress, her hair, but she wouldn't wake up. He crawled on top of her. Smoke burned his throat and eyes, and he cried until rough hands dragged him away and carried him outside.

Then his ma came out, limp as a rag in the arms of a man whose face he couldn't see. Horses charged out. The cow his ma had been milking ran from the barn, its calf following, wide-eyed and weak, the hair burned off its hide. The roof collapsed and the walls fell with it, and the smell made him retch.

Suddenly awake, Clay stumbled out the front door to the pump, his clothes soaked with sweat, heart stampeding. He splashed water on his face and chest, then straightened and looked up at the swath of stars banding the night, flecks of broken light against the vault.

Was she there? Was she watching him?

He'd never know the answer, because he couldn't bring himself to ask the God who had taken her from him.

# CHAPTER 13

Puzzled by Clay's reaction the day before, Sophie stood at the sink, staring out the kitchen window and seeing nothing but sunrise casting a crimson flare on snow-covered peaks. At every turn, he amazed her—with unbounded kindness, inexplicable timing, or surprising disclosures. Partial disclosures. Bits and pieces of a story she longed to hear and understand. And she finally admitted to herself that she really didn't know anything about this man who had worked his way into her heart.

The difference in their ages was now the least of her concerns, for he had clearly lived more of life than she. He was also clearly unwilling to share it with her.

When he hadn't returned for supper, she was not surprised. It was to be their first meal alone together, and she too felt a bit awkward about it. But after the incident with Willy, the tension between them had stretched tight as barbed wire. Perhaps time was all they needed—that old standby remedy that made women forget their birth pangs and gladly give life to another child.

Yet she'd worried. She'd fretted and stewed until she was absolutely useless, so she went out to the barn to see if his horse was gone. Duster stood half asleep in his stall, and she hurried back to the house, praying she hadn't been found out.

Another hour crawled by, then another, and near midnight she stole back with the plate she'd kept in the warmer. Potatoes, carrots, and sliced roast so dry she had to make extra gravy from bacon drippings. A half dozen cookies. Determined to feed him, she'd lifted the latch on Deacon's cabin door.

Clay's long frame stretched from head to foot of the bed, boots and all. She set the basket on the old table, then tiptoed out, no breath passing her lips until she made it back to the house, where she checked through the front window for any sign that she had wakened him.

Nothing.

And this morning nothing—other than a *thump* from upstairs that quickly brought her back to more pressing matters like breakfast. Willy had learned that she came running when he pushed over the chair. The little urchin.

Prepared this time, she carried a tray of toast and tea upstairs and quietly opened the bedroom door. From the smell of things, Willy had been busy doing more than just pushing over the chair.

"Good morning, young man," she whispered. "Do you need to use the potty?"

Mae Ann lay propped on her pillows, the babe at her breast. "At least he doesn't seem to be jealous."

Sophie set the tray on the bed beside Mae Ann. "No, he doesn't. I'm afraid he's too busy for that. I'll take him outside to the privy and get him cleaned up. Honestly, I didn't think about his needs last night."

"Do you mind changing him?"

Unbid humor bubbled from Sophie's heart, relief from heavier thoughts. "And what would you like me to change him to? A puppy? A foal? A kitten for the barn?"

Mae Ann laughed, then pressed her hand against her abdomen with a small moan.

"Oh, I'm sorry. I know better. Of course I don't mind changing his britches. That's part of the reason I'm here, to help. I'm doing laundry today, so I'll soon be disturbing you as I change the bed linen and help you with your clothes and another round of swaddling for …" Her fingers brushed the baby's downy head. "Have you chosen a name?"

"Madeline. Cade and I discussed it before he left. I felt certain she was a girl and Cade argued that it was a boy. But he agreed on the name *just in case*." Gentler laughter brushed Madeline's head as she suckled.

"It's a beautiful name and well chosen." Carved into one of the crosses atop the hill—Cade's mother's name. Sophie recalled his parents' funeral, the same day Betsy eloped with her beau. Such pain all the way around for this family, yet now new life bore a beloved name and offered another go at things.

Self-pity pinched behind Sophie's eyes, and when Madeline broke away in sated slumber, Sophie scooped her up. "Enjoy your breakfast now that she's had hers. I'll bring the cradle in from Willy's nursery and then take care of the little man."

~

Clay hadn't missed the latch lifting on the cabin door last night, nor the aroma of seasoned roast from the plate Sophie left on the table. But he couldn't eat it.

Before dawn, he saddled Duster and rode for the knoll. Unobstructed, the grassland lightened at the first wink of day, but the red-rimmed horizon promised a storm before nightfall.

His personal storm had quieted, slid away untended, and with the morning came a peculiar trait that had carried him through life with something like hope. He didn't know when it started, but he knew it was the reason he leaned toward daybreak. Maybe something his mother had told him early on, but he wouldn't dredge through the memories to find it.

Duster tasted the first breeze and tossed his head, flicking his ears toward horses grazing below. A shrill whinny from the corralled stallion answered a call from a prancing white mare that swished her tail and tossed her head. Betsy's Blanca.

Parker should wait until early summer to breed the pair, but the stallion could tear himself up breaking out of the round corral and through fences. Unless Clay moved Blanca completely out of range to, say, the Price farm. However, that was no guarantee either with the way the wind blew.

He could also turn them out together and tell Parker there'd be a late-spring foal next year. *You're in charge*, he'd said.

At the nudge of a boot heel, Duster made his way down the north slope toward the yearling's pasture and fenced-off hay, stockpiled against a late storm. Spring blizzards were all too common in Colorado.

It was a perfect morning for skirting the ranch and getting the lay of the land. Deacon had filled him in, but getting an eye on it beat all the hearsay in the world. And if he timed it right, he should make it back by midday. If Sophie didn't have dinner on the table, he could always eat what she'd left in the cabin.

Aside from beef, she might be running low on stores, after what Deacon packed in the chuck wagon. A good excuse to check on Maggie in town, ask about her friend's acreage, and stop by the livery for veterinary calls.

His perimeter ride stretched into mid-afternoon, and by the time he made the home place, his stomach thought his throat had been cut.

Storm clouds rolled off the mountains, flirting with the rangeland. He unsaddled Duster, left him in the barn, and brought the milk cow in as well.

The stallion had worn a path around the inside of the round pen, and Clay slipped through the poles, a cotton lead behind his back. Voice low, he moved toward the center, unhurried but confident. "You want out of here, don't ya boy?"

Head up, tail flicking, the bay pranced the perimeter, nostrils flaring, one ear swiveling toward Clay and the other toward a sassy white mare a pasture length away. Thunder rolled in the distance.

"Got a big box stall for you and that gal you got your eye on."

The stallion blew and tossed his head, made another trip around the corral but in a tighter circle, closer to the center.

Clay waited, murmuring low and steady, showing the horse there was nothing to fear.

A couple more trips, and it stopped beside him, eyeballing him, flicking those ears.

Clay held out his empty hand. "Come on, fella. Let's get in out of the rain. It's fixin' to cut loose here any minute." He slid his hand along the bay's neck, and its skin quivered at his touch. He stepped closer, his tone easy and calm as he clipped the lead on the headstall, leaving plenty of slack.

Another head toss but no fight, for there was no constraint. Within minutes, the stallion followed Clay through the gate and into the barn.

After settling the horse in the biggest stall with hay and water in opposite corners, Clay screwed his hat down and picked up two more leads. The smell of rain hung heavy and thunder growled closer as the storm crawled toward the ranch.

Sophie's old mare and Blanca pressed the farthest of the near pasture, instinctively fleeing the onslaught. Clay turned his shirt collar up against the wind and walked out toward the pair, showing the leads. As he'd figured, Blanca was eager to get inside, but the old mare resisted, completely out of character for a saddle horse.

At a close lightning strike, she went straight up, eyes rolling white and wide. He grabbed for her halter, but she cut away with surprising speed and high-tailed it for the gate he'd left open, heading for the herd in the next pasture over. He let her go. He couldn't bring them all in the barn, and his priority was keeping the stallion safe as well as Parker's yearling bulls. They'd have enough sense to get in a low spot or on the off side of the stockpile and ride out the storm.

As soon as he led Blanca in the barn, she squealed. Xavier's nostrils flared and he struck at the stall door. Clay had little choice but to put them together. Better than getting them both sliced open trying to get at each other. No sense asking for more trouble when trouble was already headed their way. The stall was big enough for both horses, and he doubled up on their feed and water.

Another thunderclap, closer than the last. He checked on Duster, calm as ever, and the milk cow that was chewing her cud and looking bored. Then he grabbed hold of his hat and lit out for the house.

Rain busted loose as he made the front porch, and the door opened.

Sophie braced it against the wind, then slammed it shut behind him. She must have been watching for him.

He pulled his boots off in the jack and hooked his hat on the wall. A small fire danced on the hearth, competing with the concern in Sophie's eyes. A strong sense of what must be "home" curled his arms, but rather than wrap them around her, he ran his hands through his hair and headed to the fireplace.

Back to the blaze, he spread his stance, warming his cold fingers. Sophie stood by the door watching him, her arms folded at her waist. He'd give his saddle to know what she was thinking.

"Come sit with me." His invitation rolled out unbidden. It wasn't his house or hearth. The old leather chairs weren't his and she wasn't his wife, but he'd make do with what he had and that was a belly full of lonely.

Halfway to him, she stopped, cinching off his air. "I'll get us some coffee."

So sudden was his relief, it made his chest ache. She didn't have to say *us,* but she had, and the word looped and settled inside him like a coiled rope.

Returning with a tray, she set it on a small table between the deep-seated chairs that declared comfort and age went hand in hand. He pulled them closer to the fire and stretched out in the nearest one, feet up on the raised hearth.

Sophie poured their coffee, curled into the other chair, and leaned toward the fire, elbows tucked tight, both hands around her cup. The firelight shadow-danced across her face.

"I was worried about you."

Her voice came gentle, warming him more than the fire.

What did a man say at a time like this when he couldn't put action to his words?

A log shifted and sparks scattered.

He pulled his feet back. "You needn't have." That wasn't enough and he reached deeper. "I got your supper."

He still hadn't eaten it, and she might know that since she apparently went where she wanted when she wanted. Which suited him fine.

She glanced his way. "There will be more of the same since Deacon and Cade weren't here to eat it all on the first serving. Hash and biscuits the second time around."

"Sounds good."

She let out a little huff like she didn't believe him, and when he looked at her, their eyes met and held.

"I rode the perimeter this morning. To get the lay of the land." Not that he had to give account of himself, but he wanted her to keep talking. He wanted to be with her, hear what she had to say.

Lightning hit close, flashing through the windows, and thunder shook the house. Sophie flinched, tucking her arms tighter and sinking deeper into herself.

He straightened in his chair, making room for her, then held his hand out.

She looked him square in the eye, long enough to strangle his air, then joined him, fitting on the seat between his legs like he knew she would. He welcomed her with a quick hug, then rested his arms on the chair, giving her space. Freedom. If she didn't feel constricted, maybe she wouldn't fight the close proximity and just let him give her what comfort he could.

She sat calmly, not tense, and soon eased back against him, smelling of supper and cinnamon. Her soft warmth seeped through his chest and into his soul and it was all he could do to not wrap completely around her. Instead, he rested his hands on her shoulders and felt them give beneath his touch. Maybe this wasn't such a good idea.

Mentally scrambling for normalcy, he cleared his throat. "I brought Blanca in and the stallion."

She turned and looked up at him, close enough for him to graze her lips, but the are-you-loco? look in her eye held him off.

"I know." He angled his head away from her hair and reached for his coffee, finding it good as always. "But it's better than getting them both torn up fighting the inevitable." He probably shouldn't mention such things in her company, especially in such *close* company, but she was a farm girl and this was a ranch, and they were both in the life-giving business, though he'd never thought of it in those terms before.

"Did you get any of the others?"

She didn't have to say which one.

Dread twisted in the hollow of his chest. "Your mare took off. I aimed to bring her in with Blanca, but she bolted for the herd."

He braced for Sophie to bolt as well.

"She went home." Resignation escaped on a sigh.

His tension went with it. "She's done that before?"

A nod answered, and she held her coffee but still didn't drink it. "She's afraid of lightning and thunder. Does fine in a snowstorm—just turns her backside to the wind like a bunch of cows. But let sheet lightning paint the sky, or what we're getting now, and she's gone. I once saw her jump a barbed-wire fence."

He sincerely hoped the mare didn't try that a second time. Not at her age.

He set his coffee aside and ran his hands up Sophie's arms, returning to her shoulders. Her head tipped to one side, grazing his fingers.

Rain lashed the house with a sudden roar, matching the roar of his heart.

"Sounds like a gully-washer for sure," she said, her voice barely audible.

A thump from upstairs was anything but. He encircled her again, aware of what was coming and resenting the intrusion.

"Willy's up," she whispered.

The tousle-haired youngster appeared at the top of the stairs with a shapeless stuffed animal held tightly in one arm. "Tea, pease."

Sophie pressed into Clay and lifted her face to him. "At least he's not scared."

Her breath was sweet and full of promise, and if not for Willy watching from above, Clay would lay claim to those lips, mere inches from his own.

It was just as well he couldn't. He sure enough didn't want to spook her.

She set her coffee on the tray and stood, her smile shy, hands holding tight to her apron. "I'm glad you're safely home. You made it back just in time."

He couldn't agree more. He'd made it back to Olin Springs and Sophie Price just in time to confirm what he wanted more than anything else in the world.

~

Sophie bit the inside of her cheek, climbing the stairs reluctantly, her skin cooling already after leaving the shelter of Clay's embrace. She felt safe with him, cocooned in his gentle strength, and she'd wanted to say so much more than she had. Thank the Lord for little boys and their perfect timing.

She took Willy's hand and tiptoed to Mae Ann's door to find her sleeping amidst the storm. What a blessing. Bending close to her charge, she whispered, "Let's go have supper. Mama can eat later."

"Tea, pease."

She squeezed his little hand, and they went downstairs to the kitchen, passing Clay who still sat by the fire. "Supper in ten minutes."

He gave her a nod and a hungry look, and it took all of her self-control to not jump like a twelve-year old girl. How ridiculous could she get? He was a grown man, was probably starving, and could eat when and where he chose.

She just wanted him to choose her.

Wait. Choose to eat with her. Big difference.

While she cut up the roast and carrots, Willy occupied himself with a cinnamon biscuit left over from breakfast, a daub of strawberry preserves, and a cup of lukewarm tea. Under the circumstances, if it spoiled his supper, so be it. At least he wouldn't go hungry.

If she hadn't spent so much time at the window watching for Clay, she would already have supper warm and waiting. She really needed to prioritize her duties. Worrying over a grown man who knew how to take care of other people's livestock as well as himself should not be a priority.

But oh, what a grown man he was.

As she took down the bread bowl, her thoughts fell on her mother and Todd. Praying while she stirred up a batch of biscuits was becoming a regular habit. She lifted her family by name, asking that they be kept safe. Mae Ann and the baby, as well. Cade and Deacon. The Eisners.

And the mare—that she'd made it home. Poor thing, her world was not right unless she was in her own barn with its familiar sounds and smells.

Oddly enough, Sophie didn't feel that way about the farm any longer. In spite of loving her mother and brother, the place wasn't quite home, for a certain someone with whom she'd like to make a home of her own wasn't there.

# CHAPTER 14

Clay found the body at the fence line, tangled in the wire. A charred post and singe marks on the mare's legs told the story.

How would he tell Sophie?

Duster shied from the carcass, ears sharp, nostrils flaring. Horses smelled death and sensed it differently than people, often scouting far around a place where the dead had fallen even months before.

Clay lifted his rope and stepped down, talking low and steady to the gelding. "Easy boy. We owe it to the old girl to get her someplace private. Away from the herd."

*Away from Sophie.*

He cut the wire, then rigged a harness and tied on to his saddle horn, dragging the body through the pasture and around to the backside of the knoll where he'd earlier surveyed the ranch. He left the mare near a juniper patch, partly sheltered and away from the creek. Nature would carry her off. He didn't want Sophie to see that, though she likely knew about such things having grown up in these high parks.

He coiled his rope and reached for his saddle horn, but Duster pinwheeled, refusing to stand still. Clay pulled the coils tighter, tucked the tail in the honda, and left the rope and his gloves on the mare's shoulder. They could both be replaced.

Duster blew and stomped at his approach, but Clay swung up and topped the knoll for a clear view. The mare hadn't been with the herd, and the other horses grazed as usual. None were down.

Returning to the charred post, he spliced the wires, then circled to the bull's pasture. The yearlings and late heifers and calves were all sound. From the looks of things, the old mare was the only casualty from last night's storm.

What she'd feared had found her, but he knew better than to second guess himself about not getting her to the barn. It did no good. Maybe it was just her time. And maybe Sophie wouldn't blame him for her death.

On his way to the house, birds sang in the cedars and scrub oak like they'd never seen the sun before. Redwing blackbirds swarmed the cottonwood trees in the yard, and water pooled in small ponds, chickens skirting the puddles. He tied up at the cabin, went inside for a soap cake, and at the pump scrubbed until his fingers were red.

He'd missed breakfast, but Sophie might have saved something in the warmer for him, and his hope rose as he stepped through the front door and dropped his hat on a hook. Fried potatoes and side pork. Gravy and biscuits. He pulled off his muddy boots and socked it into the kitchen.

She wasn't there, but the back door was open and he peeked out to the porch. She was up to her elbows in wash suds, hair hanging over the side of her face, and Willy "helping," as wet as the laundry.

Clay's heart hitched and he eased back, poured himself some coffee, and found a plate in the warmer. Sophie Price warmed more than his food. He needed to find his own place and build up his business so he'd have more to offer her than a buckskin gelding and a pouch of surgical instruments.

"Mustu Cay!" Willy bounded into the kitchen trailing water in his wake.

Sophie followed, nearly as wet.

"Good morning." She pushed her hair back and smoothed her apron. "Excuse the way we look. We've been doing laundry."

She went to the stove and moved the coffee over the firebox. Willy climbed into his chair asking for tea, please. The kid needed to learn to drink coffee.

"I'm riding into town but can take the buckboard if you need anything from the mercantile. Looked like Deacon might have cleaned out your stores."

"Come to think of it, yes. There are a few things. I'll make a list."

She returned with a pencil and paper and sat down across from him, smelling like wet clothes and lye soap.

"I'd go with you, but of course that's not possible. Not for quite some time, and then probably on a Sunday to church."

She flicked him a glance.

He maintained a practiced, neutral response.

"Would you mind stopping by Maggie's and asking Betsy if she's talked to the Eisners. Find out how they're doing if you can. More specifically, Abigail, if you don't mind."

She blushed like a summer rose and he gulped his coffee, welcoming the burn.

"I shouldn't ask that, but … well … you …" Her hands flailed around, plucking words from the air.

"I'll do it," he said, trying not to laugh at her fluster. "It's all right. I'll be stopping by the livery for veterinary calls. And I want to see how Maggie's doing."

Sophie's hands and expression stilled, and she eyed him like a schoolmarm searching for a chalk thief. "You think she's not doing well, don't you."

Straight-forward Sophie had returned.

The inevitable was inevitably hard to address. Strengthened by the memory of holding her the night she wept over the Eisner's baby and the way she settled against him during the storm, he reached across the table and covered her hand. Warm, capable. Womanly.

"Maggie's up in years, and the signs are there."

Sophie flinched.

He curled his fingers around hers.

"But she's healthy and well-cared for. Loved."

And he was a coward.

He tightened his hold the slightest bit and lowered his voice. "Like your mare."

He felt realization hit. Felt it in the tensing of her fingers, the flaring of her eyes.

"I'm sorry."

She pulled hard and he let go. A sob broke from her and she covered her mouth with a glance toward Willy.

Clay had noticed a pull toy by the hearth the night before, and he leaned close to the boy. "How would you like to go in the other room and play with that wooden horse on wheels for a little while?"

Willy's face lit with the idea, and he slipped off his chair and hurried into the great room. Clay walked around to Sophie and pulled her to her feet.

She came willingly, and he encircled her, blocking out the world and storms and anything that could hurt her.

"I'm sorry I didn't get the mare in last night."

Sophie shook her head, her whisper hot against his chest. "She wouldn't have let you even with all your horse-handling skill. Her fear was too great. Too long set within her."

Something about those last words burned into him like a premonition, and he cupped her head in his hand and kissed her hair.

She wrapped her arms around him and held on like she meant it.

~

With Sophie's list in his vest pocket and his saddlebags under the buckboard seat, Clay maneuvered mud and traffic on Main Street, marveling at how each churned up the other.

Thatcher was out front of the hotel, supervising a boy washing the window and pointing out spots he'd missed. Poor kid.

The sheriff's office door was closed, and smoke twisted from the black chimney pipe.

Clay continued to the opposite end of town and turned around at the church house, stopping first at the livery. Erik's hammer sang from the back of the stable, and John pitched a fork load of soiled hay into a wheelbarrow.

"Mornin'."

The kid back-handed sweat from his forehead, but smiled when he turned around and saw who was speaking. "Mornin', Mr. Ferguson. I have a message for you here from a man whose horse ain't eatin'." He pulled a slip of paper from the pocket of his dungarees.

"When did he call?"

"Day before yesterday. But I told him you'd be by and I'd let you know."

"Appreciate it."

Clay walked back to where Erik was fitting a shoe to a twitchy gelding snubbed to a stout beam. He took hold of the horse, muttering under his breath, and ran his hand along its neck.

"*Danke.*" Erik went to the anvil for another tap on the shoe and returned with a smaller hammer. From a pocket in his leather apron, he counted out eight horse-shoe nails, put seven of them between his teeth before he bent the back leg, and pulled the hoof between his knees.

He sank the first nail, twisted off the end, and repeated the process six times. Then he clinched them all the way around, dropped the hoof, and returned the unused nail to his apron pocket.

Laying a beefy hand on the horse's rump, he walked around to the other side where he slid the clincher in a wooden box on the ground nearby and drew out a rasp. "Did you talk to the boy?"

"He told me a fella stopped by wanting me to look at a horse that won't eat."

Erik grunted as he lifted the other back leg.

Clay held the horse until the smithy finished the last two shoes, then turned it out in the corral.

"Is *gut*." Sweat ran off the big man's brow, and he wiped his eyes with a rag from the nail pocket. "Not many come, but we tell them when they do."

"*Danke*," Clay said with a grin and a finger to his hat. He returned to the buckboard, certain that John was faring better than the kid washing windows for Thatcher.

At the *Gazette,* he bought another paper, though he hadn't read the first. Evening fodder that would bring him up to date on the community. Farmers usually posted the latest remedy they'd tried and flowered things up with their opinions.

He folded the paper under his arm and braced himself for Sarah Reynolds at the mercantile. Sure as summer follows spring, she was there arranging seed packets on a table. As soon as his entry jingled the bell, she went to fluttering and following him around the store. It was all he could do not to ask if she had something in her eye. But she'd likely throw her head back so he could take a look and he wasn't up to that right now or ever.

Instead, he gave Mr. Reynolds Sophie's list and busied himself at the counter trying out gloves until he found a pair that fit. As an afterthought, he chose a smaller pair on the chance that Sophie didn't have any. He'd never seen her wearing gloves with the old mare, and it wouldn't be a bad idea for her to have them. The memory of her warm hands that morning made him want to keep them protected.

Reynolds tallied the order on Parker's ledger page and returned the list to Clay.

He paid for the gloves, loaded the stores, and drove to Maggie Snowfield's.

Betsy was pinning laundry on the clothesline and smiled when he walked around the end of a line of sheets.

"Come inside for coffee and pie. Maggie will be thrilled. Now that she's feeling better, she's been going on about the Fairfax ranch or farm or whatever it is. Sounds to me like it's a little of everything. I'm not really clear, other than the woman is moving to her daughter's in Denver."

Maggie looked better than he'd seen her since he'd been back—still thin, though she'd never been much more than a rail.

"Oh, Clay, dear. You are just the person I hoped to see." She took plates and cups from the cupboard and set the tea kettle on.

He thought of Willy.

Betsy slid the coffee pot to the back of the stove and handed Maggie a serving knife.

"My lands, but it's good to see you." She brought a napkin-covered pie pan from the counter. "They're not fresh, mind you, but canned peaches fill a crust as well as anything, don't you think?" She sliced off a quarter of the pie and passed him the plate with a fork. "I hope you like it."

He would. He remembered Maggie Snowfield's pie-making ability. The fat slice oozed all over the plate, and she sat down across from him watching as if he were judging an entry at the county fair.

"Can you stay for supper? We'd love to hear how things are going at the ranch." She cut a glance to Betsy. "With Sophie and Mae Ann. How are they doing? And that stallion Betsy told me about."

Maggie went on while he ate, and he wouldn't have been able to get a word in edgewise anyway.

Betsy filled his cup with coffee and Maggie's with tea.

"The Ladies Library Committee met this morning, and Bertha Fairfax announced her place is officially on the market. She's moving in with her daughter in Denver, you know, and she wants to see that the farm is in good hands before she leaves."

Maggie came up for air and a sip of tea.

"She also said her milk cow isn't doing well, and she'd like for you to come check on it."

Her avoidance of his eye said she'd also mentioned his interest in buying his own place.

"Depending on where it is, I might have time to stop by today before I head back."

Maggie's cheeks warmed to a deeper color and she braced her shoulders. "Wonderful." She'd found something to sink her teeth into.

"Sophie and Mae Ann?" Betsy peered at him over the rim of her teacup, wheeling the conversation back on course.

"Doin' well." He stalled for the right words in present company. "There's a new Parker on the place. A little girl, but I haven't caught her name yet." He hadn't thought to ask since that question never surfaced in his line of work with livestock. He left out the part about Sophie's mare and took the note from his vest pocket. "If you have a pencil, I'll write down how to get to your friend's place."

Betsy rummaged through a drawer for a pencil stub, and he sketched out what Maggie described rather than write down her many words.

As stuffed as a scarecrow, he took his plate and cup to the sink. "Thank you, ladies, for the wonderful pie and coffee. It will see me on my rounds and home."

Parker Land and Cattle wasn't really home, but it felt right conversationally. "Make sure you don't overdo."

"Oh, posh." Maggie brushed him off with her hankie-holding hand, and he squeezed her shoulder, confirming his observation on her thinning status. He sent Betsy a look with a tip of his head toward the door.

Good reader that she was, she followed him out to the clothesline, where she picked up a man's shirt and snapped it out. "As you saw, she *is* better, but now she'll sleep the rest of the day. Doc Weaver says it's nothing out of the ordinary, considering her age and all."

He coughed, stalling while he hunted the right words. "Sophie wants to know how Mrs. Eisner is doing."

Not put off in the least by his query, Betsy said she'd been at their shop the day before. "Abigail was downstairs. Too thin, I thought, but up and around. From what I could tell without being completely nosy, all was well."

Aware of her long-standing friendship with Sophie, told her about the mare as gently as possible.

She turned toward the line, where she pinned Garrett's shirt, then wiped her eyes with her apron.

"I've got a nice horse from the saddle string that I want to give her after I try him and smooth off the rough edges. If he doesn't work for her, I'll find another. But don't tell her."

In typical Betsy fashion, she regrouped and fired. "And when am I going to see Sophie to tell her?"

Laughing, he climbed to the wagon seat. "When's her birthday?"

The question earned him a bright-eyed answer. "June fourth."

"All right. But keep it a secret."

Swatting the air in his general direction, she huffed. "Oh, go on with you."

He clucked the gray out to the road and headed north from town, the same direction that would take him to the fella whose horse wasn't eating. He passed the church and library house with as much interest in one as the other.

The land was greening up. With storms like they got last night, it wouldn't be long before the grass was thick and rich and hayfields were begging to be cut. Two miles out, he turned onto a side road that led to a rundown barn and house. A man was breaking ground with a plow and a mule that had seen better days.

The fella stopped and dropped the lines from his shoulders as Clay drove up near the barn and set the brake. He jumped down to be greeted by an old dog that fit right in with everything else.

"Afternoon. I'm Clay Ferguson, the veterinarian you asked about at the livery. I hear you have a horse that's not eating."

The man swung his gaze over the gray mare harnessed to the buckboard. "Ain't exactly a horse."

"I see." Clay glanced at the mule a few paces out. "Why'd you say it was a horse?"

Folded arms and a quick huff set the fella on the defense. "Figured you wouldn't come for a mule."

"Let's have a look at him."

Surprised, the man hesitated long enough for Clay to walk out to the animal and eyeball the situation before looking inside its mouth. The mule's saliva was excessive and pink, and it smelled foul. "When'd you last have his teeth floated?"

"Nigh on couple years."

"Unhitch him and bring him to the barn." Clay walked back to the buckboard for his saddle bags and met the man at the railing.

Most people with horses and mules knew the teeth wore unevenly as the animal chewed. And most people did something about it or called on someone who could. This man wasn't most people.

"It's going to take us both to get this done because he's in pain. See that pink foam running around his mouth? He's bleeding. Get a stout rope and tie him to the hitch rail, then grab his tongue and hold on."

Clay didn't want to throw the animal if he didn't have to, but he would if its owner was faint-hearted. He hung his bags over the opposite end of the rail and pulled out his file. The farmer proved his salt, and the ordeal was over in a half-hour. Everyone was worn out, but the job was done.

Clay didn't expect to be paid, but he expected the mule to feel better in a day or so.

"Appreciate you comin' out." The farmer fished a few coins from his dungarees' pocket and handed them over.

Clay accepted them. "Leave word at the livery if he's not better in a couple of days, and I'll come back. Give him some soft mash until then and plenty of water." He looked out at the field. "Maybe lay off the plow for a day or so."

After washing at the pump, Clay threw his bags in the wagon and took the main road back toward town. The next turnoff wound west from the flatland and over a low saddle between two hills. The view stopped him cold.

Below lay a hidden park. More like a meadow, pristine and green, with a creek skirting the north edge and twenty or so cow-calf pairs grazing along.

From a distance, the buildings looked kept up—a small frame house and barn. Sheds, a garden, privy, root cellar. He looked again at the sketch he'd drawn from Maggie's description, hoping he hadn't got it wrong, then clucked the gray down into the meadow, following a wagon trail that crossed the creek.

Up close, he could see the barn needed work, with the main door off its runner. Corral poles were missing or broken, and the calves didn't look to be branded. They could have been run in with Parker's bunch, and might be yet, depending on what happened in the next little while.

An older woman came out from the house, watching him like a hawk watches a squirrel hole.

Clay pulled up and set the brake but spoke to her from the wagon seat. "Afternoon, ma'am. I'm Clay Ferguson, the veterinarian. Maggie Snowfield told me you had a cow that needed to be looked at and asked me to stop by."

The information loosened her stance, and she came down the front steps. "Yes, she mentioned you this morning at the library. Said you had a way with animals. I'm Mrs. Fairfax."

He climbed down and doffed his hat. "Ma'am. A pleasure to meet you."

"Follow me. The cow is in the barn."

The cow was in perfect health—aside from being dry as a duck in the desert and blind in her left eye.

He'd expected as much, knowing how Maggie might finagle things to get him out there.

The brindle shorthorn watched him with her one big brown eye, chewing her cud and occasionally swishing her tail at flies.

"When did she freshen last?"

Mrs. Fairfax rubbed the knuckles on her right hand. "To tell you the truth, it's been a year. I sold that calf to the Bittmans. My hands ache too much to milk and I can't keep up with all this work. Nor can I get any help to stay on. Not enough to do, in their opinion. They want to break horses, and all I have is my buggy mare."

"I've got something that might help your hands, if you have a small crock or canning jar."

While she went to the house, he returned to his wagon and removed a bottle of liniment from his saddlebags.

The screen door slapped behind her, and she handed him a quart jar. He poured in some of the pungent mixture, and her nose wrinkled.

"Rub a little of this into your hands each morning."

She fanned the air and made a face. "Mercy, what is it?"

"Just a little, mind you. It doesn't smell the best, but it should keep your joints from aching quite as much."

"Are you going to charge me for this?"

He schooled his face and swallowed a laugh. "No, ma'am. I'm just passing on what might be a remedy for you. But don't use too much at one time or the library ladies won't want you sitting by them."

She tilted her head back and looked down her nose at him even though he topped her by at least a foot.

"I heard you might be wanting to sell."

She gave him a stone-faced answer. "Possibly. Why? Are you interested?"

"What are you asking?"

"What are you offering?"

The woman could make a killing at poker.

"I'll have to get back to you on that. If it's for sale, I'd like a friend of mine to see it and get their opinion."

She sniffed and looked off toward the cattle, turning the jar in her bent fingers.

"Would you be interested in selling the milk cow?"

Her sharp eyes shot back to his.

He made an offer, and she accepted.

After tying the cow to the back of the wagon, he bid Mrs. Fairfax good-day, climbed to the seat, and turned around in front of the house.

She was rubbing liniment into her hand and holding her head to the side, but stepped out to him, her countenance uncertain, almost sad.

"My daughter has asked me to come live with her in Denver." Resignation edged her tone. "She and her husband have a large house and two children. I've never lived in the city." It was almost a confession. "I'm not sure I'll be happy there."

Reading between the lines on her face, he recognized doubt and loneliness. "You'll be with your grandchildren. Your family." The words bruised a spot inside him, but she needed to hear them as much as she needed the horse liniment he'd given her. "Can you wait a couple weeks before you sell?"

She looked square into the middle of him—a female Deacon Jewett to be sure—and flexed the fingers of her right hand. "For you, young man, yes. But only two weeks."

He tipped his hat and drove out of the small barnyard, one milk cow in tow.

Not exactly a profitable day. He'd spent more money than he'd made, and more than likely would be committing the stake hidden in his saddlebags if Sophie liked the place.

Dadgummit, he needed to know if Sophie liked *him* before he asked her about a home. His gut told him she did, but he had to hear it from her, see it in her eyes.

Now he had two weeks to find out.

# CHAPTER 15

With Willy down for an afternoon nap in his own bed and Mae Ann and the baby sleeping, Sophie walked out to cottonwood trees and settled on the bench. Cougar came to her with a hang-dog look.

"You miss her, don't you?" The dog laid his yellow chin on her knee and plopped on his haunches, tail sweeping an arc in the dirt.

"I miss someone too, so I know how you feel, though my association isn't as long-standing as yours."

She was talking to a dog.

She was pathetic.

A soft breeze whispered through the trees, their leaves yet small and delicate.

"He comforts me but won't let me do the same for him. Instead, he pulls away, closes up, and walks off. Something pains him terribly."

She leaned toward the dog and laid her hand against her bodice. "I can feel it right here."

Cougar sighed a not-so-sweet dog-breath sigh.

She coughed and straightened. "It's something that concerns his mother. I know he had one or he wouldn't be here, obviously. But he's never mentioned her and slams tight as a cellar door at the subject. In fact, he's never mentioned his family at all. I don't want to pry, but I'd like to know."

A sigh of her own slipped out. "The way he holds me—"

She gave Cougar a warning glare. "Don't you repeat any of this, you hear?"

With a whine, the dog dropped to its belly but kept promise-filled eyes focused on her, ears attentive to her voice.

She gripped the sides of her arms and hunched her shoulders. "Last night in the storm—and this morning—make me think there is more than kindness in his gesture. And honestly, I want there to be more than kindness. I want—"

Cougar heard the wagon the same time Sophie did. He bounded away, barking at the wheels rolling to a stop at the house.

She stayed put, watching Clay. The ease with which he jumped down and stooped to pet the dog. The way he reset his hat and took stock of the yard, skimming the barn, cabin, and corral until his eyes rested on her.

Even from a distance, she saw his mouth tick up with a smile and her pulse ticked up right along with it. "A penny for your thoughts," she wanted to say, but it would take a wagon-load of pennies to get him to talk.

Her breath stilled as she waited to see if he would join her or immediately start unloading. A kind of test, she admitted, hoping it would tell her more about him and his private thoughts.

He dropped the tailgate.

She dropped her heart.

Stupid test.

*And stupid me for setting myself up in such a ridiculous manner.*

She matched the corners of her apron point to point, smoothing out the edges and lining them up just so on her lap.

"Enjoying the sunshine?"

Startled, she looked up to see him coming toward her, his limp nearly imperceptible. Another mystery. Why did he limp? Did it have anything to do with those scars on his back?

She tucked her skirt against her leg in silent invitation. More silliness.

He sat down, not too close, and Cougar nuzzled in between them, giving Sophie room to breathe.

"Betsy said Mrs. Eisner is doing well. Thin, she thought, but up and around, helping out in the tailor shop."

*Thank God.* Sophie fingered her opened collar, inviting air into her lungs.

"Maggie was stronger too, though she tires easily and is also too thin in *my* opinion."

Afraid to look at him, Sophie nodded and smiled, relieved again.

"I gave her a cow."

Her head shot up. "A cow? You think she's strong enough to milk a cow?"

His throaty laugh sent a shiver through her insides. How would she ever be able to carry on a conversation with this man? Her sensitivity to his voice, his nearness, and the memory of his touch made her weak as a willow.

"The cow is dry. I bought it off the widow Fairfax, who's moving to Denver."

He took his hat off, scrubbed his hair, and put it back on. Palmed the back of his neck and tugged at his shirt.

"What?" Clearly, she wasn't the only one who was nervous.

His look cut sideways at her, not straight on. He stretched his arms out and palmed his knees. "She's got a real nice place. Not too far from town, but private, almost hidden away in the hills with a creek and pasture. A barn, house, and about twenty cow-calf pairs."

Her heart sank. He was looking for a place of his own. As soon as Cade and Deacon got back, he'd be gone, and that could be as soon as tonight.

Cougar looked up at her with a dusty sweep of his tail.

*Don't cry. Not here. Not now.*

"The barn and corral need work, and the calves need branding. Maybe run in with a bigger herd come fall."

He stalled.

"I didn't see inside the house, though, and I'd like another opinion on what I should be looking for."

He reached down to pet the dog. "Would you ride out there with me and look the place over? Tell me what you think?"

Was he asking the dog?

She'd never liked see-saws as a child. The up-and-down made her queasy, and that was exactly how she felt now. *Down—up—down.*

Sitting as straight as she knew how, she pulled in a deep breath. "I could do that."

He relaxed, arms and shoulders loosening. Cougar looked at him and whined.

"Maybe your ma could spend the day with Mae Ann and Willy. Or half the day. At least half a day."

*Up.* "We could go on a Sunday and kill the proverbial pair of birds with one stone."

He became that stone—motionless, silent, hard.

*Down.* Another unanswered question, but she pushed it aside in exchange for a different one. "When do you expect Deacon and Cade?"

He thawed a little. "Could be any day. But I've only got two weeks. Mrs. Fairfax said she'd give me two weeks to make an offer."

*Farther down.*

She was right. He was looking for his own place, and now she knew how long it'd be until he was gone.

The up-side was his invitation. She'd get to see where he'd be living and doctoring and branding, and, in all likelihood, training horses.

But what did it matter if she liked the house or not?

*The see-saw slammed to the ground.*

It wouldn't be hers.

~

Sophie agreed to go with him.

Clay couldn't sleep that night for playing their conversation over in his head. He lit the lamp on Deacon's table, where he sat down with a copy of the *Gazette.* But his brain wouldn't sit still, and three times he had to read a paragraph about a rancher who lost his horse to a snake bite.

If Sophie liked the Fairfax place, he'd make an offer.

If she didn't, he'd keep looking.

Plain and simple. Uncomplicated.

He started in on a letter to the editor, but it muddled when the yellow dog went berserk outside, answered by the heeler. Parker and Deacon were home. It had to be close to midnight.

He pulled on his pants and boots, rolled up his bed, and tossed it on a bunk in the extra room.

The chuck wagon crawled up in front of the barn as he stepped outside.

Deacon moved at about the same speed, climbing down from the high seat.

Clay wondered if the creaking was the wagon or the old fella's bones.

"I've got the team," he said. "Get some shut-eye. It won't be long till sunup."

"Obliged." Deacon was showing his years, and it tugged on Clay.

Parker rode up, laid reins to the rail, and unsaddled his horse.

"Welcome home," Clay said.

"It's good to be home."

"Just so you know, you've got a little filly bunkin' in your room with the missus."

Parker stared at him, fighting fatigue, trail dust, and miles to figure out what Clay was talking about.

"Born the day you left."

That nearly bugged the man's eyes out. He hooked it for the house, then stopped and looked back. "Would you un—"

"I'll take care of it. Go see your family. 'Course they might not appreciate your timing, but give it a try."

Parker nearly tripped over his feet getting across the yard to the house and must have made a racket inside, for a light appeared in the upstairs window. Clay knew it wasn't Sophie's room, for she had the one on the north end of the house.

Seeing to three horses, fetching water and feed, and putting them up was exactly what he needed to warm his muscles and weary his mind. Afterward, he fell onto his bedroll and slept until the first crow of the rooster.

A comforting sound somehow, that danged bird cracking off before dawn every morning. He probably had rooster in his blood.

In light of the homecoming, he shaved outside without benefit of a mirror and hoped he caught all the strays. Afterward, he donned a clean shirt and went to the house for the milk bucket, easing the front door open.

A yellow glow spread around the end of the kitchen wall. Sophie was running parallel with him again, up early getting things ready. He imagined her in their own kitchen at daybreak, frying steaks and making coffee.

With a shake of his head, he doused those thoughts and plastered his damp hair back.

"Good morning." She'd heard him come in after all.

The kitchen was warmer than the main room. He'd always thought it was the cook stove, but now he wasn't so sure. "Mornin'. You're up early."

"So are you." She filled a tin mug with hot coffee and handed it to him. The sight of her all fresh and awake fired through his skin nearly as much as the hot cup. He set it on the table.

"I'm always up early." Doggone it, no reason to say that.

Her profile revealed a smile, but he didn't know if it was a real smile or the tuck in her cheek. Without seeing her eyes, he couldn't be sure.

He fetched the bucket from the pantry and, on his way out, saw her fold biscuit dough over, pat it with her hands, and cut circles in it. An odd quiver slid down his back, like he'd watched someone else do the same exact thing, but that wasn't possible.

By the time he returned, the entire Parker family had come down for breakfast, Mae Ann happy as a lark that her husband was home.

Clay set the milk at the end of the counter, covered it with a cloth, and washed up.

Deacon joined them late, but no one ribbed him. He'd earned his extra winks.

Ready this time for a prayer, Clay took a seat and refrained from reaching for the steak platter. Parker held his hands out, one to Mae Ann on his left, the other to Deacon on his right. Sophie followed suit, so Clay did the same, clamping on to Willy's little hand and reaching across for Sophie's.

Without looking up she placed her warm hand in his.

He held on for everything he was worth.

"Thank You, Lord, for Your protection, for this food, and for bringing us all together. Amen."

"Amen" rounded the table and vibrated through Sophie's fingers, but Clay kept his to himself, though he did place a high value on the three things Parker mentioned.

Everyone tucked in, focused on the fare before them. Clay slid a glance Sophie's way, surprised to catch her eye. She blushed to match her ma's strawberry preserves, and his imagination stampeded with reasons. Could she really be interested in him?

"Update me."

Parker broke into Clay's daydreaming, and he shot back through recent events. "Xavier's healing up real nice and has settled some."

Parker flicked him a look.

"Had a storm two days ago. Heavy rain, lightning. I brought the stallion in the barn—that big box stall on this end." He might as well just plow right into the facts. "Brought in Blanca too, as she was pretty worked up and I didn't want either of them tearing through fences and boards."

Parker nodded while he chewed, watching his wife and newborn daughter. He probably hadn't heard a word Clay said.

Sophie held her napkin at her mouth longer than necessary but didn't look at him.

"We had a lot of lightning and lost one horse."

Parker stopped short, as did Deacon.

"Sophie's mare. She was standing next to the fence when it hit. May have been trying to jump." The crumpled body he'd found confirmed it, but he wasn't going to paint that picture in Sophie's mind.

Every head but Willy's turned to Sophie, yet she held up, eyes on her plate. Clay admired her mettle.

"We'll get you another one," Parker told her before he took the next bite.

Clay's intentions reared in opposition. *He'd* get her one. Already had one in mind, but he'd speak to Parker about that out of Sophie's hearing.

The boss cleared his throat and cut a look at Deacon. "I'll be leaving again day after tomorrow."

Mae Ann made no comment. Apparently, they'd already talked it over.

"I'll be gone a week at best, meeting with a cattle buyer in Denver and a fella I heard about who's interested in good saddle horses. Deacon's staying here. Clay, I'll need you to drive me to the train station Tuesday morning."

Lightning wasn't the only thing that struck hard and fast. "Will do."

Sophie got up and came around the table, stopping behind Willy and Mae Ann.

"Let me take Madeline so you can have a chance to eat." She held her arms out and Mae Ann handed her the baby. Sophie cradled the infant against her chest, tucking its head in the curve of her neck, then went to the other room.

Clay's brain went to figuring his next move. He'd ask Deacon to fetch Travine Price for Tuesday while Sophie rode along with him and Parker to the train. That'd give them the rest of the day to see the Fairfax place and take a leisurely ride home.

Alone.

His collar got tight just thinking about it.

# CHAPTER 16

Sophie had seen the train station several times. She'd ridden to town in a wagon. She'd known Cade Parker all her life. But she was beside herself about spending most of the day alone with Clay Ferguson. How would she do her hair? What should she wear?

That last question was an easy fix, and she laid the nicest of her two dresses across the bed. Springtime yellow with lace-cuffed mid-length sleeves and a scooped neckline. Mama had always said it brought out the gold highlights in Sophie's hair.

She scoffed. Her hair had as many gold highlights as Deacon Jewett's, and he had none.

He'd ridden to the farm yesterday afternoon to ask Mama if she'd come stay with Mae Ann and the children—and himself, no doubt—and hadn't returned until late. That meant Mama said yes.

This morning, he'd left in the buckboard before dawn. Sophie, Clay, and Cade would leave as soon as he returned.

For as much traveling as went on with this bunch, they needed a buggy like Maggie Snowfield's. A niggling in the back of Sophie's mind said it was Cade who suppressed the notion. His parents had died in a buggy accident.

She tried her hair several different ways, but without hairpins or combs, she was limited. A knock on the bedroom door startled her. Surely Clay wasn't leaving already?

When Mae Ann peaked around the door, Sophie breathed easier. "Please, come in."

"Madeline is sleeping, the angel, and Cade has Willy, so I'm free for a visit." She sat on the bed and stretched out her legs, leaning against the headboard. "I hope you don't mind. I'm more comfortable with my feet up."

"And you should be. Can I get you another pillow?"

"No, this is just right. It's nice to do something other than lie in bed, smelling of wet flannels and McKesson's baby powder, though I love Madeline more than I thought it possible to love a second child."

She watched Sophie, who saw every innuendo of her facial expression reflected in the dressing-table mirror. And the one she saw at the moment said Mae Ann read Sophie like a copy of *Peterson's* women's magazine.

"That color is quite becoming on you."

If Mae Ann said it brought out the gold in Sophie's hair, she was going to take it off.

"What are you doing with your hair?"

"I have no idea. I'm not very good with pins and combs, and I don't have any with me anyway."

"I have several you may borrow if you'd like, but may I make a suggestion?"

Sophie locked on Mae Ann's reflection in the mirror. "Please do."

"Wear it the way you are most comfortable so you're not fussing with it and distracted from more important things during your outing."

"We're just taking Cade to the train. It's not exactly an *outing*."

Mae Ann cocked an eyebrow that could have shot an arrow.

"All right," Sophie conceded. "You have a point."

"How are you most comfortable with your hair?"

"It's not very fashionable but I usually wear it twisted in a knot at my neck because I know it won't come loose and get in the way. But I'd rather pull it back with a ribbon, though that's a childish way to wear it, I suppose, and I'm certainly no child."

"Do you ever wear it in a braid?"

Sophie shook her head. "Not since I wore two of them in grade school."

Mae Ann swung her feet to the floor. "I'll be right back."

When she returned, she held a long white ribbon, a curling iron, and several hair pins. "May I help you?"

Sophie felt the blush crawl her neck. She was here to help Mae Ann, not the other way around.

"For all you've done for me, let me do your hair."

It was the warm smile that made her decision.

By the time Madeline fussed for her mother, Sophie's hair was coiled in a loose braid and pinned low on her head with ribbon running through the braid. Soft tendrils framed her face, helped along by the curling iron heated in the lamp chimney.

She actually felt pretty. "Watching you makes me think I can do it myself." She picked up her straw hat, which sat nicely without disturbing her hair.

Mae Ann gave her a quick hug. "You can. And we're finished just in time. I think I hear dogs barking, in addition to Madeline squeaking."

At the top of the landing, Mae Ann touched her arm. "Wait. I've one other thing."

She returned from her bedroom with a soft white shawl. "It's early enough to be chilly or for a spring wind to stir up rainclouds. Though in these high parks, as you know, it's best to be prepared for anything. One of the strongest storms I've seen was in the summer."

"How kind of you." Sophie was well aware of extreme weather changes and appreciated Mae Ann's thoughtfulness. "It's much nicer than my heavy cloak."

Watching the stairs, she didn't realize Clay stood at the door until she was halfway down. When she glanced up, he was staring, hat in hand, and eyes full of something on which she dare not speculate.

She should have worn the other dress. The neckline of this one revealed the flush at the base of her throat.

He stepped forward. "You're ready."

A bit disappointing.

"You look … different."

She might be sick.

"In a good way." He regarded his feet, then met her eyes again. "You look beautiful."

Did that mean she'd not yet looked very good to him and this was a shock? The see-saw lifted her heart and dropped it as quickly. "Thank you."

Though grateful for his notice and mention of it, she prayed the trip would not be an emotional up-and-down *outing*. It would not do to lose her breakfast on any leg of the journey.

Mama was not in the great room, nor the kitchen.

"She's outside talking to Deacon." Clay thumbed over his shoulder.

Of course she was. And of course he could read her thoughts. Not exactly a comforting realization.

Cade came in and dashed past them up the stairs, where he met Mae Ann at the landing with a kiss.

Sophie could not move fast enough through the front door.

Mama and Deacon stood near the buckboard, his hat pushed back, cheeks ripe as summer plums.

Everyone had someone. Sophie felt like a misplaced shoe.

"Oh, look at you." Mama took her hands. "That dress is perfect. It brings out the—"

"Thank you, Mama, for helping today." A quick kiss on the cheek stopped the chafing phrase, and Sophie lifted her skirt to climb to the seat.

Clay was beside her before the first step, and with his hands at her waist rather than her elbow, he assisted her the rest of the way. She took the second seat that Cade had built in for his growing family and saw disappointment in Clay's eyes. "Thank you, but I will be just fine here. I'm sure you two have things to discuss on the way."

Mama and Deacon each leaned slightly toward the other, though not touching. Sophie felt like the mother watching her child in the throes of young love, a completely disconcerting position in which to be. She didn't need help feeling old.

Cade blew through the front door with a storm on his face and a satchel in hand. Neither did she envy Clay's position beside him all the way to town.

Nervousness stretched the drive into eternal dimensions, yet the train had not left and was building up steam as they pulled in at the depot. She remained seated while the two men walked to the passenger car. Less than two weeks ago at this very depot, she'd watched Clay lead the injured stallion down a ramp and through a crowd as if it were the most casual of all events. It felt much longer than that.

Good heavens, but the memory stirred her all over again, nearly as much as the look in his eye from where he stood next to the buckboard indicating the front bench.

~

Clay had hoped Sophie would move up on her own and was disappointed to find her still sitting on the makeshift backseat. He offered his hand, and she took it while edging her way around the end of the bench.

The train's whistle blew, and he turned out of the depot yard and back toward town.

Sophie looked down Saddle Blossom Lane as they crossed it but didn't mention Snowfield's and Betsy. He was selfishly pleased. He didn't want to share her with anyone today, though he expected her to check on the Eisner woman. In fact, he hoped she would. It'd give him a chance to stop by Bozeman's for a picnic.

Not that he was clever enough to think of it. A fellow student at the school had shared how he'd taken his girl on a picnic and proposed, and she said yes.

Clay ran a finger around the inside of his shirt collar. "Would you like to stop by the tailor's to check on Mrs. Eisner?"

Sophie looked at him with a mix of surprise and gratitude. "Yes, I would. How did you—never mind." A smile lifted her mouth and his hopes at the same time.

He stopped in front of the store, glad to see it was open, and handed Sophie down. "Take your time. I've a couple things to tend to."

With a clear view through the front window, he waited until he saw Mrs. Eisner greet Sophie, then flicked the reins and pulled up again in the next block.

Bozeman's was running at full throttle.

"Mornin'." Hoss jerked a nod on his way by. "Sit anywhere."

Clay stood his ground and caught the man on his way back. "Can you pack a picnic dinner?"

Hoss stopped and set his coffee pot on the counter. "How soon?"

"Now."

The man laughed outright. "It'll cost you extra, but sure. I've got fried chicken, potato salad, pickles, and canned-cherry pie."

"Bear sign?"

Another chuckle. "On the house."

While Hoss packed the meal, Clay waited at the counter.

"You that horse doctor, Ferguson?"

He turned to an older gent in dungarees and a chambray shirt.

"Yes, sir."

"You know anything about farrowin' hogs?"

Visiting quieted at the nearby tables, men listening in on the conversation.

"My share. Do you have a question?"

The older man's eyes snapped as he scratched his unshaven cheek.

"My son's got a sow he's worried about. Bred January first, and she hasn't farrowed yet. You got any recommendations?"

"Are you sure of the breeding date?"

Someone snickered behind him, and the farmer glanced that way with a poorly hidden smirk. "Sure enough."

"All right, then. Since she needs a hundred and fourteen days, tell him he can plan on April twenty-fifth, give or take a day. Make sure she's got clean straw and enough room so she doesn't crush her pigs. Keep the bedding clean and give her good feed and water. She'll need to keep her strength up."

Someone snorted. "Told ya."

The farmer's humor faded, and he went back to his table amidst guffaws and rude jokes.

Clay had played the game before.

Hoss set two paper sacks on the counter and lowered his voice. "You're workin' at Parkers', aren't you?"

"For now."

"Bring back my dishes and I won't charge you extra."

"Fair enough, but it might not be today."

Hoss waved the detail aside and took Clay's money with a wink. "Have a nice time."

Clay felt every eye pinned to his shirt as he walked out, but he'd won the first round.

He put the sacks under the rear bench and covered them with one of Deacon's quilts he'd tucked in earlier that morning. Then he drove up the street and turned around at the livery.

John was on hand. "Mornin', Mr. Ferguson."

"John. Any customers?"

"Yes, sir." He pulled a note from his trousers' pocket.

Clay took the paper and dropped two bits in John's hand. "Obliged."

"What's this for?"

"Your cut for helping me get my business going."

Pride bent the boy's mouth in a smile, and he pocketed the coin. "Thanks."

Clay flicked the gray down Main Street, and as soon as he pulled up in front of the tailor's, Sophie came out. Mrs. Eisner stood on the threshold.

He doffed his hat. "Mornin', ma'am."

"Good morning." Addressing Sophie, she added, "Thank you again for stopping by."

Sophie settled next to him, more relaxed than she had been. Good news did that for a person.

He took the next corner, and she looked over suspiciously.

"I'm turning around. The Fairfax place is north of here about two miles."

Main Street gave him cause to look to the sides of the road when he was really looking at her. She'd done her hair up with a ribbon, and it was all soft around her face. If she were a filly or a heifer, he'd know just what to say about her fine appearance. As it was, uncertainty kept him lock-jawed for fear of saying the wrong thing. She hadn't been too pleased earlier when he said she looked different. Even *beautiful* had driven doubt through her eyes.

He could handle a cantankerous old pig farmer but didn't know what to say to the woman he'd set his hopes on.

The road out of town stretched lazily until they reached the turn off that ribboned over grass-covered hills. Recognizing the low saddle ahead, he slowed the gray.

Sophie took it all in, turning on the bench and scouting the land like she was looking for something. When he stopped short of the saddle, her brow wrinkled.

"Is this it?"

"Not quite."

"Then why did you stop?"

*Because I want to kiss you and ask if you'll marry me.* "I want you to get the full effect of what's on the other side."

She snugged her shawl tighter, and one hand fingered the neckline of her dress. A very becoming neckline. "I'm ready."

He lifted the reins. The gray took the cue and eased over the dip between two hills.

Sophie gasped, and he stopped again, relieved that it all hadn't been a fanciful dream.

# CHAPTER 17

Stunned by what lay before her, Sophie blinked a couple of times to make sure she wasn't imagining things.

With the morning sun still behind them, the sky ahead was cornflower blue over a long green meadow where cows and their calves grazed. A white barn and farmhouse stood off to one side like proud parents, and as Clay had mentioned, a creek skirted the north end of the little valley.

No wonder he wanted this place.

"Fairfax? You said the name was Fairfax?"

"That's right."

"More like Fair *View*. You know, fair, as in lovely. What a lovely view."

"I know."

She glanced over, expecting him to be taking in the small ranch, not her. The look in his eyes said everything she'd always wanted to hear a man say and scared her right out of her wits. Quickly, she faced forward.

He flicked the reins, and the horse started down the gentle slope. Before they reached the house, an older woman came out on the porch and waited while Clay drew up in front.

"I've had two people stop by. Guess they heard through the grapevine, but I kept my word to you." She rubbed her right hand.

"I appreciate it, Mrs. Fairfax. I made it as soon as I could."

He jumped down and offered his hand to Sophie, his eyes gentle, fingers warm.

She'd never been so turned upside down but managed the porch steps without tripping.

"Mrs. Fairfax, I'm Sophie Price. It's a pleasure to meet you."

The woman sniffed and raised her chin, glancing between the two of them as if they'd broken the law by riding out together.

"Are you Mr. Ferguson's *intended*?"

Clay stepped forward. "Miss Price works closely with Dr. Weaver as a midwife in Olin Springs and has agreed to give me her opinion about your house. Is now a good time to see it?"

Considering Clay's explanation, and after an obvious appraisal of Sophie's deportment, Mrs. Fairfax led them indoors.

Clay squeezed Sophie's elbow, but she refused to look him in the eye. The see-saw was pounding her insides.

"It's a small but comfortable home. My husband and I raised three children and enjoyed many years here until his passing." She dabbed an eye with her tatting-edged hankie, and Sophie struggled to dredge up sympathy for what she considered exaggeration.

"How is your hand, Mrs. Fairfax?"

The woman's expression shifted immediately as she flexed her fingers. "Much better. I do believe that potion you gave me has made a difference."

Clay smiled and nodded his approval, then led Sophie into the kitchen.

Cozy, with a cook stove, ample cupboards, a table and chairs, and a view of the hills beyond the house. A backdoor opened to the spring sunshine and looked out over a fenced garden. Sophie liked the kitchen much more than the kitchen's owner.

Two bedrooms, the main room they had entered, and the kitchen made up the entire house. Sophie's home had three bedrooms, a parlor, and a short hallway, but there was no comparing the Parkers' sprawling home or Maggie Snowfield's. However, the little house stood on its own merits.

"May we see the back?" Sophie held the woman's eye, daring her to refuse the request.

"By all means."

Clay opened the back door and stood aside as Sophie stepped onto a wide porch, as expansive as the front. Two rocking chairs faced the west with a glorious view of not-so-distant mountains. The sunsets must have been breathtaking.

A privy and root cellar were not far away, and with Mrs. Fairfax leading, she and Clay walked around the house to the barn. Chickens scratched in the yard. A cow bellowed from the pasture, and birds chittered in cottonwood trees and willows.

Sophie's heart swelled. She loved it all. "You have a well, I assume." She hadn't looked for a windmill, but now saw it peeking above the barn in good repair. Another point in favor.

Clay took hold of the barn's front door, off its runner and sagging against the building that needed a fresh coat of paint. Up close, the years were evident.

Sophie could relate.

She wandered away from Clay and the owner, who were discussing other aspects of the property, for she had done what he asked—looked at the house and formed an opinion. If she had the money, she'd buy the place herself, raise a gateway, and hang a sign that said "Fair View Ranch."

In spite of the bumpy ride her emotions had taken, her stomach growled. An early breakfast called for an early dinner, and it was likely after noon. She'd be starving by the time they made it home to the ranch, and she still had supper to fix. Poor foresight on her part for not putting a roast or beans in the oven before they left.

The creek drew her, and she was tempted to pull off her boots and stockings, hike her skirt, and trounce through it just to raise the owner's ire. But that wouldn't be fair to Clay. He had the chance for a fresh start and didn't need her making the woman mad.

"What do you think?"

She spun and would have fallen in the water had he not grabbed her arm. Lost in less-than-charitable musings, she'd not heard his approach.

She smoothed her skirt and ruffled feelings, and glanced past him to the quaint little house.

He side-stepped into her view, snagging her heart and attention with a hopeful look not unlike what she'd seen on Willy when he wanted a cookie. She was helpless. And hopelessly smitten.

"The house is small, but for a single man starting out, I think it's lovely."

He scowled and looked away.

Like it or not, that was her answer. He'd have to deal with it. She headed for the buckboard.

He stepped in front of her. "But what do you think as a woman who … what would you think of a kitchen like that? Or of the yard and garden, and … well, the whole place. Would *you* like it?"

Again with the see-saw. What did it matter?

Expectation drained from his eyes as he moved closer and lowered his voice to that raspy tone he'd developed in the last three years. "You don't like it."

Before he left for school, he'd simply sounded like a young man, not some deep and unexplored cavern.

She shivered involuntarily.

"No. I mean—that's not what I'm saying."

"Then what are you saying?"

She folded her arms, wishing she hadn't left Mae Ann's shawl on the seat so her hands would have something to hold.

Meeting his earnest gaze, she had to tell him the truth.

"I would happily live here myself."

~

Swallowing a whoop was the hardest thing Clay had ever done. Right up there next to not kissing Sophie Price on the mouth in front of the snooty Mrs. Fairfax. Hopefully, there'd be plenty of time for that and more *after* he signed the deed.

He laid a hand on Sophie's shoulder, and nearly buckled at the slight tilt of her head. Holding tight rein on his manners and good sense, he gave a light squeeze and went to make Mrs. Fairfax an offer.

After the expected dickering over price, she accepted when he held out his earnest money and mentioned he'd be paying in cash. Her tone changed considerably as she rolled the bills and tucked them into her apron pocket. "I'm leaving all the furniture other than a few personal items such as my sewing machine, dishes, and such. I'm sure you understand."

"I do."

"Includes the buggy, buckboard, and livestock. I certainly don't have any use for them anymore." She gazed out over the pasture, then back at the barn. "As soon as you bring the remainder of the money, I'll sign the deed over to you and you can file it."

"Thank you, Mrs. Fairfax." He offered to shake on the deal, and her hand went slack on his next words. "May I ask a favor?"

Satisfaction thinned in light of her natural suspicion. "And that might be?"

"I've brought a picnic along in hopes that Miss Price and I might eat at the north end of the property, on the other side of the creek where the path crosses."

The woman nearly burst into tears and he took a step back, fearing she'd launch herself at him. "Are you all right, ma'am?"

She waved a frilly handkerchief with one hand and pressed the other to her lips. "You go on ahead, young man. Never mind me."

Fighting for composure, she pocketed the hankie and drew herself up. "I will telegraph my daughter as soon as I receive your payment, and you can move in when I'm gone, which should be within the month." Turning for the door, she paused. "Congratulations. I wish you well."

Within the month. And he hadn't said anything about proposing.

He stepped off the porch and surveyed the land around him. Everything he saw would be his. The buildings. The pasture. The animals. His gaze slid toward the creek, where a woman in a yellow dress stood like a spring flower. She was what he wanted most of all.

Thankfulness rose in him like a blister. Sophie would call it a blessing. He couldn't form the words, though an ache started beneath his ribs and spread across his chest. He rubbed it with the heel of his hand and climbed to the wagon seat.

She watched him approach, and when he reined in and extended his hand, she stepped up and took her place beside him. An omen? Or just the everyday nature of things. He didn't put stock in omens, but life gave signs of health or disease, and they could be trusted.

"Hungry?"

She flattened a hand to her stomach. "Starving, I'm sorry to admit."

"Good."

She puffed out her disapproval.

He chuckled.

"Look under the seat in back."

She turned around, which moved her closer to him, and reached for the quilt. "You went to Bozeman's."

"Yes, ma'am, I did. Fried chicken, bear sign, and a couple other things. Plus the quilt to sit on, though I can't account for any critters since it came off Deacon's bed."

She laughed like she was happy—a lighthearted sound that shivered down inside him.

He turned off the path onto a green patch for the horse, jumped down, and offered his hand. As Sophie reached for it, he circled her waist with one arm and scooped her legs out from under her with the other. She clamped on to his neck in alarm, and he spun her around just to hear her laugh.

"Clay Ferguson, what's gotten into you?"

She had. All the way into that deep, dark corner he'd shut off from the light of day. She made him feel almost whole.

"Put me down. Mrs. Fairfax is probably watching from her front window."

"Doesn't matter. The place is mine. Fair View Ranch."

He said it without thinking, without considering her reaction to the idea until her hand clapped over her mouth and her eyes grew round as dollars.

Reluctantly, he set her down, then gently held her by the arms. Touch would tell him what she was feeling whether she trembled or tensed or relaxed. He'd felt her do all three.

Together with her eyes and her voice, touch would tell him what she was thinking.

She made to step back, but he wouldn't let go. Her gaze dropped to the thick grass where they stood, and he hooked one finger under her chin and lifted it.

Eyes shining, she brushed beneath them, her fingers trembling.

"What is it?" he whispered.

"How do you do that?"

Now he was worried. "Do what?"

She took the hand that lifted her chin and held it in both of hers. "Know what I'm thinking."

He cupped her face and lowered his mouth to hers, skimming her warm lips. She didn't pull away, but laid her hand on his chest, right over the spot that burned like living flame. Encircling her as he had before, he pressed her close, this time kissing her deeply. And this time her arms went round him and her fingers fanned out on his back.

Internal reins pulled hard, and he broke from her sweet lips, resting his head atop hers but still holding on. Her racing heart matched his and stampeded all his words against his skull. He had to corral them and cut out the right ones.

The perfect ones. Those she wouldn't refuse.

He took a half-step back, sliding his hold down her arms, keenly aware of the rise and fall of flushed skin above her ruffled bodice. "Sophie Price, will you be the mistress of Fair View Ranch?"

Her breath caught, and her eyes said she needed to hear more. But what? What did a woman want to hear from a man? What did that man say?

Maybe he wasn't clear enough, was trying too hard to impress her rather than saying what was on his mind.

"Would you marry me?"

She closed her eyes and his heart dropped. How could he let her go? How could he go without her?

"Yes."

Less than a whisper, it shuddered through him. He touched her face. He had to see the answer in her eyes.

She smiled and blinked at pooling tears. "Yes, I will marry you."

Lifting her, he swung her around—

"But only if …"

He stopped, aware that she was pushing against him, that she had a condition. He set her down and waited to be shot by a firing squad. It couldn't be any worse than the sudden jerk on his soul.

She fussed with her dress, and her crooked smile tugged at her cheek. "Only if you let me eat before I faint dead away."

Her playfulness did things to him. Things he couldn't act on now. But feed her—that he could handle.

Needing to touch her, he brushed the back of his hand against her cheek. "You drive a hard bargain, Miss Price, but I'll concede."

She spread the quilt close to the creek, and he set the paper sacks in the center. She opened one and took out Bozeman's idea of a picnic: a paper-wrapped pickle, tin cup full of potato salad, another one with cherry pie squashed inside, and two pieces of chicken also wrapped in paper. The last bundle held bear sign.

Clay's sack held the same, plus two cloth napkins Hoss must have stuck in as an afterthought, and two spoons. Good man.

Sophie folded her hands in her lap and waited.

His stomach knotted, and he laid his hat crown down on a corner of the quilt.

He couldn't do it.

She tipped her head, asking why.

He couldn't tell her.

Clouds scuttled across her face, but she reached for his hand and bowed her head. "Lord, what a beautiful place this is. Thank you for our food and this time together." Her voice dropped to a near whisper. "Thank you for Clay. For bringing him home."

With a squeeze of her fingers, she looked up. "Amen."

For the first time in his memory, the foreign word clawed up through his throat, sharp as an unsheathed cougar. "Amen."

# CHAPTER 18

The pain etched on Clay's face marred all traces of his earlier joy, and Sophie's heart broke for him. Had he never been loved? He'd not used the word when he spoke to her of marriage, though she believed he did love her. His kindnesses to her and his affection revealed his feelings. *As did his kiss …*

But something was terribly wrong deep inside him. It had risen to the surface when she'd mentioned his mother and again today when she assumed he would ask God's blessing on their meal.

It was a perfect meal that he had gathered in his cowboy way, and she would not have changed a thing, other than the cause of his obvious agony.

Again, the plea returned. *Talk to me, Clay.*

The buckboard climbed to the top of the rise, where he reined in and turned to look at the land he'd claimed. She turned as well and linked her arm through his. He covered her hand, his fingers strong and callused yet soothing. Much like him—strong and soothing yet callused against sharing his pain.

Doubt began circling like a hungry wolf—head low, eyes fiery and fierce, waiting to pounce and tear away what she held precious. If Clay didn't share his deepest hurts with her, how could they share their day-to-day lives, certain to be shot through with pain as well as happiness?

The ride back to the ranch was quieter than she'd hoped. Such a perfect opportunity to talk privately, yet Clay sat entombed in unshared thoughts.

She had to try. "Did Mrs. Fairfax drive as hard a bargain as I did?"

He looked straight ahead, but the corner of his mouth hitched, the first crack in his defenses. A deep rumble in his chest hinted at laughter, and he slid her a glance, eyes once more filled with warmth. "Not nearly."

Relief sighed from her like wind through a pine, and she scooted closer. Bold, Mama would say. *Absolutely necessary*, Sophie would answer.

"Will she give you time to talk to the bank or have you already?"

Nosy? Yes, if he hadn't proposed marriage. Under the circumstances, she felt she had the right to know if the man she was marrying was also going into more debt than he could carry.

"Nope."

Nope, what? Had her simple *yes* to his proposal shortened his speech to single syllables?

"Don't need to. I'm paying cash."

He straightened a little as he said it, the first hint of actual pride she'd seen in him.

"Cash? You have enough cash to buy a small ranch?"

The deep-chested laugh rolled out and he wrapped his arm around her, pulling her even closer. "Are you wonderin' if I robbed a bank?"

He was toying with her, and she didn't appreciate it. She stiffened slightly. "I know you wouldn't do that, but it's about all I know of you."

They came to a dip in the road, and he lifted his arm from her shoulders and took the reins in both hands. "It's from sale of the family farm out east, past La Junta."

Silenced for a moment by the sudden influx of information, she began forming pictures of his childhood. He had a family after all. At least a mother and father. Siblings?

"Do you—"

"I don't talk about 'em."

End of conversation.

He snapped the reins, and the gray picked up its pace on the straightaway. The door had closed, and she was left outside.

If this was a glimpse of what life with Clay Ferguson was going to be, she had some serious praying to do—another thing he didn't share with her. Maybe she had accepted his proposal too quickly, too rashly, befuddled by the beauty of the Fairfax place and her affection for him.

Pulling up out of the dip, the mare jostled them back to level road. Was affection cause enough to give her life and strength to a man who held back from her?

One thing she knew for certain. If she ever had children of her own, she'd steer them away from see-saws.

~

Of all the outright stupid things Clay had done, gambling wasn't one of them. The next morning, he added it to the list. He was gambling on Sophie not pressing him about his life prior to Olin Springs.

His gut said he was a fool and she'd win.

His gut—or rather, his nose—said he also needed to wash the clothes under his bunk, and no way in ten was he going to ask her to do it. He gathered everything in the sheet from his bedroll and dropped them by the pump handle outside. When she'd agreed to marry him, it was understood that she'd be doing his laundry, but not this side of "I do."

Deacon was checking on late heifers in the north pasture. Clay found a bucket in the barn and the soap cake he'd used for shaving and set to scrubbing. A couple shirts, a pair of trousers, socks, and whatnot. He draped it all over the hitch rail to dry.

Things went just fine until he slipped inside for a cup of coffee and returned to find his whatnot missing. Didn't take long to see the yellow dog dragging them through the dirt.

"Hey! Get back here!" He went after the mongrel.

It must have misread his intentions, for it took off like a brand-singed calf huntin' its mama.

He was about to go get his rope when he caught Sophie in front of the ranch house holding her sides and laughing.

Busted.

She went inside and returned with a soup bone that she tossed to the dog. It dropped his drawers at her feet.

*Don't pick 'em up. Don't pick 'em up.*

She picked them up. Dainty-like, holding a corner with two fingers and looking him dead in the eye. No question, she was still laughing.

He gathered what pride he had trailing him and walked over to retrieve the item.

She backed out of reach. "This is why we have clotheslines. Meet me around back with the rest of your clothes and I'll show you how to pin them on the line."

He hadn't bothered to grab his hat and could feel his ears burning bright as Christmas candles. To Sophie's credit, she didn't say anything.

By the time he joined her with the rest of his wet clothes, she'd rinsed the dirt out of his under-riggings and hung them out in plain sight.

She wasn't laughing any more, but that crooked smile nearly wrapped around her ear. "This is also why the line is in *back* of the house, so things are kept more private."

He tossed everything over a wire and moved in for a private kiss, but she handed him a bunch of wooden clips from her apron pocket and side-stepped him. "Watch and learn."

The way she spread the shoulders of his shirt made him wish he was in it. She pinned it to the line, proving she'd done it a hundred times—the same way he'd trim a horse's hoof and think nothing of it.

She tossed him the second shirt. "Your turn." Arms folded, she watched him like a schoolmarm. "Not bad." And with that, she left him standing there with a bunch of oversized toothpicks. "You're on your own, cowboy."

Dadgummit.

At least Deacon was gone.

The next morning, so was he. An hour before it broke light, wearing clean clothes and riding Duster with his saddlebags full of promise. He figured he could call on the widow Fairfax, sign the deed, and get to the land office in Cedar City by mid-afternoon. He'd be back to the ranch well after dark, but he didn't want to be gone more than one day. He'd ride all night if he had to.

The only thing he didn't like about his plan was the temperature drop and the feel of snow on its way.

Dawn broke thin and gray as he topped the low saddle to the widow's ranch. Her small herd was still bedded down, a sure sign that rain or worse was coming. He trotted into the yard and laid reins to the hitch rail.

Mrs. Fairfax greeted him at the door.

"It's going to storm," she said, leading him to the kitchen and the inviting smell of coffee and baked goods. "But I had a hunch you'd be here sooner rather than later."

The deed and other papers were on the table, and a crate sat off in one corner full of packing straw and china dishes. The woman was as eager to get on with life as he was.

"What did she say?"

Stalling, he took a seat and tried the coffee before realizing she was talking about Sophie.

"She said yes." He swirled the brew in his cup. The next pot of coffee made in this house would be by Sophie's hand.

"Good." The widow nodded as if she'd just set the world back on its axis.

Maggie and her manners kept him seated without rushing things along too much, but Mrs. Fairfax understood he was trying to make the land office in Cedar City before it closed. She waved from the front porch as he rode away, nearly all the money he had in the world stuffed in her apron pockets.

With a stomach full of coffee and some kind of sweet bread he hadn't expected, he skirted Olin Springs and cut a trail south. A napkin full of Sophie's biscuits rode in his saddle bags, supper on his way home.

Still not home, really. But she was there, and that made the ranch home for the time being. The blister in his chest throbbed, like it had been off and on since she'd said she'd marry him. Sweet, brave, compassionate Sophie Price was going to be his wife. That realization alone lit a fire in his belly and gave him more reason than doctorin' ever would for building a life and a future.

But she was also inquisitive, and she wasn't going to take him at face value. He knew that as well as he knew Duster was a six-year-old buckskin gelding. Not after what she'd seen the day he patched the cabin roof. It busted open a whole barrel of questions for her. Questions he didn't want to take out and examine one by one, tearing open wounds patched over like that roof. Too long he'd worn a poultice of avoidance, and he'd had no cause to peel it off until he saw the questions in Sophie's eyes.

She'd gently probed to understand, pressing him for his secrets. And like the stallion constrained in the stock car, it was only a matter of time before something gave way—the padlock on his past or her patience.

Later. He'd look at it all later.

Duster sensed his mood and took the trail at a good clip. A client in Olin Springs had mentioned a small town about a half day's ride, Lockton. Said folks there had call for a veterinarian, but Clay couldn't make the detour today. He'd telegraph the livery there and see if enough folks needed his services to make it worth a separate trip.

The wind picked up at his back, and he raised his coat collar. Cloud cover bottomed out as he rode into Cedar City, but the land office was still open. He recorded his deed, answered the clerk's questions about work as a veterinarian, and promised to come back for a few days. The man's horse needed its teeth floated, and he'd said a couple ranchers might be interested in talking about treatments.

When Clay left a half hour later, the temperature had dropped again. He pulled his slicker on over his canvas coat and vest and swung to the saddle, turning Duster into wind carrying the promise of snow. He passed the Stratford Hotel on his way out of town, tempted at the thought of a hot bath and soft bed. But a tug on his gut made him keep riding.

Preacher Bittman would say that meant it was a good time to pray.

Clay snorted. Problem was, he didn't know how, and he'd made that clear as creek water at the picnic with Sophie. Dadblastit, today was not the day he wanted to rehash all the things he *couldn't* do.

No sunset to speak of that evening. Just a slow fade as wind-churned clouds quilted the sky. Trooper that he was, Duster kept his head down and plowed on. Snow flurries cut their trail off and on after full dark. The wind shifted, but it didn't come a blizzard like Clay feared it might.

Time was hard to measure when everything that told it was missing. He pulled his hat farther down and his scarf up over his nose and mouth, trying to remember what blue sky looked like. Duster knew the way home, and Clay knew enough to give the horse his head.

When they rode into the yard, all the ranch-house windows glowed with yellow light, as well as the two lanterns beside the front door. The hair on his neck raised, and he tied up at the rail instead of the barn and stepped inside on a wind gust.

Sophie, Deacon, and Mae Ann all turned at the same time, their frantic looks dulling to disappointment when they saw him.

Sophie ran to him as though he was the cavalry come to save the day. "Willy is missing."

A sob broke from Mae Ann, and Deacon put his arm around her shoulders.

Clay gripped Sophie's arms. "Where have you checked?"

"Everywhere."

He looked at Deacon.

"The barn, out buildings, even Pine Hill and the cabin." The old cowboy gave Mae Ann a quick squeeze. "I'm going out again."

But the slight jerk of the foreman's head said he didn't hold much hope.

Clay drew Sophie to the hearth and tugged his hat off. "Where did you see him last?"

Mae Ann's breath broke on her words. "At the kitchen table."

Sophie looked down as if ashamed. "We were all there, drinking coffee and talking about, well, things."

He knew what she was referring to, and it cheated him for her to be sad. But it cheated him more for Willy to be missing, and anger churned behind his ribs where the blister had been. "Do you know what time that was?"

"With the clouds settling, we ate early. About four, but it felt like dusk," she said. "The last thing I remember is him asking where you and his papa were."

Gut shot by double barrels couldn't hurt more. "What time is it now?" He answered his own question with a glance at the mantel clock.

"We looked everywhere twice," Deacon said. "In every cranny a kid could crawl. But we'll look again."

"All right. I figure six hours." He plowed his fingers through his hair. "How far can a three-year-old go in six hours in good weather?"

They all stared at him.

"A man can make three miles in an hour if he walks steady. Let's give him one, which means the farthest he could have gone was six miles from the house, but not in a storm. He wouldn't have the endurance. He's got to be around here somewhere closer."

Mae Ann strangled a cry and covered her face.

"Deacon and I will ride a perimeter mile and keep circling in until we find him."

His teeth clenched tight enough to snap a horseshoe nail. "And we'll find him."

He shoved his hat on, then pulled Sophie in for a quick embrace and whispered against her hair. "Listen for two shots. Two shots mean we found him alive."

Her eyes rounded in fright, but he jerked his head toward Mae Ann.

On his way out the door, he swore a silent oath against what Sophie must have felt like when the Eisner baby died.

*Not this time. Not when I can do something about it.*

He and Deacon stopped at the cabin where he buckled on his .45, checked the load, and dropped extra cartridges in his vest pockets.

Deacon did the same.

Snow fell in fits and spurts as they rode a mile out from the yard, measured by fence line and pasture, and stopped.

"One shot found." Clay swallowed against a boulder in his throat. "Two shots alive."

Deacon screwed his old hat down and they turned in opposite directions.

Clay didn't think about his childhood. Didn't *want* to think about it. But he needed to think like a three-year-old right now. Since he'd been one, it was all he had to go on.

Where would he search if he was looking for someone? *For his mother.*

The spot inside his chest stung like a scab ripped off. *I'd go where I thought she was.*

Willy knew where the people in his life went. The barn, the corrals, Deacon's cabin. Upstairs. But he hadn't been in any of those places.

Would he try to get under cover from the snow and wind? Had he fallen in a hole or crawled into a coyote den?

Chances were he'd travel downwind from blowing snow, not into it, which would put him southeast of the house and barn—the way Clay was headed.

With the wind at his back, he pushed into every juniper clump he came to. Most of the area was open range. Rocks peppered outlying areas, like the patch of boulders along the trail to the Price farm, but he found nothing.

In an hour he met Deacon and they tightened their circle, closer to the barn and house.

"Wil-ly!" Deacon's holler was small and faint, yanked by the wind. It'd sound the same to the boy, if he heard it at all.

Clay pulled his scarf up over his face and kept riding, feeling like he rode in mindless circles for no reason. Snow was drifting, so the ground was clear, but how much of a trail would a three-year-old kid leave?

His oath came back to him, as empty as the night. *Not when I can do something about it.* Cold fear cinched his throat. He couldn't do a blasted thing.

Dread squeezed his lungs, and the cry came of its own accord. "Oh, God, show us where he is."

The words didn't make it past his scarf, where his breath froze, hanging like icicles before him as he covered another hundred yards. At least he thought it was a hundred yards. Riding blind made it easy to lose all sense of direction and distance. How would a little boy know where he was going or *should* go? Would he just lie down and curl up in a ball? Hunker up next to a rock and freeze to death?

*God, no. Please.*

Another cry tore out of his chest and died on the wind. "Help us. Help me. I can't do this on my own."

*The yellow dog was gone.*

Like a gunshot, the words drew him up and he looked behind him for—what? The yellow dog was gone. What did that have to do with anything?

A spark lit in the back of his brain, and he whirled his horse around, squinting through the dark and blowing snow and off his trail in what he thought was the direction of the knoll. The wind hadn't shifted until *after* dark.

# CHAPTER 19

Head down, Clay hunched his shoulders and heeled Duster straight into the icy cold screaming off the mountains. The gelding reached through it, pushing against the wind's knife-edge, climbing toward the knoll.

The red sandstone stood colorless and bare, blown clear of snow, but not the brush around it. The scrub oak at its base bowed with a heavy load where snow had swirled over the rock and sucked back against it. Clay remembered that brush. The dog had bellied in under an arched branch, following a rabbit's scent. But now there was no opening. Just a snow-covered mound.

The dirt had blown clear. No tracks to read. No clues to say whether it was just a pile of snow blown in or a cougar taking shelter. Clay tugged his right glove off with his teeth, pulled his .45 and stepped down, holding the reins with his other hand. He eased closer to the lump. Toed it with his boot. Felt a growl.

Cocked the hammer.

A head raised, and yellow eyes challenged him.

Recognition hit, and the dog's ears flattened with a whine.

Clay's heart slammed into his ribs, and he eased the hammer up and holstered his gun. Another whine, and he knelt and reached in around the dog.

"Papa?"

The frightened little voice burned through Clay like hot steel, and he pulled Willy from the dog's sheltering cradle.

"It's Mr. Clay, Willy. Take hold round my neck."

He unfastened his slicker and covered the boy, then stepped up to the saddle.

Reaching under his slicker, he drew his gun. "It's going to be loud, Willy. Hang on."

The dog flattened its ears and looked away.

Clay fired once and then again, hoping—no, praying—the wind carried the sound to those who needed to hear it.

With a catch in his voice and a quick arm around Willy, he looked at the yellow dog. "Let's go home."

~

Sophie's head jerked up at the incongruent noise. A gunshot?

She held her breath, straining to hear above the crackling fire and wind buffeting the house. *There—again.* Her pulse spiked. Was it her imagination?

Mae Ann slept in the other chair, feet tucked beneath her with still enough room on the seat for her precious boy to snuggle with her—if he'd been there. Madeline lay swaddled in her arms. Dare Sophie raise a mother's hopes over what might only be a tree limb snapped by the storm?

She added wood to the fire and sat on the hearth, facing the door, willing it to open and Clay to stride in strong and tall with the boy in his arms. *Oh, God, show him the way to Willy.*

But for the wind and fire, all was silent, and it was silence that had alerted her to begin with. An uneasy feeling that afternoon when the birds stilled and the sky turned to slate. Something had been missing. A consistent noise or presence that suddenly wasn't there. And that presence was Willy.

The front door crashed open and she cried out.

Mae Ann sat up with a start.

Clay blew in, his yellow slicker flapping at his legs but tight around his middle and bulging. He came straight to the fire where he knelt and set two small booted feet on the hearth. "You can let go now, Willy. You're home."

"Papa?"

Sophie swept the baby from Mae Ann's arms and sobbed as the mother fell to her knees in front of her son, doing the same.

Deacon came next, slamming the door behind Mae Ann's dog, which ran across the threshold and shook snow from its back.

Deacon pulled his boots off in the jack, then pegged his slicker and hat on the wall, as did Clay. Gun belts hung from both men, and Sophie shivered at the sight. Life in the high parks often came to a standoff between man and predator. Thank God, tonight's bullets had signaled survival.

She hurried to the kitchen with Madeline tucked against her and dumped old coffee grounds into a tin on the counter.

Clay followed and drew her into his arms, holding her as if he feared she might blow away.

"Thank God," she whispered. Something had happened out there in the wind. Something that cut clean through him. She sensed the difference but didn't ask. Patience was not her strong suit, yet she waited, one arm around him in gratitude, Madeline cloistered between them in the other. Prayer rose silently from her soul that he would tell her.

"Sophie, can you bring me some towels?"

Clay kissed the top of her head. "I'll get the coffee going."

Still holding the baby, she laid her other hand against his cheek, red and cold as ice. "Thank God. Thank you."

His cold lips took hers with sudden urgency and shot icy fire through her veins. She lingered a moment, then gathered every length of toweling she could find in the kitchen. At the hearth, mother, son, and dog formed an unusual trio. Willy's boots sat beside him, his clothes not as wet as she'd expected. The dog, however, was shivering uncontrollably, soaked to the skin.

"Koogu hepped me," Willy said, patting the dog's wet head.

Mae Ann rubbed Willy's hair. "Would you get him some dry clothes from upstairs, please?"

"Of course."

When Sophie returned, Clay had joined them and was rubbing the dog with another towel.

Remarkably, Madeline slept through all the tromping around, but Sophie's arm was nearly numb. She gave the dry clothes to Mae Ann, then sat facing Clay but next to Cougar who smelled more like wet *cougar* than wet dog. "What happened?"

The muscle in Clay's jaw clenched and he shot a look to Deacon in the other chair, then back to the women.

"When I found them, the dog was curled around Willy, covered in snow. No telling how long he'd been like that. They were tucked in under a scrub oak on the knoll. This side of a patch of red rock."

"That's not far," Mae Ann said, her voice breathy and full of tears. She helped Willy get his arms in the sleeves of a dry shirt, and between errant sobs, hugged him and kissed his cheeks, red and chapped from the cold. "Maybe a half mile. Was it on one of your circles?"

"Twice that hound earned his keep." Deacon's crusty voice caught an edge on the last word, and Sophie looked over to see him rubbing his mustache with the back of his hand.

"He warned Cade when Mae Ann was in a fix up at the old farm a few years back."

Mae Ann wiped her eyes and kissed Willy's head, then kissed the dog's head too.

Clay hadn't answered her question.

Sophie touched his arm. "What made you look there?"

He covered her hand with his, strong and hard and still cold. "I took Willy for a ride up there the day his sister was born. Showed him his pa's land. The yellow dog went with us. Tonight Willy must have gone looking for his pa."

His voice got thick and he shook his head like he couldn't talk.

"And Cougar went with him," she whispered, throat squeezing with gratitude for the Lord's unlikely guardian. But she couldn't wait, she had to know. "What made you think to look there, off your planned search area?"

Clay swallowed and pushed his hand through his hair, then looked at her with a hundred words in his eyes. Not one came out of his mouth.

She balled her fingers into fists, wanting to press the point. Impatient curiosity roared as loud as the wind, but she held off in front of the others and added her question to a list that was growing longer by the day. The moment was one of victory and relief, and she'd not spoil it to make a stand on principles.

She turned to Deacon. "Where's Blue?"

The old fella huffed. "In his hidey-hole at the barn is my guess. That's where I'd be in this storm."

"Cougar will stay here tonight." Mae Ann rubbed his coat again with the dry end of a wet towel. "Do we have a soup bone or anything for him?"

"I'll check." Sophie handed Madeline to her mother and flexed her arm on the way to the kitchen, as well as her sensibilities. Why wouldn't Clay talk to her? Why were words so difficult when he did everything else with patient precision? What was he hiding? The questions were growing like nettles and just as stinging in their irritation, but she shoved them down and set about scraping leftovers into a pie pan for the dog.

Few things conjured comfort like hot coffee on a blustery night. She carried a tray of tin cups and cookies to the hearth, then returned for the pie pan and set it before the shivering dog.

Deacon's eyes lit up at the sight of sweets, and he helped himself to a handful.

In the wake of such intense relief, fatigue slid up behind her and sank into her bones. Mae Ann had to feel the same, and Sophie encouraged her upstairs with the children. The night would be short, and they all needed as much sleep as they could get.

At the landing she looked down at the men and dog by the fire. Only one was watching her. True to her nature, she was half one emotion, half another—gratitude and vexation. The see-saw wavered between the two. She pressed her fingers to her lips and tipped them toward the weary man who watched her.

He fisted his hand and held it over his heart.

~

From the old leather chair, Deacon snored like a locomotive. Dawn whispered at the window, and Clay took the coffee pot and mugs to the kitchen. He'd never shut his eyes.

He tugged into his coat and boots and set his hat, and at the creak of the door hinges, the yellow dog trotted out into the snow ahead of him.

Cougar. Heck of a name for a dog, but it had the yellow eyes and big feet to go with it, as well as the good sense to shelter Willy.

*Why?*

The single word spiraled up from a dark corner Clay rarely looked in. *Why* was one of those questions he didn't ask unless it had to do with sick or injured livestock. In those cases, *why* could lead to a cause and therefore a remedy, at least a comfort. But asking *why* where people were concerned had never given him anything but more pain.

Why had his mother died in the fire?

Why did his father beat him? Curse him?

Why had he let the fire-crazed horses run out of the barn and over Clay in their panic to flee?

The cold knifed through his pants and into the leg that hadn't been properly set.

Only once since he'd left his childhood behind had he asked a man why, and that man was Garrett Wilson. Why had he trusted Clay after he'd drunk himself senseless, nearly shot up the bar, and landed in Wilson's "Iron Bar Inn," as the sheriff called it.

Garrett's answer rang as plain on this cold morning as it had four years ago in that jail cell—*Somebody needs to.*

That's when things started to change for the better.

Clay's boots crunched through six inches of crisp white that had fallen after the wind died last night. Everything lay still beneath it, and no birds sang in the trees.

Something was different about the morning. More than just a fresh start—more of a relief. A memory cracked through the shell of his heart like a hatchling, and it frightened him as much as the futility of his search frightened a prayer from him the night before.

A prayer that had been answered.

No way in a hundred would he have thought to ride up to the knoll. He and Deacon wouldn't have circled around to it for a couple hours, maybe more. The clear morning sky after the storm might have set that red sandstone off in the perfect light, but it would have been too late by then. The probability twisted his insides.

*Why?*

He pulled his gloves on and tromped across the yard, around the barn, and away from the word where he could stand out in the open and watch the sun rise.

Like every sunrise before, it drew him. They always had, though he didn't know—there it was again—why. He dipped his head until his hat brim cut the line where sky met land. And at the moment white light broke the edge, the blister in his soul split open with the sound of her voice.

*He's faithful, Clay. Look at that sunrise, so fresh and perfect. It's His mercy, brand new every morning.*

The pain sent him to his knees, and he clutched at his chest. Lanced by forgotten words, the blister drained through his every pore and ran down his face like acid.

All these years he'd hidden from the memory, the loss, the tenderness of his mother's voice. It wasn't worth the impossible price it cost him to remember. Yet she'd drawn him without his knowledge. He could no more break his connection to her than he could his connection to dawn.

"Oh, God." His voice came strange, strangled. Breath burned his lungs as if it were his first and last. He suddenly understood the source of thought—of the dog, the knoll. The recognition of God's presence in the storm shattered Clay to the core.

"You told me where to look."

Another gasp, tight and searing. "You found him. Because You love him."

He dropped back on his boot heels, squinting against the blinding light reflecting from every crystal for miles around, stunned by the beauty, but more so by a truth that far out-weighed all the unanswered whys of his life.

"You found *me*."

# Chapter 20

Saturday morning, Sophie slid a perfect chocolate cake from the oven and set it on the counter to cool. Mae Ann made the best cake on the Front Range, and Todd had frequently reminded Sophie of that fact ever since he'd tasted Mae Ann's efforts years ago. But Sophie's butter-cream frosting made tree bark edible, so she didn't mind offering her cake to the Parkers while Mae Ann was in confinement.

If she could call it that. Nothing very confining about the woman seeing her husband off and coming down to the kitchen for meals. It was all Sophie could do to keep her from helping with the cooking.

Abigail Eisner had been another one quick to return to her normal routine, though Sophie felt, under the circumstances, that it was best for Abigail.

None of the men had been on hand this morning for breakfast, including Willy, whom Mae Ann insisted sleep with her the last two nights. After the emotional drain of him having gone missing, they'd stayed abed most of yesterday, and Sophie took a light dinner up. Aside from that, she'd had the kitchen to herself, but today her mind was scrounging for where everyone was. Clay in particular.

He and Deacon were probably looking after late heifers or checking on the young bulls. Riding fence line or looking for injuries among the horses, or one of the other hundred things that kept ranchers out at all hours.

Images of the Fairfax ranch rose with a quickening in her breast, and she marveled again that Clay had been thinking what she was thinking about changing the name, as if he knew.

Like he'd known where Willy was. Her instincts told her the Lord had answered everyone's prayers, possibly even Clay's, if he'd prayed. But again, he wouldn't tell her. Ire whipped through her like the butter, sugar, and cream she was beating into frosting.

Well, she knew a few things too, and one was how different Clay had been when he came through the door with Willy snugged tight in his slicker. Oh, how she longed to hear the real story. The story of Clay's heart that he kept to himself.

Lately, she looked forward to meals more than she ever had before, because they brought Clay nearer. So had Mrs. Fairfax's tiny kitchen, and Sophie's imagination had soared uncontrollably at what it would be like to be the mistress of that cozy home and to share it with Clay.

It was a shuddering thought, and it rippled through her, tying all her hopes and dreams together in one big bow. And that's where doubt settled in—right under the bow.

What if he never opened up to her? Never shared his past. Never told her what had made those brutal scars on his back or the reason he limped. The reason he didn't talk about his family.

Could she marry him knowing nothing? Even Mae Ann as a mail-order bride had known *something* of her betrothed before agreeing to marry him sight unseen.

That night, habit had her boiling water for baths until she remembered that no one would be riding into town for church. Deacon hadn't even shown up for supper, and when she asked Clay of his whereabouts, he merely hitched the side of his mouth and gave her a warm look. Many more of those warm looks and she wouldn't have to heat water at all.

Sunday morning she woke to melting ice dripping from the eaves and hurried down to start coffee and hotcakes. Everyone joined her, and she could see Mae Ann's longing for her husband in her eyes.

Deacon showed up with a trimmed mustache and no spurs. Apparently *someone* was going to church.

"You're looking mighty sassy this morning," Clay said over his syrup-drenched hotcakes.

Seated directly across from Sophie, Deacon watched her over the brim of his coffee cup.

What was that about?

Setting his cup on the table, he straightened the slightest bit. "Miss Sophie."

He never called her that. Oh dear. She knew what he was going to say, and part of her didn't want to hear it. Not here in front of Clay and Mae Ann.

She scooted her chair back.

"I got somethin' to ask you."

Reluctantly, she remained seated.

"I 'spect you know how I feel 'bout your ma, and if'n it seems right to you, I'm gonna speak to the preacher today."

Mae Ann grinned like a schoolgirl, and Clay slid her a sideways glance.

No one said anything, but every eye turned to Sophie, including Willy's.

After a moment, Deacon cleared his throat and started to say something else.

She interrupted his intensions. "It is truly thoughtful of you to consult me, Deacon, but Mama is a grown woman and she knows her own mind. I dare say she's like a girl when you're around, so I'm sure you both will be very happy together."

It took every ounce of her fortitude not to look at Clay. They hadn't spoken of a wedding or mentioned any plans at all since the picnic.

As happy as Sophie was for her mother, the dread of her life was coming to pass. Mama would be a bride before she was. "If you'll excuse me, please."

She fled upstairs to her room at the end of the landing, feeling all of twelve. Was there no end to this emotional see-saw? Falling across the bed, she buried her face in the quilt and held her breath. If she didn't breathe, she wouldn't cry. And she mustn't cry. Not over this.

At a gentle tap on her door, she groaned, not unlike Mae Ann had in labor.

Another knock.

Sophie sat up and fingered hair off the sides of her face. "Come in."

Mae Ann entered with Madeline and sat on the edge of the bed. "Is it your mother and Deacon, or is something else troubling you?"

Against Sophie's deepest wishes, tears broke free and she buried her face in her apron. Mae Ann's arm around her shoulder merely brought more.

Not much was hidden between women who shared the birthing process, and that included fears, faults, and dreams. So close in age, she and Mae Ann had become more than patient and midwife.

"It's everything. All at once." Sophie dried her face, not surprised that giving voice to her pain eased it a little. "Deacon's been sweet on Mama for a long time. She twitters like a spring robin when he's around. And why shouldn't she? Papa's been gone for years now, and she's worked hard to keep the farm. Who knows if Todd will stay on, or if he even wants to, and I'm often gone tending to women when their time comes."

She laid a reassuring hand on Mae Ann's arm. "Don't think for a moment that I begrudge time here with you. But Mama needs someone with her as well, and Deacon is who she wants."

Madeline fussed, and Mae Ann unfastened her bodice. "Your mother is a fine woman, and she's done a notable job raising you and Todd and tending the farm. Deacon is blessed that she'll have him."

The baby latched on and soon the contentment of a nursing child wrapped around the three of them.

"And?"

Sophie glanced up.

"You said *everything*. That usually means more than one."

She was worse than Betsy, and her matter-of-fact tone brought a weak smile to Sophie despite the open wound. A sigh broke free with words in its wake. "I am ashamed to admit this, but it hurts a little to see Mama married before me."

Mae Ann cooed at Madeline and brushed her cherub cheek with a finger. "Did you and Clay discuss a wedding date?"

Sophie rolled the hem of her apron. "No. It seemed foolish to ask so quickly on the heels of saying yes."

Mae Ann looked out the window as though viewing the strange past that brought her to the Parker ranch. "Our proposals and weddings aren't always as we imagined they would be."

A tattered breath caught Sophie in the chest, and she considered the events that had led to Mae Ann's marriage. "I'm sorry. I'm one to talk."

Mae Ann gave her a tender smile that encouraged Sophie to spill even more of herself. "Make that I'm the *only* one to talk. Though I feel like Clay and I have grown somewhat closer, he doesn't share anything about his past or his family. The day he proposed is the day I learned he paid for the Fairfax place with money from the sale of his family's farm, and only because I asked him point blank. Yet when I started to mention his parents and siblings, he cut me off."

Mae Ann clearly understood, based on the compassion in her eyes. "Give him time. I have a sense that he is one who must build up trust before he reveals the unseen."

The words pricked Sophie. She had lived her life trusting, yet lately had been faced with trusting God when things fell apart. She didn't know who or what Clay trusted, or if he even trusted her. The bow around her dreams began to loosen.

"I believe you and I need a turn in town," Mae Ann said. "What do you think of taking the buckboard in to church this morning? Do you think it's too soon for Madeline?"

At mention of her name, the baby noisily broke from nursing and looked up at her mother as if awaiting an answer.

Sophie stroked the silky head. As much as she'd enjoy seeing Betsy, she did not agree with Mae Ann, who was already bristling against confinement. "Give her another week. And yourself. The trip and the exertion of greeting everyone will be tiring. One more week of rest will do you both good."

~

When Deacon rode off, Clay turned the stallion out in the round pen and Blanca back with the herd. He shook out a loop on the sorrel he'd cut from the herd earlier and saddled it. Cold-backed, it humped up a couple times, but soon remembered what it meant to have a man in the saddle.

They rode out of the yard and circled around to the north pasture, the horse taking in the scents and sights. It flicked its ears at the cow-calf pairs and responded quickly to the touch of heel and rein. But he wanted to see how it was with Sophie. How they worked together before he'd trust it with her.

Parker would be back from Denver on Tuesday, and depending on what Mae Ann needed, Sophie might be gone soon after. If it were up to Clay, he'd take her to town, get Pastor Bittman to say words over them, and move to the Fairfax ranch. But he hadn't talked to her about it, and he suspected she wanted a wedding and a get-together with her friends.

And he needed to talk to her about other things, like what happened.

But it was easier planning chores around the place he wanted to complete. Cleaning it up some. Painting the barn and a few other odd jobs that needed doing. He didn't want to live there without her, but he might have to for a while.

He circled back to the barn, saddled Duster, and left both horses at the rail.

Sophie was in the garden. She pushed loose hair from her eyes and watched him approach.

"I've got something to show you."

He could watch her break a slow smile any hour of the day, any day of the week. "You have the time?"

"I do."

He liked the sound of those words.

She pulled off her work gloves and laid them on the gate post, then walked beside him to the barn. Her notice landed on the sorrel and she moved around to the rail where she could look it in the eye.

The horse swished its tail, calm as Duster, but followed her with its ears and tested her scent.

She rubbed under the forelock and along its neck. "Nice-looking fella."

"Take a short ride with me?"

Surprise caught her around the eyes, and she looked back at the house before picking up the reins. "Just a short one."

Testing both her reaction to the horse and its response to her, Clay turned Duster away from the rail and swung up.

Sophie hitched her skirt above her boots and stepped up pretty as you please. Confident but light-handed with the reins, she drew around, sitting easy in the saddle.

"The stirrup leathers are the perfect length. How did you—" She shook her head and the crooked smile looped her cheek.

He'd never seen her on anything but the old mare and was pleased with how she handled the gelding. In this case, the rider was as good as the horse, not the other way around. He pulled a pair of leather gloves from the back of his waistband and held them out.

"For you."

She hesitated, glancing from the gloves to his face and back again before taking them. "Thank you."

They fit as if special made for her, and he was more than a little proud.

"Show me the knoll?" She looked in a westerly direction as if she knew where it was.

He didn't want to take her there. That was where he'd laid her mare to rest on the other side, and she might figure that out in the warmer temperatures. But she was already riding that way.

He loped up beside her. "You been out here before?"

"Not exactly. I've wondered about it though—that red rock that shoots up like a sentinel. The shortcut to the farm runs on this side of it, but I've never taken the time to ride closer."

An easy walk took them up the rise. Rabbits darted across their path as they approached, and quail flushed out from under the scrub oak.

Sophie drew rein. "Is that where you found Willy?" Her voice was quiet, almost reverent.

He hadn't been back since that snow-blinding night, but the alcove was clear. An arched branch, inviting in its symmetry and just the right size for a small boy and a big dog.

"That's it."

She looked at him then, not with a glance, but something inside her reaching for him with more than her eyes. "We prayed, Mae Ann and me. We prayed you'd find him."

Clay swallowed the strange taste, still new in his experience and not yet something he could put into words. "Your prayers were answered."

She waited, her question shouting through the silence.

The sorrel's nostrils flared, and it tossed its head, uneasy with the rise of rancid flesh on the breeze. Clay turned Duster back the way they had come, hoping Sophie would follow his lead and not catch wind of the smell.

At the barn she stepped down and ran her hand under the horse's neck, laying her head against it. "It felt good to ride again."

Clay didn't know if she was talking to him or the horse, but it didn't matter. "He needs a name."

She stepped back, set her hands on her slender hips, and cocked her head. "He's a handsome thing. As shiny as a new penny."

Clay flinched, and she saw it. "What?"

"You can't call him Penny."

"Why?"

"That's a girl name."

She snorted and covered her mouth.

He unsaddled the horse, brushed him, and exchanged the bridle for a length of rope around its neck and handed her the end. "Put him in that front corral."

She didn't move. Just looked at him.

"Please."

Her easy smile lifted, and she led the sorrel inside the corral, where she drew him around, slowly pulled the rope off, and stepped back without turning away.

After she came out, Clay closed the gate behind her. "Happy birthday."

She cut him a side look. "What did you say?"

"Happy birthday. It's early, but you need a mount and neither of us might be here when the fourth of June rolls around. I wanted you to have him. But you can't call him Penny."

Again she covered her mouth with one hand and hugged her waist with the other.

If she puddled up, he didn't know what he'd say, so he moved in and wrapped his arms around her.

"You are a kind and thoughtful man," she whispered against his chest. "But mysterious."

He tightened his hold, not ready to walk through the door she'd opened again.

~

Tuesday morning Clay saddled the sorrel and led Parker's Cricket into town where he met Parker at the depot. As Clay suspected, he looked happier to see his horse than a buckboard.

A couple horses were led out of a stock car and down the ramp by handlers, one a finely bred filly that Parker watched with a keen eye.

"I've been meaning to ask," Clay said. "Why'd that fella back East send Xavier on the train without a handler?"

Parker's face clouded over. "Someone was supposed to be with him. That oversight nearly cost me a horse."

He glanced at Clay. "No luck to it that you were there."

Clay agreed, but turned the conversation. "Mind if we stop by the livery? John's been taking messages for me and earning himself some pocket money while he's at it."

John had no calls that morning, which suited Clay, and they were soon riding to the ranch, sunlight warming their backs. Conversation carried over the dry clop of hooves on hard-packed earth, easier shared when not looking each other eye to eye.

"I bought the Fairfax place."

"That's a nice little ranch. Good feed, water. Her husband passed some years ago. I might have bought it myself if it'd been closer."

"She's got about twenty head, all with calves. I'd like to run them in with your herd this fall if that suits you."

Parker chuckled. "Goin' into the cattle business, are you? Got anybody picked out to help you run the place?" He slid a knowing look in Clay's direction.

"As a matter of fact, I do."

Parker laughed outright. "You sound like Deacon."

"He talked to the preacher on Sunday, but we haven't heard." Clay needed to do the same, but first he had to talk to Sophie. Really talk to her, about more than when to set the wedding date.

Parker didn't say anything for a while, just sat the saddle staring down the road with what looked like the past on his mind.

"I knew it was comin'. Can't keep a man like that forever, though I came close. But since I won't let him top off the rough string anymore, he set his sights elsewhere. Probably hurt his feelings, but I didn't want to see a bronc go over backwards with him and drive a saddle horn through his belly."

A sober picture, but Clay had seen that and worse.

"You wouldn't be interested in the job, would you? Stayin' on as foreman?"

Parker didn't give up easily.

"Not now."

They kicked into an easy lope the rest of the way, and when they reined in at the barn, Clay brought up the sorrel.

"I'd like to buy this horse."

Parker stepped down and loosened his cinch. "That's a good little pony. You'll need more than your buckskin now, but I expect you know that."

"It's for Sophie."

Parker glanced at the ranch house, other things clearly on his mind. "Good choice."

They settled on a price—much less than the horse was worth, but Clay didn't argue. It would have been an insult.

"We had some excitement while you were gone. Mae Ann'll tell you. It all turned out good, but it was a tight spot for a while."

# CHAPTER 21

Wednesday morning, Sophie set potatoes, eggs, and coffee on the table, then took her seat with Clay, Mae Ann, Willy, and Cade. Deacon came in with an unusually slow stride, on purpose, she supposed. He had an announcement, but he didn't need to say a word. It stained his face like red on a rooster.

Cade bowed his head. "Thank you, Lord, for taking care of my family while I was gone."

He paused and Sophie held her breath, knowing why. When he started in again, his voice was breathy and hoarse.

"Thank you for watching over Willy and bringing Clay when you did."

Another pause.

"Amen."

Sophie imagined God blessed the food even though He hadn't been asked. It seemed a minor thing next to Willy's rescue. She peeked under her lashes to find Clay watching her. She hadn't taken his hand across the table and felt childish.

His brows pulled together, a question weighting his features.

Now he knew what it felt like.

More childishness, but her doubts outnumbered the days she had left at the Parker's. In spite of his birthday gift, he'd dodged her curiosity again. Was curiosity such a bad thing where her future husband was concerned?

She might have to give the horse back to him.

Deacon didn't dig in like he usually did but coughed and wiped his perfectly trimmed and clean mustache with a napkin. "You're all invited to the weddin' Sunday after service."

He looked at Sophie and gentled his voice. "She said yes."

Sophie blinked several times before getting her voice to cooperate. "I knew she would. Congratulations, Deacon."

The old man puffed up like one of her mother's fried fritters in hot grease and reached for the potatoes.

Sophie hid behind her coffee cup and stared at the table, feeling completely conspicuous. She also felt Clay watching her with that protective edge he sometimes carried.

Even though she knew it was coming, the suddenness of Mama's wedding caught her hard. *Mama's wedding.* The words flipped her right off the see-saw and she landed hard. She'd said yes too, but there was no celebration in her heart. And with Cade home from Denver and Mae Ann quickly regaining her strength, she was no longer needed.

The next day, she packed her things and tethered her bags to the handsome horse Clay had given her. "Penny," she murmured.

One ear flicked back.

"Pen."

He eyed her then and whiffled his breath against the palm of her hand.

"Pen it is. In light of your masculine sensibilities."

Cade and Mae Ann joined her in front of the house, Willy in Cade's arms, Madeline nestled in Mae Ann's. They promised to do exactly as she had instructed them.

"That includes resting," she urged, hugging Mae Ann. "As if I were here hounding you to do so."

Turning to Cade, she gave him her sternest look. "I knew you before Mae Ann came along, so I know you can cook and take care of the kitchen. See to it that you help in that way."

"Yes, ma'am," he said, taking her hand and closing her fingers around an envelope.

Mae Ann hugged her husband's waist. "Thank you for everything, Sophie. We'll see you Sunday at the church."

Clay was strangely absent when she turned Pen out of the yard for the pasture shortcut, and it was just as well. It was easier this way. Leaning over to pat the horse's neck, she felt like she had a part of him with her. But this part didn't have much to say either.

The red sandstone stood guard west of the shortcut, and as she neared it, Clay rode out from around the knoll and joined her on the deer trail. He stopped, facing her, straight-backed and on alert, his hat tugged low but not so low she couldn't see his eyes. So blue and earnest, they threatened to steal her breath.

In deep, dark contrast, his voice bridged the narrow distance between them. "What is it, Sophie? What's wrong?"

Her hackles rose that he would ask of her what he wasn't willing to give himself, and she braced her shoulders. She hadn't wanted a standoff, but it had come down to that.

"You want to know, but it's not important to you that I want the same. How can I marry you if I don't know you or anything about your past? Even Mae Ann knew something about Henry Reiker before she came out here from Missouri, and she was a mail-order bride. I want to *know* you, Clay, share your past with you as well as the future. But you won't talk to me. You won't share yourself with me. You won't even tell me what happened the night you found Willy."

His eyes never left her, and her skin stung. Her lungs tightened. "I'll send Pen back with Todd tomorrow."

His brow pinched in question.

She leaned over and patted the gelding's neck. "I call him Pen. But you can call him whatever you want now."

"No." The word came harshly, and his horse stepped forward until they were close enough that his knee brushed her skirt. "He's a gift. I gave him to you."

Her heart was shattering. She had nothing left to say, but she refused to cry in front of him. Lifting the reins, she touched her heels to Pen and he responded quickly, so much more quickly than her old mare.

They loped along the creek, and taking her bearings from the windmill, tiny and frail-looking in the distance, she cut across the grassland. Her heart was only slightly heavier than her satchel tied to the saddle, for she'd left most of it in pieces at the knoll.

She drew up before she reached the barnyard and sat looking at the old house. Deacon would probably spruce things up if Mama asked him. He seemed to think the sun rose and set in her smile.

Tears charged and Sophie squinted against them. She'd not go home to her mother weeping over her own tattered emotions. She'd not rob her of the happiness that had finally come her way.

She walked Pen to the barn, where she unsaddled him and turned him out with Todd's horse. Clay was right about one thing. She wouldn't send Todd with Pen to the ranch tomorrow. She'd wait until after the wedding.

The hum of Mama's treadle sewing machine greeted Sophie when she walked in the back door, and she followed it into the parlor.

"Sophie!"

Her mother opened her arms in welcome, and Sophie stepped into them like a lost child.

"I'm so glad you're home."

"I couldn't stay away, Mama." She knelt on the floor beside the chair. "I couldn't miss helping you get ready for your wedding day."

"Oh, that." Her mother's face broke into her spring-robin look, and her cheeks flushed to match the dress lying across her lap.

"What a lovely color. It suits you."

Mama hadn't had a new dress in ages.

"I'm just reinforcing the waist and cuffs, then I'll add a little lace at the neck." She looked at Sophie, her brows knitted. "You don't think that's too much, do you? This isn't some big fancy affair, just a simple exchange of vows. I don't want to be pretentious."

"*Mama.* You're getting married, for heaven's sake. The bride has every right in the world to be beautiful."

Laying a hand against her mother's weathered cheek, she smiled. "Has Deacon not told you how beautiful you are?"

At that, her mother blushed deeper. "He said I'm pretty as a filly in a flower garden."

"High praise, coming from that cowboy."

They laughed and chattered like close friends rather than mother and daughter, and Sophie convinced her to put on the dress and parade through the parlor. Then Shopie did her hair up, trying different styles and promising to weave wildflowers through it Sunday morning.

When Todd didn't come in for dinner or supper, Sophie became concerned.

"He's staying at Deacon's cabin so I can get ready and have a few days to myself."

Laughing, Sophie took up an apron. "That's more consideration than you've had in years, I dare say. Sit there at the table and attach that lace you want. I'll fix supper."

In the next few days, Sophie helped her mother wash and prepare her clothes, press her wedding dress, and give the house a good spring cleaning—a lot to do in little time. But Mama and Deacon had no reason to wait. They'd known each other for years and were well-suited. They were not youngsters, and companionship would soften the approach of their later years.

Life would be much the same around the farm, since Deacon was there most of the time anyway, but things would be very different for Cade and Mae Ann. Deacon had been more family than employee, nearly a surrogate grandfather. What would Cade do without him, and who would ever be able to fill his shoes? Or boots, as the case may be.

One person came quickly to mind, but he'd recently bought his own place and would be even farther away now.

On Sunday, Sophie was up at dawn cutting flowers from the garden and those that grew wild along the fences. She kept thoughts and questions of Clay to herself. It was Mama's day, and she'd not detract from that.

While she did up her mother's gray-streaked hair, they ate biscuits with butter and honey and drank more coffee than anyone should be allowed. But jitters were jitters, and sipping hot coffee was better than stewing the morning away until they set out for town.

Bittersweet her mama's marriage and bittersweet her fondness for Pen as she tied him to the back of the farm wagon. She needed him for just a little while longer. With Cade Parker's generous gift, she could get a horse from Erik at the livery. And maybe he would let her leave Pen there until Clay picked him up.

"Deacon told me about what happened to the mare, poor old girl." Mama climbed up to the seat. "Are you borrowing this handsome fellow from the Parkers?"

Sorrow crawled into her heart and curled up in a corner. "He's an early birthday gift from Clay."

Mama's quick glance said a mouthful, but Sophie managed to keep conversation off herself and on the pending event.

The day was as bright and clear as Sophie's hopes for her mother. Todd and Deacon met them at the church, Deacon in a clean starched shirt, string tie, and a smile that stretched his mustache from ear to ear. The shirt bore a crease pressed into each sleeve—Mama's signature touch.

He handed Mama down, and Sophie drove the wagon around back, where Betsy and Maggie Snowfield waited with garlands of spring flowers and slender branches from Maggie's apple trees. Sophie joined them, too distracted to sit through the sermon anyway.

"Here," Betsy said. "Hold this while I wrap the back of the seat." She handed Sophie one end of the garland. "Can you stay over tonight? We haven't visited in ages, and now would be the perfect opportunity."

"I concur," Maggie said. She laid more garland along the top of the tailgate, eyes sparkling with conspiracy. "Or you could stay two days. All week?"

As spry as she used to be, the woman seemed to thrive on social activity and get-togethers.

"I might take you up on that, Maggie," Sophie said. "I'd feel rather uncomfortable at the farm with Mama and Deacon newly married and all. They should have *some* time to themselves."

Which was exactly the reason she had brought Pen. Being the spinster daughter was bad enough without being a tag-along too.

When they finished with the wagon, they slipped inside and squeezed together in the back pew. Pastor Bittman was preaching from the Sermon on the Mount, reminding folks how God sent sunshine and rain on both the evil and the good, and how people should love their enemies.

The closest thing Sophie had to an enemy was Clarence Thatcher. She shuddered, drawing Betsy's glance in their cramped seating. Enemy or no, Sophie could not fit Mr. Thatcher in the same sentence with the word *love.* Clay, on the other hand, fit as neatly as the riding gloves he'd given her.

Oh, Lord, what a fix her heart was in.

~

Mama had hoped everyone would leave as they usually did after the service and not make a big fuss, but that wasn't to be. Everyone stayed.

At the back of the chapel, Sophie took her mother's hands in both of hers. "I love you, Mama," she whispered. Her mother's true beauty shone from the inside out and filled Sophie with pride as well as hope that she would someday bear the same inward loveliness. "You are a beautiful bride."

Her mother's grip tightened, and she swiped at her eyes.

"The Lord has someone for you too, Sophie. Never doubt it. We may not understand His timing, but we can count on His faithfulness to give us what we need if we wait for Him."

Sophie had heard the sentiment all her life, more frequently after her father passed than before. And though it stung to admit it, she knew that the Lord's answer might not necessarily be a husband.

Pastor Bittman honored Mama's request with a brief and quiet ceremony, hardly a ceremony at all. Sophie stood beside her mother and Cade beside Deacon as they repeated their vows. After a sweet kiss and embrace, Mama and Deacon waited as congregants went outside where the Women's Society had sweet punch and lemon cake set up under a tree. The ladies were determined, it appeared, to not miss out on any opportunity to celebrate. Weddings were not an everyday occurrence, and the more reasons for celebration, the better.

Sophie helped herself to cake and looked for Clay, disappointed that he hadn't come. She forked off a corner bite and glanced up in time to see Mrs. Fairfax working her way through the crowd. Hoping to escape the woman's regard, Sophie turned quickly—right into Clarence Thatcher, sloshing his punch against his green brocade waistcoat.

"Oh! I am so sorry." Instinctively, she pressed her napkin against the spill. He leaned into her efforts, so close that she detected alcohol on his breath.

She took a step back, mortified. "My apologies." Betrayed by the heat climbing her cheeks, she cringed at his probable misreading of her embarrassment for feminine ardor.

"My dear Miss Price, do not bother your pretty head." His voice slid around her like a snake through grass. "I have other attire." With glimmering eyes, he boldly considered her dress and hair, leaving her with the same slithering sensation. "You look absolutely ravishing today."

She coughed at the bite of lemon cake stuck halfway down her throat.

He took her elbow and steered her toward a shade tree. "Wait here while I get you a glass of punch. I had my chef create it especially for this occasion, and I am sure you will be delighted."

She was sure she was going to be sick. How dare he even speak to her after his cruel remark at the hotel. And how clumsy of her to bump into him and then appear remorseful. Lord help her, Clay would not be coming to her rescue this time.

"Miss Price." The widow Fairfax appeared as if by divine appointment. Sophie nearly kissed her. "What a lovely bride your mother makes." An eyebrow raised. "Even if she *is* beyond marrying age."

From the corner of her eye, Sophie saw Mr. Thatcher returning with the promised punch. She linked her arm with Mrs. Fairfax and made a sharp turn.

"Thank you for showing Mr. Ferguson and me your property the other day. It is a lovely place that you have kept in good repair. I do hope you will enjoy your new home with your daughter as much as you did the one here."

The woman leaned into Sophie's blatant flattery, though the wish for her future happiness in Denver was sincere. Patting Sophie's arm with a gloved hand, she whispered, "And I hope you and Mr. Ferguson will be as happy there as my Albert and I were."

~

Clay had dropped rein on the south side of the church and taken up position at the back of the sanctuary. He picked out Deacon and Travine, Garrett, the Reynolds and their daughter Sarah. Sophie, Betsy, and Maggie sat in the last pew, but they hadn't heard him slip in. Every seat in the place was filled. Either word had gotten out about the wedding, or Pastor Bittman had honed his skills in the last few weeks.

"The Lord tells us to love our enemies," Bittman said. "That's not so easy."

Clay's left knee throbbed. Fine sermon topic for a wedding day.

Words jumped at him from the pulpit—"those who hate us … spitefully use us … persecute us."

The skin on his back twitched, and he straightened from the wall.

"Why should we love our enemies?" the preacher asked.

Good question. Clay's recent revelation of God's love had been a comfort. But this?

"So we may be sons of our Father … "

*That's asking too much.*

He escaped through the open door, lungs screaming for air. He squeezed his shoulders and flexed his neck, twisting out a tight kink.

*You're nothing but dirt. Just like your name—dirt!*

The taunt snapped against him, rope on raw skin, and he balled his fists, fighting a vengeful impulse. He'd never raised his hand to the man who beat him, but he'd finally left—days before he'd ridden into Olin Springs four years ago.

He made the cottonwood tree at the fence and fell against the rough bark, temples throbbing with his heart-beat.

*Sons of our father.*

He'd spent most of his life aiming for the opposite. How could Bittman preach something he didn't know anything about? There had been no father. No pa, no one to teach him what a man did—other than drink and hate, curse and kick.

Music filtered through the haze of pain, and some-one called his name.

He came round with a fury that set the girl on her heels. Sarah Reynolds. He shook his head, trying to clear the fog, and wiped a hand across his face, drawing sweat in his palm. "Beg pardon, miss."

"I—I wanted to ask you a question about Filbert."

He shifted his weight to both feet, squared himself. "Filbert?"

"Yes. My new puppy." She took a step back. "I was going to ask if you might look at him and tell me if you think he is doing well."

Uncertainty stained her features as well as her tone. "But I can see that you are otherwise detained, so—good-day." In a swish of skirts, she joined her parents, glancing nervously over her shoulder as people filed out of the church.

Several men headed for him. Farmers and ranchers who plied questions about their livestock. The talk brought him up from a dark pit and back to daylight. Back to purpose and direction. Not until one of them mentioned food did he realize he'd missed the wedding.

The others paired off with their wives and closed in on a table spread with cake and punch. Everyone had stayed for the nuptials, even the widow Fairfax, who was dabbing her eyes with a hanky.

He searched for Sophie and found her talking to Clarence Thatcher.

Suddenly, he wasn't hungry. His hands balled into fists again.

Thatcher took her by the elbow and steered her—without resistance—toward a bench in the shade.

Blood pounded in Clay's temples. His breakfast threatened to make an appearance. He cut around the side of the church, grabbed his reins, and swung up. Main Street was empty, and he buried his heels in Duster's sides.

# CHAPTER 22

Clay had failed to show up for her mother's wedding.

How could he? Clarence Thatcher was there, of all people, and she still cringed at the memory of his touch.

And then Mrs. Fairfax's comment about Sophie's future happiness with *Mr. Ferguson*. That hadn't helped at all.

Pen waited drowsily where she'd left him, and after every remnant of the wedding was gathered and put away or taken home by church matrons, she rode to Maggie Snowfield's.

Clay's absence weighed down the selfish side of her heart's remains. The side that fought jealousy. Lord help her, how could she be jealous of her mother's happiness? Yet without Clay there, she felt twice the loneliness.

She slipped in the back door of Maggie's kitchen like an intruder. No one greeted her other than the tell-tale fragrance of lemon cake baked earlier that morning. Regretfully, it brought Clarence Thatcher to mind. She might never eat lemon cake again.

Maggie was likely resting. Betsy and George too. Heaven only knew where Garrett was, for his dog wasn't tied to the garden bench.

She'd been invited to stay, she reminded herself, yet she felt she didn't belong. Nor did she belong at the farm. Though Deacon had spent at least half of his time there, it would now be his home with Mama as his wife. Everything would be different, she the outsider. The unwanted party in the home of a newly wedded couple.

She felt ill.

As quietly as possible, she took the stairs to the room she'd last occupied and eased the door closed behind her. She pushed the curtains aside, and late afternoon light cut through and into her eyes.

Of course Clay hadn't come to the wedding. Not after what she'd said the evening before. *Unless he'd been called away.*

She straightened, a sliver of relief darting in like sunlight from the window. Certainly, that must be the reason. He'd been called upon by a rancher, or farmer, or Erik at the livery to an urgent situation. She would do the same for a woman in need.

The tightness in her stomach eased a bit, and she set her carpet bag on the bed and unpacked her clothes. With no intention of going downstairs for supper, she laid her dress over the back of a chair, removed her stockings and corset, and slipped into a shift. Leaving the curtains open, she raised the window, then took several quilts from the bench at the foot of the bed and layered them atop the mattress.

The sheets were cool against her legs and she curled into a ball, waiting for her body warmth to spread to her coverings.

The curtains lifted with a breeze, so different from the brutal winds of the recent storm. She shivered, thankful for Willy's safety and how Cougar had shielded him. For Cade's return, the reuniting of Mae Ann's family. Mama and Deacon's new start in life. And the little white house and ranch Clay had bought—*Fair View Ranch.* Her mind's eye easily saw a sign hanging above a wide gated entry. She also saw herself in the kitchen fixing breakfast, the aroma of fresh coffee filling the small space as morning light crested the hill beyond the pasture.

The image was unbearable. So were the memories of Clay's tenderness—the way he squeezed her shoulder on occasion, held her after he'd found Willy … *kissed her at their picnic.* Yet a wall remained between them that he was not willing to remove.

She wanted to yell and rant, shake her fists, and stomp out her frustration. She wanted to demand he open up and share things with her. Yet that wasn't how it worked, was it. One did not demand trust and intimacy.

She slid farther beneath the quilts and rolled to her side, releasing her hold on what she wanted, letting her dreams slide down the side of her face and onto the pillow.

~

Dawn came clear and cloudless, just as it had the last four days. Clay stood near the snub post in the round corral, watching the stallion circle at an easy trot, no hitch in its gait, no favoring of the back leg sliced open in the stock car a month before. A wicked scar cut across Xavier's gleaming coat, and Clay doubted it would fade much over time. But the horse was sound, its purpose unhindered. It had healed well.

The black was waiting for Clay at the barn, their morning routine settling in as habit. Clay had spent more time with Xavier and the sorrel than this horse, so he was making up for lost time before Parker let him go. His month was nearly over. He tacked up, swung to the leather, and rode north.

The first breeze freshened, perfumed by pine off the mountain. He breathed deeply, with eyes as well as lungs, taking in the beauty of the lower range that blushed with new grass and fiery paint brush.

On recommendation from one of his instructors at the college, he'd apprenticed with a horse doctor in Missouri. Working with everything from draft horses to pony pets of the wealthy had taught him more than he'd learned in two years at veterinary school. Had he stayed in that part of the country, he could have had a lucrative business. But the West called, Colorado in particular. These high parks and a gal with summer-brown hair more specifically.

Until last week, he'd thought he had all three.

He squeezed Clarence Thatcher from his thoughts and his heels to the black, cutting down an easy slope to the bull pasture at the bottom.

Drawing rein, he counted heads, spotting a calf with every animal except one.

Alarm snaked up the back of his neck, and he counted again. A calf with *every* animal except one.

A yearling bull was missing.

He dropped into the pasture, where he checked corners, low spots, and behind the stockpiled hay. Slowly, he rode the perimeter, a clear image of Sophie's mare in his head, though he knew he wouldn't find a similar fate.

But larkspur and wild iris would kill an animal. He scoured the pasture for sign of the toxic flowers, and that's when he saw the busted third strand on the west side—an open door to the high country and trouble.

The black took him home at a good clip.

~

With Deacon gone, Clay and Parker were on their own. Blue trailed Parker, and this time Cougar wasn't locked in a stall. The lush grass held no sign of the bull's recent passage, but they found a flattened spot not far from a shallow pond where a bear had bedded down. The hair on the back of Clay's neck rose, and he slid the Winchester in its boot, checking for easy access.

Parker carried the same.

If the bull had bogged down in a wet spot, it'd be bear bait, as well as easy pickings for coyote and cat.

They climbed the edge of the park toward aspen and pine, but the dogs gave no sign in the timber. Turning back, they followed a low ridge that sloped into a gully where willows clustered in the bottom. Three deer raised their heads, watched for a moment, then bounded up the opposite side.

Clay pointed out a dark patch at the far end where the ravine drained into a thicket. Could be the bull or deadfall, hard to tell from a distance. "What do you think?"

"Let's take a look."

Blue caught wind of something and shot off like a dart, Cougar fast on his heels.

The closer they rode to the thicket, the more racket the dogs made, running back and forth, growling and yapping.

Clay spotted the bull bogged in a quagmire, sunk up to its belly, but the dogs weren't after it.

The hair on his neck rose.

The bull bellowed.

Branches snapped like gunfire.

A bear crashed through the thicket.

One swipe of its claws sent Blue flying with a yelp. Cougar ran around behind the creature, snipping and slashing, drawing it off Blue.

The grizzly never made a sound. Just lumbered after Cougar, the silver-tipped hairs on its shoulders rolling with each swipe of its massive paws.

Both Clay and Parker drew their rifles, took careful aim, and fired from the saddle. The bear lunged at Cougar, then toppled headfirst to the ground, motionless.

Clay's heart hammered in his chest, the beat echoing in his throat and temple. His hands were sweaty. He booted the rifle, then reined the black around the end of the wash and toward the grizzly. Not keen on the smell, the horse shied and danced a wide circle in spite of Clay's spurs.

Parker held his rifle on the bear in the unlikely event of a sudden resurrection.

Convinced it was dead, they dropped a loop on the bull's head and another around its backside and pulled it out of the bog. When it came clear, Parker flicked his loop off, recoiled and threw another around the head.

With two ropes and the predatory smell of bear behind it, the young bull had no trouble finding its home pasture.

Parker ran it in a corner, where they tied up a leg and dropped it. Clay checked it over for injuries, satisfying himself it was no worse for wear, but with a warning.

"We'll need to keep an eye on his feet. Depending on how long he was in that bog, he could end up with hoof rot."

After fixing the break in the fence, they mounted and headed for the barn. Blue wasn't with them.

"I'll go look for him," Clay offered.

Parker pulled his hat lower, shook his head, and turned back. "See you at the house."

Weren't too many things closer than a man and his dog, and no matter what Parker found, it needed to be him that found it.

Clay rode up the back of Pine Hill, past the ponderosa and the two crosses beneath it. There were no guarantees in this country that a man would make it home at night. If it wasn't a blizzard, it was lightning. Bears or mountain lions. A hoof in a badger hole and a bad fall. He realized it more now than ever.

He also realized he'd faced that bear without a second thought, eerily calm in the moment. But he couldn't share his scars with a woman he loved.

~

When Clay walked through the front door without Parker, Mae Ann came out of her chair on the run. He caught her by the arms. "He's all right. He's not far behind, bringing in Blue."

She collapsed against him and he led her back to the chair.

Willy looked up from where he played on the floor with a pull toy. "Papa?"

Clay squatted next to him and ruffled his hair. "He'll be here in a minute."

"Did you find the bull?" Mae Ann's voice betrayed her real concern that far outweighed whether they'd found a lost bovine.

"We did and we got him back. Fixed the fence as well. Your husband is safe, he just needed to do this on his own."

She stiffened, eyes tightening with alarm. "What happened? Is Blue hurt?"

"Let's just say he's got a big heart."

Understanding his message, she worried her collar. Willy must have read the gesture, for he left his toy horse and climbed into her lap.

"Mind if I make some coffee?"

She looked up, confused, like she didn't know how to answer. "Yes. I mean no. I'll start some for you."

Clay lifted a hand. "I'll get it. You just rest."

The front door blew open, and Parker trudged in with the bloody dog and laid it on the hearth.

"Willy, come help me make coffee." Mae Ann took her son by the hand, dragging the wide-eyed boy to the kitchen.

Blue was barely breathing. Four long gashes opened his right side, ribs stark white against the flesh.

Clay went for his saddlebags. When he returned, fresh towels and a pan of warm water waited beside the dog. He clipped blood-matted hair from the lacerations, and Blue whined weakly when he sterilized the area. A good sign.

"He may be alert enough to feel this, so hold him as still as you can."

Parker nodded, his face pale and drawn.

An hour later, bloodied water filled the pan next to the bandaged dog. Clay sterilized his needle and scissors and returned everything to the leather pouch.

Mae Ann brought in a tray of coffee and biscuits.

"No bones were broken, no arteries severed, but he lost a lot of blood. We've done all we can," Clay said. "It's up to the Lord now."

The last phrase felt odd on his tongue. He'd never said it before because he hadn't believed it before.

He took his bags to the cabin, unsaddled the horses, and turned them out, pleased with how the black had held up under rifle fire. When he got back to the house, Cougar was lying on the front step. He lifted mournful eyes and let out a long low whine.

Clay stooped to rub his back and sides. "Give him time, boy. He's got to heal up and he's no youngster. You did good today. Real good."

Clay stepped over the dog, pegged his hat on the wall, and washed again in the kitchen. Mae Ann had a late dinner cooking on the stove, but he doubted any of it would be eaten until that evening.

Parker had started a fire on the hearth, more out of something to do than the need for warmth. But there was no telling how the night would turn. It could be snowing again by morning.

It was well after dark when Mae Ann took Willy upstairs and Clay stretched out in her chair. Parker sat in the other, nursing cold coffee and staring at his dog. Praying, Clay figured.

The fire crackled, a comforting sound. Clay added a couple more logs and brought in hot coffee.

"Blue was my father's dog."

The graveled comment came low and quiet, more of a thought than spoken words.

"It took some time before I stopped hating him. Same with my father."

Shock roused Clay from fatigue as well as his assumptions. He'd figured Parker Land and Cattle hadn't had much trouble, at least among the people. No operation ran smoothly when cattle were involved, but a family spread—well, that always gave him a homesick feeling for what he'd never known and wished he had.

"You didn't know that, did you?" Parker tore his weary eyes from the dog and looked at Clay.

"No, sir." Deacon had mentioned Parker's pa being hard to get on with, but he hadn't mentioned the dog.

Parker huffed and turned back to the fire. "My father and I rarely saw eye to eye. Then he and my mother died in a blizzard and I blamed him. *Hated* him. For years. Took a while before I didn't see or think of him every time I looked at Blue."

He leaned forward, elbows on knees. "Not until Mae Ann came along was I able to forgive him."

Unsettled by the confession that hit too close to home, Clay sensed Parker wasn't finished.

"Hate will kill a man. Eat him alive from the inside out."

The skin on Clay's back twitched.

"Forgiveness carries a high price, but it's worth it."

No words came. Clay had nothing to say or give. Only an ache in his leg, a burning in his chest, and what he thought he hadn't heard Bittman say last Sunday—

… our Father *in heaven.*

# Chapter 23

Daylight sneaked into the predawn sky and birds chittered in the cottonwoods as Clay saddled Duster. Parker wanted him to stay on while Deacon was gone, and he'd agreed to give him a week, with a day to follow up on veterinary calls.

The gelding was eager to ride, liking the way morning tasted and the scent of cedar and sage. But Clay didn't like not having Sophie around. He missed the sound of her laughter, her crooked smile, and the way she felt in his arms. The way *he* felt when she was in his arms. But she'd given him an ultimatum.

And Thatcher had rushed the gap.

The gelding stretched into a lope, cued by tension in Clay's legs. He'd believed Sophie had no use for the hotel owner, and bile stirred his belly over what he'd seen on Sunday. But he'd been so off kilter after Bittman's sermon, he might have seen wrong.

Clay thought he'd stopped listening after "our Father," but it curled around him last night like Cougar around Willy in the storm. *Our Father in heaven,* Bittman had said. Not my father or *the father*, but *our*, implying family. What would that father be like? Certainly unlike the one he'd known growing up.

The sun winked above the horizon, and he dipped his hat brim. *New every morning.*

The words came each day now, his ma's gentle voice so full of faith and promise. She'd known that Father and had tried to show Him to Clay. Would have shown him more if she'd lived.

Guilt swept in like a low-bellied cloud, smothering what little hope had sprouted. He been two years older than Willy when the barn caught fire and his world with it.

Everything was different after that—everything except what his ma had said and he'd forgotten, drowned by his father's drunken rages, the cursing of his name, and the burden of blame.

~

Olin Springs lay half asleep. Merchants swept the boardwalk in front of their businesses, and smoke curled from a few chimneys. Bozeman stood outside in a clean apron, his broom a toothpick next to his bulk. He nodded as Clay rode by. Coffee and bear sign would have to wait until after the livery.

"Mornin', Mr. Ferguson." John leaned his pitchfork against a stall. "Buster Lockhart was just here in a panic about his milk cow. She's havin' a hard time of it, and he thinks her calf is comin' breach."

"Just here? Where's he live?"

"'Bout a half mile north out of town, right turn off the road."

Clay tossed him a coin. "Obliged."

"The widow Fairfax was in too. Erik said to tell you if you stopped in."

"Appreciate it."

Clay found the smithy at his forge, stoking the fire.

He stabbed the poker through the coals and glanced up.

"*Frau* Fairfax takes the train tomorrow and wants you to drive her. She moves to Denver."

Sooner than Clay had figured. "I can do that."

"You bought her place."

"That's right."

"*Gut*. You will be closer."

Clay waited another minute, but Erik was a thrifty man with words as well as money. When he picked up an iron blank with his tongs and shoved it in the fire, Clay knew he'd said his piece.

Morning was still cool beyond the livery doors, and Clay left Bozeman's bear sign behind and rode north to Buster Lockhart's farm. The man was right about his cow, and it took so long to turn the calf, Clay figured it'd be dead. He figured wrong. He and Lockhart threw their backs into a final pull, and a good-sized bull calf slid out onto the straw. Clay cleared its nose, rubbed it down with straw, and let nature take over.

New life was one of the more pleasant aspects to his work, but his clothes didn't look so pleasant when he reined in at Mrs. Fairfax's hitch rail.

"Ma'am," he said, tipping his hat, the only part of him that wasn't soiled. He'd washed as best he could at Lockhart's, but it hadn't done much for his shirt.

"Didn't recognize you." She gave him a once-over, then eye-balled his horse. "Him either."

"No, ma'am. I imagine not."

"I'm leaving tomorrow."

"Yes, ma'am. Would you like me to drive you to the train?"

She pulled her hankie out and folded it over a couple times. "It leaves at eight sharp. Or as sharp as can be expected."

"I'll be here."

"I have trunks to load."

"I'll be here early."

She looked at his trousers and shirt.

"Delivered a calf at Lockhart's. Haven't had a chance to clean up yet."

She sniffed and dabbed at her nose. "I'll see you to-morrow, then."

He tipped his hat again and reined away from a woman who was leaving behind everything she'd known and loved. He hoped her daughter understood that.

Bozeman was clean out of bear sign, and Clay was too dirty to sit among folks trying to eat. He rode back to the ranch wondering if Deacon had a copper tub for bathing. After turning Duster out, he settled for the creek and a soap cake.

The next morning he unsaddled Duster at the Fair-fax ranch and left him in the corral. He harnessed the widow's buggy horse, about the same age and condition as Sophie's old mare, and hoped it didn't keel over before he got the buckboard around to the front of the house. But he had no choice. Duster didn't pull, and they didn't need a rodeo on the way to the train.

Several bags and small crates waited on the porch. So did Mrs. Fairfax.

"Mornin' ma'am. Looks like you're ready to go."

She stared at him as if he were daft, then went inside. "Come help me with my trunks" wafted through the screen door.

He figured the old horse wouldn't bolt but set the brake anyway and found two steamer trunks waiting in the main room, open and half empty.

"Everything goes inside," she said. "I don't want to worry about losing something important. I'll fill one and you fill the other with what's on the porch."

She was as frugal in her packing as she was her conversation, and they were soon driving up the lane toward the dip in the hills.

"Stop."

He obliged her, and she turned in the seat and looked back on the ranch just coming to life in the morning sun, fresh and verdant. Cow-calf pairs grazed, unaware that their recent owner was on her way out. A rooster crowed, the windmill creaked, and thin clouds stretched pink above the mountains.

"All right." She turned back around, stiff as the wagon bed.

At the depot, Clay hefted her trunks to the platform and waited while she went inside for whatever it was she needed. He'd already seen her ticket clutched tightly in her right hand. The liniment must be working.

When she returned, her eyes were red-rimmed.

"Are the library ladies seeing you off?"

She considered her ticket and straightened the crumpled edges. "I'm not fond of lengthy, tear-filled farewells. I said my piece at the last meeting, as did they." She looked at him. "You don't have to stay."

Relieved by her down-to-earth attitude, he relaxed. But he'd stay. Wasn't right to leave a woman in her situation alone.

She raised her chin and looked off in the distance. "Thank you for driving me in."

He doffed his hat and held it against his leg. "I'm happy to. Appreciate you lettin' me buy your place and not some other fella."

"I hope you and Sophie will be as happy there as Albert and I were when we were young."

He squeezed the crown of his hat and did his own looking away. "That remains to be seen."

Mrs. Fairfax scoffed. "My boy, if that is what you think, then you are as blind as that one-eyed milk cow I sold you."

The woman's candor caught him off guard, and he blurted out his argument. "I saw her with … someone at the church after the wedding last Sunday."

He'd said too much, but apparently Mrs. Fairfax hadn't.

"Did you also see her drag me by the arm, rambling on about my home, adeptly dodging the advances of that pompous Thatcher fellow?"

No, he hadn't.

The train whistle blew, and he set his hat at the conductor's boarding call. He ushered the widow to the passenger-car step, where she turned and bore into him with forge-black eyes.

"Wake up, Mr. Ferguson, before you lose that young woman."

She disappeared inside, and moments later he was still staring as cars slid past, not really seeing them, chewing on what the widow had said.

With the clarity of the train whistle, he charged to the wagon, turned it around, and glanced down Saddle Blossom Lane. He'd take the wagon back, get Duster, and come settle things with Sophie Price. Tell her what she wanted to know, what she had the right to know.

And then he'd tell her that he loved her.

~

A week's reprieve with Betsy and Maggie was just what Sophie had needed. But she couldn't stay forever. She'd have to go home sooner or later and adjust to life on the farm with Todd and Mama and Deacon. Bittersweet at best.

"Penny?"

She straightened an embroidered napkin atop the press board on her lap, assuming Betsy meant her horse grazing in the pasture behind the barn. "What about him?"

Betsy huffed. "A penny for your thoughts, silly."

Oh, that. Of course. She had none that were anything but gloomy, for she thought only of her future as a spinster and the whereabouts of Clay Ferguson.

"Nothing you'd be interested in." Seated close to the stove, she exchanged her iron for a hotter one and continued pressing wrinkles from an embroidered napkin.

Betsy punched down bread dough and flipped it over. "Try me."

Wasn't that what friends were for? Sharing misery as well as happiness? She pressed the iron over a corner cluster of pink roses, clearly Maggie's favorite flowers. "I haven't heard from Clay since I left your brother's more than a week ago, before the wedding."

Betsy covered the bread bowl with a tea towel and took a pan of sugar cookies from the oven. She scooped several onto a plate, and set them on the table with two teacups.

"You don't know where he is?"

Sophie helped herself to a cookie too hot to eat and dropped it on her saucer. "It's not just that. I don't know *anything* about him. His background, his childhood, his life before he crossed trails with Garrett four years ago. He won't talk to me about anything from his past."

She looked up. "When he bought the Fairfax place, he just walked right up and gave Bertha cash for the whole kit n' caboodle."

Betsy's eyebrows rose appropriately.

"He said the money was from the sale of his family's farm. But when I started to ask about his family, you know what he said?"

Irritation built up a head of steam in the retelling, and she lowered her voice in a sarcastic imitation. "'I don't talk about 'em.' And that was that. Didn't say another word about mother, father, siblings, old dogs, or crazy uncles."

"He has a crazy uncle?"

Sophie rolled her eyes and broke the cookie in half, not sure if the question was offered in commiseration or mockery.

Betsy sat down with the teapot, her lips curved in a secretive way that irritated Sophie. If her friend knew unshared secrets, she'd be madder than a hornet. "What are you not saying?"

Honey-brown tea filled one cup and then the other. "You sound like I did before I married Garrett. I wanted to know about his past and he wasn't as forthcoming as I thought he should be."

"What'd you do?"

"I listened to Maggie."

Sophie stared, frustrated and about ready to walk out.

"She said Garrett didn't have to give me a detailed account of his life before I entered it, and she asked if I had done so with him. Barring unacceptable things such as him being a scoundrel or ruffian, a mean-spirited soul, or on the wrong side of the law, she asked if I needed to know every little thing in order to love him."

After sufficient time for Sophie to ponder, Betsy peered over the edge of her teacup. "Do you love Clay?"

Sophie stalled at the blunt question. She'd thought she did. "I'm not sure." She frowned and dragged her hand across her forehead, trying the erase the uncertainty.

"You insist that you don't know anything about him, but I believe you do."

"How can you say that?"

"I heard it in your voice when you first told me he was the horse handler who led Cade's stallion off the stock car without incident."

Sophie felt a flush rise to her cheeks.

"Then there was the evening he carried you inside after Abigail Eisner lost her baby. And the look on your face when you learned the two of you would be living at the ranch at the same time."

The door buzzer rang.

Betsy removed her apron. "I'll see who it is."

Whoever it was, they had lousy timing. Sophie snatched another cookie from the plate and strained to hear conversation from the front of the house. If it were Clay, he'd come around to the back door, not ring that infernal buzzer. Maggie was napping with George in her room, and Sophie hoped it hadn't disturbed them.

The door closed and footsteps entered the parlor, soon followed by Betsy's heels clipping down the hallway. She didn't sound happy.

"Clarence Thatcher is here to see you."

Sophie choked on the cookie.

Betsy ran cold water in a glass and handed it to her. "He said it was urgent."

Based on her tone, Betsy didn't believe him.

Sophie pressed a floral-cornered napkin against her lips, watching her friend. "You sound unconvinced."

Betsy snorted—an endearing trait that brought back sweeter times from childhood.

Sophie set the press board aside. "I'll see what he wants."

Smoothing her skirt, she tread as lightly as possible on the hallway's hardwood flooring. When she stopped at the parlor door, their visitor was standing at the window, arms crossed. Not an urgent posture.

"Mr. Thatcher."

He spun at her voice, obviously surprised by her arrival, but also pleased.

She stepped into the parlor and he met her, taking her hands without invitation. She pulled but he held tightly.

"Please, Miss Price, you must come with me to the hotel. An out-of-town guest there is in distress with her first child and insisted upon a midwife."

Sophie extricated her hands and clasped them behind her, out of his reach.

His brows peaked as if pleading, and his demeanor suddenly exuded the urgency he had mentioned to Betsy.

"Why did you not send for Dr. Weaver?" she said. "His office is near the hotel."

"As I said, she insisted on seeing a midwife. And she is in distress." He lifted a hand toward the doorway. "Please, come with me. I've brought my carriage so you won't have to walk."

"I can ride."

"But that would take time saddling the horse, and she is … well … " His eyes took on an air of hesitancy, as if he couldn't bring himself to say what needed to be said.

*Or didn't know.*

"Does she have family with her, a husband or relatives?"

His mouth pursed in a moment's uncertainty, but he quickly rallied. "Not that I am aware of. But she is in—"

"Distress. You mentioned that."

If there really were a woman about to face childbirth in a strange town with no family or friends, Sophie wanted to help in any way she could. She had never refused her services, though she'd known all of the women beforehand. Could she refuse a woman in need simply because she didn't know her?

"I'll get my satchel."

His stance eased, an unspoken tension sloughing off. "Please hurry. I'll wait here for you."

*You most certainly will.*

She hurried to her room for her satchel, then stopped in the kitchen. "He says there is a woman newly arrived at the hotel who is about to give birth and is requesting a midwife."

Betsy untied the apron she'd put back on. "I'll go with you."

"That's not necessary. It's only a few blocks away and he brought his carriage. I'll send word if it looks like we need Dr. Weaver."

"Who will you send?"

"The clerk. I'll send the clerk." A chill shivered through her at the image of the sour man.

"Sophie—"

"Don't worry, Betsy. A woman needs help. It's what I do."

Thatcher stood at the front door and opened it when Sophie entered the hall.

As he handed her up to his carriage, the strangest sensation washed over her—as if she were stepping into a lion's lair.

Following the quick—and silent—trip to the alley behind the hotel, he parked and led her through the kitchen and restaurant to the lobby, where he paused at the front desk and whispered something to the clerk.

The bespectacled man flashed a look at Sophie that she couldn't read, then gave his employer a quick nod.

"This way, Miss Price." Thatcher indicated the stairs, not the hallway to their left and the ground-floor rooms. That fact, and the commanding tone of his voice, raised a flag—as if he were leading a military campaign.

What happened to the pleading hotelier calling on behalf of a guest?

Her grip tightened on her satchel.

After climbing the long staircase, she stopped at the second-floor landing. Abigail Eisner came to mind. A woman on the threshold of childbirth would not deliberately choose a hotel room accessed only by stairs.

"Please, Miss Price, this way."

She straightened, assuming her most dignified air. "Surely you would not give a woman in the family way a room on the second floor."

He looked sharply at her, resentment narrowing his eyes before a placating smile tipped his mouth. "She insisted upon the utmost privacy, and the second floor assures that."

Again, his hand extended, indicating the hallway of closed doors. "After you."

The back of Sophie's neck crawled, and she glanced down at the carpeted steps she'd just climbed, then back to him. "No, Mr. Thatcher, after *you*."

Clearly annoyed by her resistance, he quickly schooled an ingratiating expression and smoothed the front of his gold brocade waistcoat. "As you wish."

He stopped at the last door on the left. A small plaque on the door to the right read "Bathing Room." The velvet-curtained window at the end of the hall looked out onto grassland sweeping into the foothills.

Sophie had not considered that the town ended so abruptly on the west side. Her skin tightened.

Thatcher withdrew a key from his waistcoat pocket and, without knocking, turned it in the lock.

Her stomach turned with it. Something was wrong—and it had nothing to do with a woman in the throes of childbirth.

She ran.

At the landing, he yanked her back by her hair. She swung her satchel at his head, but he ducked and knocked it from her grasp.

Twisting her arm behind her with surprising strength, he pressed his mouth against her ear.

"We have things to discuss, Miss Price." His hot breath chilled her to the bone, heavy with alcohol and sickeningly sweet. "Such as your unseemly dismissal of my offer of kindness at the wedding. Your *mother's* wedding."

He snickered on the word.

"It could have been *your* wedding had you not repeatedly scoffed my attentions. You scorned me, Sophie. You should not have scorned me."

She opened her mouth to scream, and his free hand clapped cruelly over it.

Biting his fingers, she clawed his face with the nails of her free hand.

He swore and slapped her until her vision blurred. A metallic taste filled her mouth.

Again he covered it, this time pinching off her nose. She dug at his fingers, fighting for air.

*Oh, God, keep me from fainting.*

His eyes gleamed with arousal. "Now, now, Miss Price. We mustn't alarm the other guests."

# Chapter 24

**D**uster trotted onto Maggie Snowfield's property and Clay dismounted at the hitch rail by the barn. The sorrel gelding he'd given Sophie grazed in the pasture with Lolly, both swishing their tails in the clear afternoon light. The peaceful setting gave him hope for a similar outcome with Sophie.

He'd prayed—a concept still new to him—and rehearsed what he wanted to say, irritated that he could talk to Mrs. Fairfax, pig farmers, and cattlemen without hesitation, but not to the woman he couldn't live without.

He plowed his hand through his hair and reset his hat, then knocked on the back door before stepping inside. Only proper not to barge in on everyone without them knowing he was there.

Betsy looked up hopefully, then wilted with disappointment.

"You were expecting Garrett, I see."

"No." She twisted her hands in her apron. "I was expecting Sophie."

His insides twisted as well. "But her horse is in the pasture."

Betsy pushed hair back from the worry on her face. "I know. He insisted on driving her to the hotel since it was so urgent."

Clay's hackles rose against the name he knew was coming. "Who insisted?"

Apology wrinkled Betsy's forehead. "Clarence Thatcher."

He was halfway to his horse before her next word.

From the back step, she yelled, "He told her there was a woman in need of a midwife."

"Not exactly," he hissed under his breath. "More like a man in need of an undertaker."

Duster hit Main Street at a dead run, where he scrambled around the corner and slid up at the hotel. Clay was on the ground before the gelding stopped. He crashed through the front door, startling the clerk into apoplexy.

Reaching across the counter, he lifted the man by his shirt front, holding him close enough to bite his glasses off his face. "Where are they?"

Trembling, the fella pointed up the stairs with his left hand.

Clay shook him. "What room?"

"Last room, left side," he choked out.

"You'd better be right."

Clay dropped him like a sack of rocks and took the stairs by threes. At the landing, Sophie's satchel and its contents lay scattered across the thick carpet.

Clarence Thatcher was a dead man.

At the end of the hall, Clay kicked in the door and it slammed against the wall.

Thatcher whirled, a panther's snarl on his face until he recognized Clay. He stumbled back against the bed, where Sophie clutched her bodice and scrambled out of the way.

"She—"

Clay smashed his fist into the sniveling man, splattering blood on the green velvet bed covering. The next blow sent him sprawling across the floor, his nose gushing red down the front of his waistcoat.

Thatcher curled into a ball, whimpering.

Clay grabbed him by the collar and lifted him to his feet.

*Hate can kill a man.*

Every rope lash, every taunt, every blow he'd ever suffered came to life in his fists, and he landed them with vicious force in Thatcher's face and throat and stomach. He'd taken as much and more from his father's drunken abuse, but he'd not let this slime touch Sophie. He'd kill him first.

"Clay!"

He hesitated, left hand gripping Thatcher's collar, the right drawn back, cocked and ready to explode.

"Clay—this isn't you!"

The words cut through the ringing in his ears.

"Stop! Please—stop!"

It was the cry in her voice that caught him. The pleading.

Crouching on the bed, blood trickled from her lip, and she clutched her bodice, torn and revealing red marks on the tender flesh beneath it.

He tightened his grip on Thatcher and lifted the unconscious vermin for another blow.

Sophie covered her face and wept.

Thatcher slipped from his grasp and fell to the floor.

Clay fell to his knees in front of her, took off his vest, and wrapped it around her.

Tear-stained and trembling, she flung herself into his arms. He stood, lifting her from the bed, cradling her against him as he carried her through the door.

Garrett Wilson ran down the hall toward them, hand on his gun. "The clerk came for me—said someone was being murdered." He glanced at the broken door then back. "Sophie, what are you doing here?"

Clay's hold tightened, his voice hard and thick. "Ask the sniveling snake in that room."

~

Sophie didn't want Clay to let her go. She wanted to stay in his arms forever. Safe, protected. But when he stopped where her satchel lay, she relinquished his refuge. "I need to collect my things."

Gently, he set her on her feet, so unlike the raging wild man who had crashed through Thatcher's door. A shudder ran up her spine.

Clutching his vest across her torn bodice with one hand, she gathered unrolled bandages, scissors, and other items and dropped them into the satchel Clay held open.

He knelt with her, watching her as if she were of great value, his breath jagged, eyes dark as gun metal.

Betsy had been right. Sophie *did* know him. She knew him by knowing what he *wasn't*—a killer.

She laid her precious herb packets, lapel watch, and soft flannels in the satchel and folded her hands over Clay's cut and bloodied knuckles. Tears welled afresh, but she looked up so he'd see her heart. She knew he had that capability—reading a soul through the eyes, for she'd seen his tenderness with a frightened horse, a lonely widow, herself.

Only a whisper could she wrench from her throat, so intense was her gratitude. "Again, your timing was impeccable."

He wrapped his arms around her, crushing her against his chest. His heart still hammered, whether from exertion or anger she couldn't tell. Likely both.

"I was foolish to go with him. The signs were there, telling me something wasn't quite right. But when I thought of the chance that a woman really was laboring for her life and the life of her child, I couldn't refuse."

A feral groan rumbled from Clay's chest and bled into her own. She clung to him, thanking God for His rescue. For the man He sent to her aid. For the fact that Clay—at her request—had relented from killing her attacker.

She captured his right hand in both of hers—already swelling. Blood clotted along the cuts opened with the force of his blows. She brushed her lips across the sun-browned skin on the back. "Let's go to Maggie's, and I'll look after your injuries."

With his other hand, he tilted her chin upward. "What about you?" His eyes tightened at the corners and his voice dropped to a cavern's depth. "Did he hurt you?"

Holding his gaze, she shook her head. "He wrenched my arm, and my lip cut against my teeth, but he did not *hurt* me." She tugged Clay's vest tighter, and her voice thinned to a whisper. "Much."

Clay's whole body tensed and the muscle in his jaw bulged. He was still angry enough to inflict more punishment, and part of her wanted him to. The other part was glad Garrett showed up when he did.

Her fingers grazed his unshaven cheek. "Let's go home."

He turned his head and pressed her fingers against his lips, setting the see-saw on a dizzying race from fear to relief to longing. "We'll go to Maggie's first. There's something I need to ask you."

~

Clay swept Sophie up and carried her downstairs and through the lobby without a glance at the clerk. From the corner of his eye, he saw the man still shaking behind the counter—a coward who knew all along what Thatcher's intentions had been.

He should come back and work him over too.

Sophie's words rose at the edge of his mind. *That's not who you are.*

He tugged her closer and kissed the top of her head nestled at his neck. How could she say that when he'd not responded to her gentle probing into his past?

Outside, he clicked his tongue at Duster, who waited untethered at the hitch rail, and the gelding fell in behind, following them all the way to Saddle Blossom Lane and Maggie Snowfield's. They snagged more than a few curious looks as they passed, but Clay wasn't letting Sophie out of his arms until she agreed to be his wife.

Not that he'd coerce her. It'd still be her choice, of her own free will. And if she chose not to, he'd sell the Fairfax place and move on. He'd never be able to live there without her.

Duster turned aside in the apple orchard, nibbling at grass sprouting beneath the trees. Clay continued around to the back steps and tapped his boot against the door.

Sophie turned the knob, then smiled up at him. A good sign.

"Oh, Sophie, you're hurt!" Betsy charged toward the door. She'd been crying, and Clay didn't feel too bad about that. He needed to cool down some before he stopped blaming her for letting Sophie go with that slimy excuse for a human. Though he knew Sophie did pretty much what she wanted, especially when it came to helping someone.

"Clay, I'm so sorry." Betsy's voice broke.

He gave a quick nod, unable to talk to anyone other than Sophie. He eased her into a chair, noting her lip, swollen now, and new red marks rising on her face and neck. It was all he could do not to go back to the hotel and finish what he'd started.

"I'm not going to break, Clay."

Afraid that he might, he took a knee before her.

She touched his bent leg fencing her in at the table. "Let me up so I can see to your injuries." Her voice was stronger.

"Bossy thing, aren't you?"

A schoolmarm glare made a brief appearance but melted as he cupped the side of her face and ran his thumb over the permanent hitch in her left cheek.

She turned her head away, but he gently turned it back. "I know you see a scar here." He touched it again, caressed it.

Her chin quivered beneath his touch.

"But I see a smile. Anticipation of joy."

At last, her lips pulled into the real thing, and she grasped the hand that held her chin. He turned it so his fingers were on the bottom, hers on top.

Surprised his hat hadn't come off at the hotel, he set it crown down on the table.

Betsy brought a damp cloth to the table, and at a sober glance from Clay, she scurried from the kitchen. The woman definitely read sign.

Finally alone, he focused on Sophie. "The widow Fairfax is gone. I'll be moving into the house."

He stroked the top of her fingers, and she watched the slow sweep of his thumb.

"Making repairs on the place. Branding calves and hauling that one-eyed milk cow back."

Her mouth turned up, but she didn't look at him.

"Watching the sunset from one of those rockers on the back porch and reaching for you so I can touch you like this."

Her breath caught on a gasp and the pulse at her bent wrist quickened.

"Will you be there?"

Her fingers tightened, and she looked into his eyes till he knew she could see clean through to all the past he'd hidden from her. All the scars that cut deeper than flesh.

"You're the best thing that ever happened to me, Sophie Price, and I've loved you for a long time."

She bit her lower lip, then flinched, fingering her mouth with a frown.

He corralled his thoughts, focused on her and their future. "I want to live the rest of my life with you, protect you, provide for you. Work alongside you and share the Fair View Ranch with you if you'll have me."

Her eyes welled.

"I know there's a lot I need to fill you in on, and if you want to wait until after that to give me an ans—"

"Yes."

He closed his mouth, afraid he'd not heard right.

"Yes, Clay Ferguson. I will have you, and be your partner, and take your hand when you reach for it."

Her gaze washed over him like morning on the high parks. "I'll even milk that old cow because I love you."

Her breath came warm and inviting as she touched her tongue to her swollen lip.

He read sign too.

Gently he kissed her, seeking to cause her no pain.

And he didn't know if it was her willing response that shook him clear to his boots—or the light that broke through him fading every shadow in his soul.

# Chapter 25

It was either share the hay loft with John at the livery or take Garrett's old room behind Maggie's kitchen. No deliberation required.

Clay tossed his bedroll and saddle bags on the narrow quilt-covered bed and did something he hadn't done but a few times, all in recent days.

He thanked God.

That morning after church, he'd asked Bittman about what his ma had said. He wanted to know if the words were something she'd come up with or if she'd read them.

The preacher led him back inside, took his Bible off the lectern, and turned right to them.

"It's a powerful verse, Clay, one worth memorizing. Lamentations 3:22 and 23."

He read the whole thing, and Clay choked up on the first line—"It is of the Lord's mercies that we are not consumed."

He fisted his hand, the skin still raw but covered with Sophie's tender care and bandages. He'd been nearly consumed by hate when he found her, and that hate would have killed both himself and Thatcher. Just like Parker said, it was eating him from the inside out.

Thankfulness came easier than forgiveness, but he was working on it with God's help, Bittman's, and Sophie's. Parker was right about that too—it came with a hefty price, but a price Clay was willing to pay.

Sore and bruised, Sophie hadn't gone to church. Neither had Clarence Thatcher. Doc Weaver spent quite a while stitching up the hotelier before Garrett planted him in a cell at the jail house. A sign hung on the ornate door across the street: "Soon Under New Management."

Maggie opened her rooms to a few of the displaced guests but kept this one for Clay, and a knock at his open door brought him round.

"Dinner will be on the table soon. Are you hungry?"

The look in Sophie's eyes reduced him to more than hunger. He was starving for her, and by the sudden flush in her cheeks, she must have read his desire.

"Yes, ma'am. But can I tear you away from your kitchen duties for a leisurely walk in the apple orchard?"

She fingered the coiled braid at the back of her neck and gave him a shy glance. "They won't let me do anything to help, so I think I can fit a stroll into my schedule."

Blossoms had given way to full leaves, and the grass around the trees grew ankle deep, brushing Sophie's skirt as he led her to the center of the tiny orchard. He'd earlier relocated the iron garden bench, after tying Pearl in the barn, and it waited for them, secluded by trees and birdsong.

Sophie smiled up at him, pleased with the surprise, and took half of the narrow seat, tucking her skirt beneath her in invitation.

He accepted, took her hand in both of his, and started with the fire. By the time he recounted finding Willy and the memory of his ma's voice the next morning, tears washed Sophie's bruised cheeks and trailed into her crooked smile.

"How could he blame you, a child, for knocking over the lantern?"

Clay wrapped an arm around her and drew her closer, drinking in the scent of her hair and the soft yield of her surrender. "I've asked that question a thousand times every year that I've lived, and I still don't have an answer. I doubt I ever will. But now, since God broke through my stubbornness and hate, it's not as important anymore."

She eased away and looked up at him with an uncommon passion. "I have one thing to say, and then we never have to speak of it again."

Stirred by her gentle fervor, he swallowed hard and took hold of his fledgling faith. "And that is?"

"Your name. Other than your eyes, it was the first thing I noticed. It made me think of God's creativeness."

If she'd slapped him, he couldn't have been more surprised, but she gestured around them, sweeping an arm toward the trees.

"Think about it. Everything He made—trees of every kind, animals, mountains, clouds—everything—He spoke into existence. But man He *formed* from the dust of the earth, from clay. Made him pliable in His hands. Touched him. Breathed life into him."

Her gaze returned to his with an intensity he'd not seen a woman wield. "That's a very intimate moment with the Creator, and *you*, Clay, get to wear the reminder."

~

On the first Saturday in June, Sophie stood before the cheval mirror in her room at Maggie Snowfield's. Abigail Eisner tucked and folded the beautiful cream-colored dress that flowed gracefully from Sophie's waist in a skirt wider than fashion dictated. But she had requested the simple square-necked bodice, lace sleeves, and fuller skirt. She needed it for riding Pen home to the ranch with Clay. Their ranch.

He hadn't balked when she said she wasn't interested in a wedding trip. Hotels held no appeal to her—or to him, for that matter—and they agreed that their new home was where they wanted to be.

Abigail smiled up at her in the mirror, a threaded needle sprouting from her seamed lips ready for a last-minute stitch. Mama loosely braided her hair according to the directions of Mae Ann, who held Madeline in one arm and little George gently between her knees. He was enraptured with the infant girl, and Sophie watched him in the mirror, wondering if his would someday be a tale of love at first sight.

Willy was with the rest of the men doing whatever Betsy told them to do at the church. Such a picture of possibilities splashed in Sophie's imagination.

Maggie bustled into the room as lively as ever, though Sophie suspected the little woman would sleep the afternoon away.

"I have something borrowed and blue," she said with an endearing look at Mama. "Your mother is sharing you with me for this occasion, and I dearly appreciate it, having no daughter of my own."

Sophie's heart squeezed at what Maggie had shared of her infant son, and she loved her own mother even more for her generous spirit.

Maggie offered a soft blue hankie edged in white tatting. "I carried this at my wedding, dear, and I'd be honored if you would carry it at yours."

Moved beyond words, Sophie pulled away from everyone fussing with her hair and dress and hugged the little woman. "You are a dear," she whispered, "and I am honored."

When each person was finished with their appointed task, they stepped back to admire the finished product. Sophie had never felt so obviously the focus of attention and was a bit discomforted.

Mama must have known, and she slipped forward, lifting her hands over Sophie's head. A fine gold chain with a small oval pendant dropped from her fingers and she fastened it at the base of Sophie's neck.

Tears threatened as she fingered the treasured keepsake, her mother and father's wedding portrait. "Oh, Mama."

"Don't cry. You want to look your brightest so you can put your own lovely wedding picture on the other side of the locket." She finished by tucking wild sunflowers into Sophie's hair and pulling soft tendrils loose around her face.

"Now you are complete," Maggie announced with her customary cheer. "In that lovely dress you have something old, something new, something borrowed, and something blue."

But those treasured gifts were not what made Sophie feel complete. The other side of her heart waited for her at the church. The man she'd loved without realizing just how much. A man who was courageous enough to not only rescue her from attack but share his deepest wounds with her and the painful story behind them.

She would have loved him even if he'd told her nothing, but now she understood what cruelty had formed his childhood, driven his desire for kindness in his work, and been redeemed when God broke through his pain with the promise of light and mercy.

Anticipation of joy, indeed. She fingered her own scar, blessed beyond measure for how Clay saw her imperfections.

Maggie left in a rush and returned with a long burgundy velvet cloak. "Put this on, dear. I know it's warm out, but you don't want to muss that lovely dress on your way to the church."

Such an elegant garment made Sophie wonder again about the woman's mysterious past before coming to Olin Springs. She really needed to temper her curiosity, though that might be a part of her that she never completely controlled.

Todd waited outside with Maggie's buggy, looking pleased and polished and ready to drive Sophie to the church. As they neared, she marveled at the tables and chairs spread across the church lawn, each decorated with fruit jars full of sunflower bouquets and filled with food. The Women's Society had been busy preparing a meal, no doubt at Maggie's bidding.

A garland hung above the church house door, and inside more sunflowers adorned the end of each pew. But most breathtaking of all was the handsome horse handler who waited beside Pastor Bittman at the front of the church, his shirt starched and creased, new trousers, and a handsome new vest bearing a sunflower boutonniere. She couldn't suppress a grin, realizing he had succumbed to Betsy's insistence that he sport a flower on his person.

A touch at her elbow turned her toward Deacon, who had taken his place beside her. With a fond tug on her heart for her own father, she gladly accepted Deacon's arm as the church organist began to play.

Betsy and Garrett took their places at the front, and it seemed an eternity before she joined her hand with Clay's and stood before Pastor Bittman.

The humming of her heart drowned most of what the kind man said until he repeated the words Clay had shared with her.

"Through the Lord's mercies we are not consumed, because His compassions fail not. They are new every morning; great is Your faithfulness."

Surprised by the gold band Clay placed on her finger but not the promise-filled kiss he pressed to her lips, she held tightly to his strong arm as they walked out of the church as man and wife.

Dinner was a festive affair with every imaginable dish on hand, including a beautifully decorated cake from the storekeeper's wife, Wilhelmina Reynolds. But summer heat pressed through the shade trees and Sophie was soon ready to leave the party behind.

Clay, attentive as ever to mood and gesture, motioned to Todd, who soon appeared before the church with Pen and Duster, both horses festooned with garlands around their necks and bright sunflowers twisted into their manes and forelocks. Pen shook his head but didn't try to rub the garlands off on the fence.

She laughed and squeezed Clay's arm. "You let them put flowers on these manly horses?"

He scowled and flicked at his own. "Just this once," he said leaning close, his voice banked low and warm.

She desperately needed to get out of the heat.

To the applause of those gathered, Clay linked his hands for her booted foot. "I know you don't need my help, Mrs. Ferguson, but for the sake of those looking on … "

"I am most honored, Mr. Ferguson," she said and easily swung her leg over the back of the saddle when he hefted her aloft.

As they reined their mounts around, Sophie looked back to see her mother beaming, tears glinting from her cheeks and Deacon holding her close. Maggie, Mae Ann, and Betsy all waved, as did everyone who wished them joy.

*Anticipation of joy.* The phrase wrapped around her like the garland on her horse, twining in and out of her heart with every step. When they came to the turnoff, Clay's blue eyes bore into her with all the intensity of a perfect summer's day, and they both lifted their horses to an easy lope until they crested the low saddle. The pins in her braid had loosened and she shook her hair free, scattering sunflowers around her.

Below them, the ranch lay invitingly lush and verdant, the creek running full from recent rains, calves fattening for market in the fall.

And above them, atop a new gate post and crossbar, hung a hand-carved sign that said "Fair View Ranch."

Clay sidled Duster up against Pen and his leg pressed her as he leaned in for a heated kiss that left her weak kneed and slack-reined. With the same penetrating look he'd given her that first day at the depot, he lowered his voice to a most intimate tone.

"You are the fairest view on this place, Mrs. Ferguson. Welcome home."

# Epilogue:

# April 1886

Sophie squeezed Clay's hand as he helped her from the buggy. It was so much easier than climbing down from the buckboard, though she could have managed perfectly well driving herself. But he would not hear of it.

He needed to check in with John at the livery, he'd said. Clay "checked in" with John every time she made a call. The last time she'd seen the boy he was sporting a hat that looked remarkably like Clay's and a proud smile that said he'd saved his "appreciation" money for just that purpose.

With one hand holding her satchel, she pressed the other against the only remaining curve of her waist and arched her back.

"Tired?" Blue eyes searched every inch of her face for truth. Feigning unlimited endurance was futile.

"A bit."

He frowned.

She lowered her chin and looked up at him through her lashes, a delightful tact she'd learned early in their marriage. It completely undid him.

He deliberately looked away. "I'll be back in a half hour. That's plenty of time."

She scoffed and brushed her lips across his unshaven cheek, which he quickly turned to capture her kiss with his own. If such ardor held through the years, they would have a passel of children and need a bigger house.

Abigail Eisner met her at the bell-topped door to the tailor's shop, her infant son sleeping soundly in her arms despite the jingling welcome.

Sophie lightly touched his olive complexion with the crook of her finger. "How is little Isaac today?"

Abigail kissed his downy head. "For the moment he is quiet."

Sophie smothered a laugh and followed Abigail to the apartment at the back of the haberdashery. Clay and John had remodeled the long, narrow shop, moving the couple's living quarters downstairs and Hiram's sewing and fitting area upstairs.

They had even installed two handrails, one on either side of the curving stairs.

Sophie seated herself on a stout wooden chair, ensuring her ability to rise again, and took the sleeping babe while Abigail prepared tea.

When she returned, she set the tray on a table nearby, then reached for Isaac and placed a cloth-wrapped parcel in Sophie's hands.

"For you and all you have done for us."

The young woman had no way of knowing that Sophie's calling ministered to her own heart as well as others' as she learned more completely the value of weeping and rejoicing with mothers, regardless of their circumstances.

At Abigail's anticipatory posture, Sophie loosened the ribbon from a perfectly hemmed flannel that would serve her own child in the near future. But what it held brought sudden tears to her eyes and gripped her heart to the point of cutting off what little breath remained in her crowded lungs.

A cross-stitched sampler unfolded to reveal a verse from Abigail's Scriptures, one that Sophie knew was found in her own, yet was often overlooked.

Therefore God dealt well with the midwives:

and the people multiplied, and waxed very mighty.

And it came to pass, because the midwives feared God,

that he made them houses.

Exodus 1:20-21

Sophie struggled for words and pressed the sampler against her breast, allowing her tears to flow unchecked. "Thank you," she managed to whisper. "I will cherish it."

When Clay called for Sophie, Abigail saw her to the door, past customers admiring Hiram's work on a recently completed man's suit, and she promised to call again in a week unless things progressed as she expected.

"You've been crying," Clay said as he handed her up. "What's wrong?"

Rather than walk around, he climbed in after her and stepped over her bulging self with his long, strong legs. "What happened? Is everything all right?"

Taking one of his rough, sun-browned hands, she held it to her lips, then pressed it against her heart, and looked into his dear face. "Everything is perfectly all right," she said, watching as he read her eyes, finding truth within them, and finally relaxing.

"Then why are you crying?"

Of course a man would not understand a woman's emotions at all times, especially when they appeared to contradict and fluctuate as hers did so frequently these recent days. But she would try to help him. She would always try.

"Because, my dear husband, His mercies are new every morning."

~

Thank you for reading Book 3 of the Front Range Brides series,
*An Impossible Price.*

If you enjoyed Sophie and Clay's story, I would so appreciate a brief review on your favorite book site – just a sentence or two.

You might also enjoy The Canon City Chronicles series, beginning with *Book 1, Loving the Horseman.*

**Receive a free historical novella when you sign up for my Quarterly Author Update: https://bit.ly/3b4eavB**

# ACKNOWLEDGMENTS

It takes many hearts, hands, and hours for a book to come to completion, and for this I am grateful. I'd like to thank advance readers Nancy Huber, Jill Maple, Cindy Pottenger, and Amanda Beck; my editor Christy Distler; and you, the readers, for allowing Clay and Sophie's story to flow into your hearts. Most of all, I thank our good and loving God for pouring this story into mine.

Thank you for reading Inspirational Western Romance. If you would like to leave a brief review on your favorite book website or other social media, it would bless my boots off!

# About the Author

Bestselling author and winner of the **Will Rogers Gold Medallion** for Inspirational Western Fiction, Davalynn Spencer can't stop #lovingthecowboy. When she's not writing, teaching writer workshops, or playing on her church worship team, she's wrangling Blue the Cowdog and mouse detectors Annie and Oakley. Connect with her online via:

Amazon https://www.amazon.com/Davalynn-Spencer/e/B002EZUEZK

BookBub https://www.bookbub.com/authors/davalynn-spencer

Website https://davalynnspencer.com/

Blog https://davalynnspencer.com/subscribe/

Newsletter http://eepurl.com/xa81D

Facebook https://www.facebook.com/AuthorDavalynnSpencer

Twitter https://twitter.com/davalynnspencer

GoodReads https://www.goodreads.com/author/show/5051432.Davalynn_Spencer

Pinterest https://pinterest.com/davalynnspencer/boards/

~May all that you read be uplifting.~

Made in the USA
Coppell, TX
17 May 2025

49505861R00173